OVERNIGHT TO INNSBRUCK

And beings in love's tunic scattered to the four winds
For no reason at all
For no reason that I can tell.

Denis Devlin, from 'Little Elegy'

Overnight to Innsbruck

Denyse Woods

SITRIC BOOKS

First published 2002 by
SITRIC BOOKS LTD
62–63 Sitric Road, Arbour Hill,
Dublin 7, Ireland

A CIP record for this title is available from the British Library.

1 3 5 7 9 10 8 6 4 2

ISBN 1 903305 06 3

ACKNOWLEDGMENTS
*Warmest thanks to Michael Palin, Sir Alex Stirling, Sally Ann Baynard,
Cormac Gordon, Antony Farrell, Brendan Barrington, Liam Carson and Jonathan
Williams.*

Set in Adobe Garamond
Printed by Betaprint, Clonshaugh, Dublin, Ireland

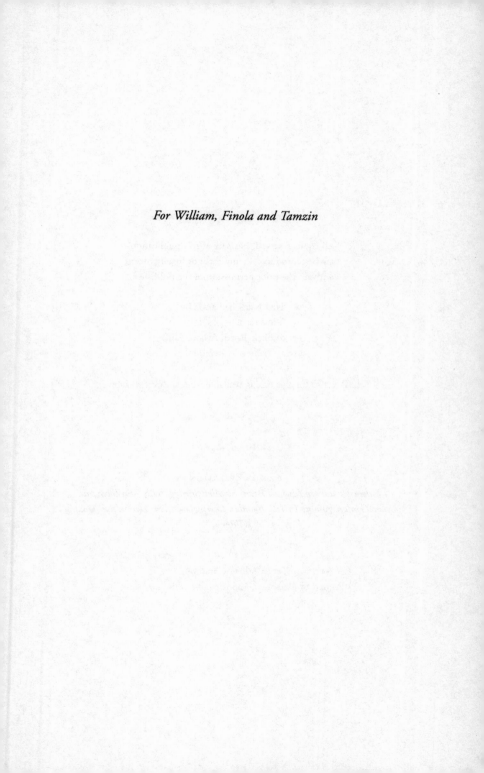

For William, Finola and Tamzin

OVERNIGHT TO INNSBRUCK

Roma Termini

The train stood at its appointed platform, belching.

I walked towards it, drenched, and looked for the carriage as numbered on my ticket. Straggled hair stuck to my cheekbones, the hem of my skirt slapped around my calves, and my haversack had absorbed so much rain that it was like carrying a water tank on my back.

I had come to Rome without meaning to. In Toulon station, four days earlier, I had decided on a whim to take the first sleeper that came through that evening, and woke up in Italy the next morning. It didn't actually matter where I was. What mattered was that I was nearly twenty-six, the cut-off age for the Inter-Rail Card, and this was my last chance for a truly cheap holiday. Rome would do as well as anywhere else – or would have done, had this not been such an unseasonably wet September. Instead of walking through sun-drenched streets licking gelati and dipping my toes in the Trevi Fountain, I had squelched through the Sistine Chapel and shivered over cappuccinos in stand-up bars until, with no hint of steam rising off the Italian pavements, I shared a taxi to the station with an American sailor who told me he had mislaid his aircraft carrier.

It was therefore a combination of whimsy and bad weather that led me to the Innsbruck train that night in 1987. Certainly I had no particular desire to see Innsbruck. I selected it, as I did every destination, according to the night-time network of continental railways. Trains offered cheap accommodation for me and my like, and since I had not slept well in my *pensione* I needed a long trip during which to recover. The overnight haul to Austria would allow me eleven hours of slumber.

I had reserved a berth, which was not quite in keeping with the image upheld by my travelling contemporaries, but it was the only way to ensure that I spent the night in a horizontal position. When I found the right carriage and stepped in, the corridor was heaving with people and haversacks. I joined the fray. Most compartments were packed – giggling girls, lovers ensconced behind closed doors, students huddled around poker games – so I was relieved to find that my own was almost empty. I stepped in, and looked up. The only berths worth having are the high ones near the ceiling. They offer headroom and some privacy, while other passengers struggle around in the confined space below, where the only options are to lie down or get out. But even the upper reaches must be shared, and on this occasion the top right-hand couchette, an arm's length from my own, was occupied by a broad-shouldered man, whose whole being seemed to have laid claim to the cabin. He lay face to the wall in a black shirt and faded jeans, and his haversack, tucked away at his feet, had an Irish flag on it. That suited: the Irish were congenial, good for passing time. I looked forward to sharing my Roman salami with him and swapping the usual tales of where, when, and were the lavatories clean, but just as I was about to hurl my haversack up there, he coughed and sniffled. He had a thick cold. Thanks, but no thanks. For the first time ever, I settled for the bottom berth on the left, as far away from him as I could get.

I dried my hair and feet, spread my sleeping bag out to dry on the middle berth, then took out my picnic and watched haversacks bob along the corridor. Since turning in such a narrow passageway with a pack on your back is impossible, it was often a case of three steps forwards and four steps back, as in some ritualistic dance. My companion for the night hardly stirred, moving about only in the discomfort of his cold. There would be no swapping of travellers' tales here. When the chaos in the carriage had ebbed, I went out to stand in the corridor, my ears gathering all at once the quips, asides, rebuffs and laughter of our multilingual population.

At eight twenty-five, the train jolted forward.

My fellow passenger had turned off the light as soon as I stepped out, the message patently clear. Like a cat put out in the cold, I stood by the window for a long time, watching the lights go by, and thought about Saul. Again. I had been thinking about him so much that his image had grown fuzzy. Was his hair quite so fair? His face so unblemished? Was this his grin, or was I now confusing it with that of a previous boyfriend? As for his voice, I had lost that entirely. At some point in the two weeks since I had seen him, the exact timbre of his voice had been lost to me, which was hardly surprising. I had known him for only three days when I left London – sixty-three hours to be exact – but in every moment of idleness since then I had revisited each one of those hours, dwelling on some more than others. Sometimes I wondered where our few days of love would lead, but most of the time I knew. There was something about Saul; something about us. There was a sense, an acknowledgment shared, that this was no passing whim, and Saul had even promised that, while I was away, he would speak to his girlfriend of two years' standing and tell her that he had moved on. Standing on the train that night, with Italy rushing past me, I sent him courage across the continent to do it kindly, and well.

I stepped back into the compartment, pulled the door shut and lay down, placing the coarse brown blanket over me. I read for a while, but soon discarded my book and switched off the dim reading light. Then it was only a question of waiting for sleep as the train streamed swiftly through places unseen. Falling adrift to the soft chuckle of my transport was a luxuriant way of sleeping and waking. I would sleep in every town between Rome and Innsbruck, would be carried for miles unconscious. I could feel all but see nothing, could hear only the soothing rattle of the carriages as they chased each other eagerly towards the Alps.

*

The compartment door slid open with a clunk.

The train had stopped. The night-time rumblings of a large station had replaced the mumble of the undercarriage. Florence, already. Midnight, then. There was commotion in the corridor as fresh passengers boarded; someone was looking into our compartment, but thought better of joining us and moved on, only partially closing the door. I turned into the dark corner. It was comforting to be one of those already ensconced, and it was even better to know that I had slept deeply for the first time in three nights. I waited to slip back into that glorious blank, and might have done so but for the stationmaster shouting on the platform and our steward directing human traffic at the end of the corridor.

'You, you,' he called. 'Here. Bed in here.'

A young woman passed our door. '*Grazie.* Thanks.' But the steward was directing her into an apparently unappealing compartment, because she called after him, 'Em, excuse me? Any chance of somewhere a little less crowded?'

There was a sudden movement on the top berth.

'Everywhere crowded,' the steward snapped. 'You make reservation?'

'No.'

'You want empty couchette, you reserve! You pay!'

I rolled onto my back and was about to close our door when the man with the cold reached down and pushed it fully open. He was going to give them a piece of his mind, and mine too, I hoped; tell them some people were trying to sleep around here.

'So I'll try another carriage,' retorted the woman in an Irish accent, and the man above me said, 'Christ.'

'Every carriage busy tonight,' said the steward, dismissing her as he scurried past our door. 'Everywhere full!'

'Well, thanks so much for your help,' she called after him.

'Christ.' The man up top dropped heavily onto the floor beside me and leaned out of the compartment. 'Frances! Fran, is that you?'

The stationmaster cried out. Whistles screeched. I turned my head towards the door; beyond my roommate's legs I could see a short stretch of corridor. Straining to hear above the hum of the station, I waited for the woman to speak.

'Jesus wept. Fran!'

'My God. Richard.'

She came closer. Her sandaled feet, the frayed hem of jeans around her ankles, stopped within my line of vision. 'My God.'

The train was moving. It had slid imperceptibly out of the station, the only evidence of motion the lights passing the window.

'When I heard your voice, I thought I must be dreaming,' Richard gushed.

Her muttered response was smothered by the train's increasing speed, and then, nothing. They stared at one another. She dropped her black holdall.

'Fran, how the hell … how are you?'

Nothing.

He shuffled on his feet, confused by her inertia and anxious to disturb it. 'God, it's so great to see you.'

Her reply was sharp, but indecipherable. The carriage rocked to the beat of the wheels.

'Look, come in here.' His voice, thick with the congestion of his cold, was giddy, breathless. He reached for her holdall. 'There's loads of room. It's only me and her. We can go up top.'

Come on, I thought, *get in here where I can hear you properly.*

She seemed petrified. Petrified, I fancied, by the unexpected resurgence of some old and awful grief. They must have been lovers, I thought. This was clearly an oft-anticipated incident, which, for all their longing, neither party could ever have been ready for.

I lay mesmerized, and uncomfortable. My neck was jammed to the right, my eyes straining to see the woman, and I realized that I was trying not to breathe, as if pretending to be not merely asleep, but actually dead.

He threw her bag up to his berth, then climbed after it to stow it away on the shelf over the door. 'Fran?' he said softly.

She stepped tentatively towards the compartment and stood in the doorway.

'There hasn't been one day,' he said, 'not one day in four years that I haven't wondered and wished and ... well, hoped to see you again, so please come up here and tell me how you've been.'

She stood. He lay. I listened.

Then she said, with rancour, 'Where *the hell* did you get to?'

After a moment he replied, 'I could ask you the same question.'

From that point on, my curiosity so vigorously aroused, I hardly moved a limb for the rest of the night.

They told their stories. They interrupted one another, often at first, but mostly each remained silent, transfixed by the voice in the dark and the tale it told.

For me, it was like falling into a vivid dream. The darkness, the rhythm of the bogies rattling across the sleepers, and the soft voices overhead transported me I knew not where at first, until I became aware, not of Ireland, as I expected, but of the barren deserts of the Sudan.

one

I

Frances stared at the desert, her mind as empty as the sandy expanse, her thoughts reduced to slow motion by the heat. There was nothing for her to do, except stay in that sleepy, timeless state for as long as possible. She was tired, still; her bones ached and her throat felt starched. Richard was off sulking somewhere, so she pulled her feet around her and looked out. The desert went on and on, an endless unattractive continuation of dirt and dust. It was like looking at infinity, she thought.

The argument she had had with Richard edged into her mind. She had never seen him so angry, and she wanted to set things right. She wasn't ready to apologize, quite, but a few hours spent ignoring each other in the same compartment, with no third party to alleviate the tension, should eventually harmonize things, and by the time they came to share another tin of warm meat they might even be talking again. That was what usually happened. Sheer exposure drew them back into cordiality. Frances wanted to get on with that process, but until Richard came back, she could only reflect. His outburst had had the desired effect: he had forced her to take stock. She tried to see the desert through his eyes, to feel this journey through his limbs. There was nothing out there, she told herself, nothing even in the swirling sand that trailed the locomotive. It was romance to think otherwise, and yet Richard had always given in and followed her fantasies with her.

Until now. Now it was her turn to follow, to live his life for a change, and so, after this trip, she would go with him to London, where she would come to a halt, even though she had thousands of miles left in her. She worried that if she didn't go their way, those unspent miles would revisit her, much later, when she and Richard had settled into their little home and were shackled by all the chains of domesticity. She feared she would rot if left in one place for too long, that the normality which Richard craved would corrupt something in her, just as her own yearning for diversity would damage everything he aspired to. This was what haunted her, and what Richard never understood.

She looked at her watch. Twenty-five past four. The air stagnated with stuffy determination. She was thirsty; her tongue felt desiccated. Richard might come back with tea, but as time passed she began worrying that he was actually stuck in the foul toilet, ridding his system of some nasty bug. He might also be walking around trying to cool down, in more ways than one, or he could be chatting to the two Australian blokes further along the carriage. Frances went back to daydreaming. After Cairo, she would see little more of North Africa and would never sit like this in the snug of a railway compartment, so she had to make the most of what was left to her.

But Richard's absence began to niggle. She got up and leaned out the door, looking up and down the passageway. Further along, a Nubian man – the only Sudanese person in the first-class carriage – was bending over to look out of the low window. He stared at Frances, his black, wet eyes scarcely moving, as if to challenge her, but it was only curiosity. Sitting down again, she wondered how long Richard had been gone. She had slept for an hour at most and was now impatient to make up with him. These rows were getting out of hand; there had been too many already. It was time to come clean, own up; time to try to explain to him that it was not only the dread of forsaking her travels, of conceding to the humdrum of unexceptional existence, that was making her cantankerous. It was anger too, and a sense of betrayal.

She had never dared tell him before, but in Richard she had

fallen for the wrong type of man and she blamed him for that. The first time she had seen him, in a café in Hamburg, he had had a rucksack by his feet and a map in his hand and she thought he was like her – one of that unkempt band of wandering backpackers who saw the world as an unending banquet to which they needed no invitation. Frances had already been at the banquet for years and intended to stay much longer, for there was no end to the courses placed before her, and no satiation either. There were certain risks that had to be avoided, love and diarrhoea foremost amongst them. Love, Frances and her ilk agreed, could be as much of a death knell to their rambling lifestyle as chronic dysentery or a dose of hepatitis, because falling for a native or for the lure of a cosy den could bring them to a standstill. Frances accepted this; she was aware of the dangers of romance, but she didn't see Richard as a threat because she thought he was like her. A nomad.

He did not disillusion her. He was bumming around Europe at the time, so they bummed around together and fell in love somewhere between the islands of Paros and Ios in Greece. By the time Frances found out that Richard wasn't like her at all, it was too late. She had fallen for a tourist.

She felt betrayed and cheated. Not then, when she was barely twenty-one and too besotted to care, but now, when she had to pay the price of that mistake. Although it had been her mistake, she blamed Richard. She resented him not only because he had now given her an ultimatum, had drawn a line in the sand, but because he had insinuated himself into her life under false pretences and then expected her to accept the consequences without rancour, or even regret.

His disappearing act had worked; by now, she had even found enough humility to apologize. But first she had to find him. She wandered the length of the carriage, looking into every compartment. The only other foreigners, the two lads, weren't around. That was a good sign. Perhaps they had gone to the restaurant with

Richard. She hurried on through three carriages until she reached the dining car, fully expecting to find Richard sitting at one of the bare Formica tables sipping a glass of tea. He would look up when she arrived, his brown eyes still angry, but mostly hurt, so she began formulating a conciliatory opening, a gentle explanation. *You silly dope. I love you. I want to be with you, but it isn't easy giving up all this other stuff...*

Richard was not in the dining car, but the Australians were. They stood out like rubbish beside a monument – their shorts and singlets obscene alongside the gallabiyas of the elegant Sudanese – but they looked like salvation to Frances. Richard couldn't be far away. They must have seen him.

'Hi.' She almost fell over them as the train lurched. 'Have you seen my friend anywhere? He's tall and dark—'

'Tall and dark?' said one, grinning. 'That's a bit difficult. Sounds like every other person on this train.'

'Yeah,' said the other. 'If he was small and white, he'd stand out a bit, you know?'

They laughed at their own wit.

'He is white, but not small. You must have seen him in first class?'

'Yeah, we were talking to him last night. Richard, isn't it?'

'Yes! Have you seen him anywhere?'

''Fraid not.'

'Damn. He's wandering around and I can't find him.'

'Can't have gone far, though, can he?'

Frances wiped her face with her scarf. 'I suppose not. If he comes by, would you tell him I'm looking for him?'

'Sure.'

Back in their own compartment Frances allowed reason to hold unease at bay. There was nothing to worry about: people don't vanish from moving trains.

The carriage was quiet. Apart from the Australians, the Nubian and themselves, all the first-class compartments were empty. She stuck her head out the paneless window, eyes firmly closed against the sting of flying sand. Richard was pushing his luck. He had made his protest and it had registered accordingly, but doing a disappearing act on the Nile Valley Express was neither fair nor funny. Wherever he was, however bad their argument had been, it was cruel to stay away for so long. She pulled in her head. 'Damn. Now there's going to be another bloody row.'

The Nubian, who had been standing farther along the corridor, walked past her door, looking in, his white robes and turban giving the impression of a ghost slipping past.

Frances sat for another half hour, fuming. So she had not, perhaps, been an ideal travelling companion recently, but did she deserve this? And even if she did, Richard was always the peacemaker, the conciliator, the one who couldn't bear conflict to drag on. But this time, she knew, had been different. His outburst had been out of character, out of proportion, and so his recovery must also take longer. Frances cursed herself for being too selfish, too self-absorbed. She had trivialized his ambition, scorned his aspirations, made light of his strength of purpose. Because he had a career to nurture, she had called him a stick-in-the-mud; because he wanted a home and family, she had accused him of being unimaginative. That had been too harsh perhaps, but falling for Richard had been an incomprehensible lapse of judgment. He was that bad dose of hepatitis she should have avoided; the debilitating dysentery that would make her go home. Why had she not seen it before it was too late?

She could no longer sit still. She went looking again. Second class was not as tightly packed as it had been before Atbara, but it was very crowded. Frances pushed her way through the carriages, knocked on the doors of lavatories, and pressed on, her irritation increasing with every foot that accidentally tripped her, with every toe she stood upon. By the time she was forcing her way through third class, sweltering and sweaty, reason began to lose its hold. Where was he? Before stepping across to another carriage she stopped to catch some breeze, but the relief was mild and momentary. Unease began to slide up her legs, preceded by a hunger-like tremor. She tried to catch her breath and calm herself; she must not faint. There was no longer any excuse for this. Richard would know that she would worry, and how on earth was she to find him on a train with several thousand people on it?

Her hands were shaking as she forged her way through more carriages. In third class, passengers were sitting on hard seats, jammed together in one great mould and lulled into a sleepless doze by the relentless swaying of their bodies. Some eyes followed Frances as she came through, but in a long-sleeved cheesecloth top and baggy cotton trousers, she was adequately covered. Audibly cursing Richard, she carried on. He was probably back in their compartment by now, with his feet up, while she was a dozen carriages away, struggling at every step. Her eyes jumped from face to face, which made her dizzy, and at the end of each carriage she had to step into the furnace of sunlight and negotiate her way across couplings to the next one. She had never felt sick on a train before, but now she did. She wished everything would stop moving. By the time she reached the end of the passenger coaches she was numb with confusion. Where was he? In the freight cars? In the engine? It was too ridiculous. This train, the only source of food, water, and shade for hundreds of miles, was like a moving oasis, carrying its population through territory so inhospitable that even a murderer would think twice about getting off.

The sight of the desert stretching out behind the train filled her with horror. Could he have fallen off and gone under the wheels? Could he be lying back there in 120° heat with a broken neck? *No.* He could not have fallen off unnoticed. There were too many people in the corridors, too many people by the doors. Someone would have seen, would have pulled the cord.

And yet something very close to fear made Frances hurry back through the carriages again. He might have moved compartments in a fit of pique and be lying on one of the high bunks in first class;

she had not properly checked their own carriage. It took her nearly fifteen minutes to get there and when she did, she looked in every empty compartment. Up at the top berths, under the bottom berths, out of the windows, in the lavatories again. Nowhere.

Weak with disappointment, she collapsed onto the bench seat. It was then, as she caught her breath, that she noticed that Richard's knapsack was gone.

The sound of her panting drummed in her ears.

She jumped up, looked under their seats, climbed onto the upper berths, searching frantically. The last time she had seen it, the knapsack had been on the seat near the door and Richard had been sitting opposite, with one foot on it. That was before they had started arguing. He had not, she was certain, taken it with him when he stormed out, but since he carried his money in the knapsack, he might have come back for it to go to the dining car. On the other hand, since it also held some clothes and belongings, he was just as likely to pack it away near Frances so that he wouldn't have to lug it around.

She sat down. Nausea rose in her stomach. This was like trying to find her way in the dark; like being in a ghost house at the funfair. The exit was there, but she couldn't see it, and every time she put her foot forward the surface dipped away, causing her to stumble.

Outside, the brown and blue of day had been mixed into the dull grey of evening. The desert drew a thin line along the horizon. There was no beauty in it, and even the approaching night offered little reprieve from the damning heat that made Frances's head pound without remorse. The Sudanese man who stood guard outside her door moved away, and soon he and the tea man could be heard saying their evening prayers at the end of the carriage, their prayer mats spread out near the toilet door. Their rhythmic incantations fell in behind the measured sound of the wheels squeaking across the sleepers.

The impending darkness made Frances set off again, pushing through carriages, bumping into people, falling against seats, banging her knees on doorways as she pulled them open. Faces everywhere, looking up, looking out, looking at her, but never the right face. Every carriage seemed stuffier than the last, the smells of food and humans causing bile to rise in her throat. At the end of one carriage, she inhaled a lungful of sandy air.

By the time she returned to base, panic had cut her off from all things familiar. Nothing was right. The airlessness and dimming light made her feel truncated, as though her exhausted body was not connected to the mind that raced in every direction, hitting a wall at the end of every line it took. She couldn't see the desert, though she stared at it. Hot from rushing and cold with sweat, she tried to calm herself by breathing deeply, the way her aunt had taught her to do when she was fussed. This helped her to think straight, spurring her to take out the map. The last stop had been at Abu Hamed. Frances remembered coming into the town, but not out of it. Not long after Richard's furious exit, she had stretched out on the seat so that when he came back – ashamed by his loss of control – she could pretend to be asleep and would not have to speak to him. However, after seething and thrashing about, she had soon worn herself out, and although she was aware of Richard coming back – she had opened one eye as he sat down – she was soon genuinely dozing. She remembered, vaguely, pulling in to Abu Hamed and hearing the cacophony outside, the local people coming aboard to hawk goods and food, and it must have been then, she supposed, that she had actually fallen into a deep sleep, for she could recall nothing beyond that point. She had slept for over an hour, and as it was now after six, they must have left Abu Hamed at around four. Could Richard conceivably have left the train there? But why? Because of one argument amongst many others? It made no sense. She tried to shake off this thought, to put it away, but the questions persisted. Where was he? What had she done to warrant this?

It had to be due to some weird corrosion of her imagination. The desert was getting to her, causing her to hallucinate. Richard was on the train, somewhere. He had to be. He couldn't have been kidnapped or dragged away with yellow fever — she would have heard the scuffle — but could he have fallen out of one of the carriages? The thought recurred over and over. Could he be back there in the sand dying of thirst?

Night had come, and it made her surroundings shrink. She had less space, less air, nowhere to look. The man in the corridor hovered near her door, glancing in occasionally from his great height at her frenzied head-shaking. In her increasing paranoia, his face acquired a menacing look. Did he know something? Was he hiding Richard? He had seen her rush about — had he also seen Richard leaving?

Frances opened another bottle and drank, allowing water to dribble down her neck and inside her shirt. Richard's knapsack was gone. What did that mean? They were travelling light. She wore her documents in a money-belt, which she rarely took off, and they shared a small rucksack for the few clothes they had needed for their week-long detour to Khartoum, but most of their belongings were in another rucksack, which they had left in storage at their hotel in Aswan. The train often stopped between scheduled stations, because of sand on the tracks and even to let people disembark, but why should Richard get off anywhere? They were going to Aswan and Cairo. They were on their way home. He finally had what he wanted. Surely he could not have been so angry that he had got off? No. Therefore he must come back. He must be somewhere, camouflaged in the mad amalgam of bodies pressed together in other carriages, and before this went beyond reason he would return with a perfectly plausible explanation as to where he had been.

He didn't.

2

Frances sat in a stupor. Richard was no longer on the train. This was the only conclusion she could reach, and if he wasn't on it, then he must have got off it. His knapsack was gone. Everything came back to that. He had picked up his bag and got off the train. Voluntarily, wilfully. And he had done so because she had driven him to it. It was no longer a question of Richard punishing her, but of leaving her. He had threatened it, and now he had done it.

The Nubian gentleman walked past the doorway again. Frances suddenly found the courage to call him. She unzipped her money-belt, grabbed her wallet, pulled out the photo of Richard she had carried with her for three years, and held it out to him. He looked at it quizzically. English was quite widely spoken in the Sudan, but it would be just her luck to be travelling with all the non-speakers in the country.

'Excuse me, but have you seen this man? He was here, with me here.' She pointed at the seat. 'And, well, he seems to … have gone somewhere. Did you see him?'

He took the photo and studied it in the bad light. He nodded. He clearly recognized Richard as the man she was travelling with.

'I don't know where he is,' she said.

'You have go look?' he asked, raising his chin to the left and then the right.

He knew very well she had. She had been whirling around like a tempest. 'Yes. I've been down the whole train. I can't find him!'

He looked at her kindly, his eyes no longer threatening, but he was shaking his head. He glanced over his shoulder and summoned the tea man, who was coming along the corridor with a kettle and glasses. They showed him the photo, but he also shook his head: 'Muta'assif.'

The Nubian raised his palms at Frances. 'You wait.' He strode down the corridor and returned some minutes later with the young guard, who still managed to look fresh in his brown uniform in spite of having been on duty since they left Khartoum twenty-six hours earlier. He was holding Richard's photograph.

'Madame. You have problem?'

In a semi-coherent rush of words, Frances told him about Richard's disappearance.

'Okay, okay,' said the guard, raising his hand to slow her down. He asked her some questions, then moved along to the next carriage, with Frances on his heels, and spoke to some men standing around the door. Delighted to meet intrigue in the midst of crushing boredom, other passengers gathered around; the discussion was lively and loud as the photo was passed from hand to hand. Everyone had an opinion, but Frances understood nothing. As she peered around the guard, several pairs of eyes looked at her, nodding as the photo went from one to the other. Some clearly recognized Richard; he had come through their carriage several times since leaving Khartoum.

Then one man pushed his way to the fore of the huddle and spoke at Frances in Arabic.

'I don't understand. English?'

He shook his head. He gesticulated towards the door. He bent his elbow and threw his arm forward. Out. Then he did it again.

Frances grabbed a door frame for support. 'He got off?' Her limbs shook. 'Is that what he's saying?'

The guard spoke to the passenger. Frances tried to swallow, but her mouth was so dry that the reflex hurt her tongue.

'Yes,' said the guard. 'Your friend he get off.'

Her eyes filled. 'My God. Where? Where did he get off?'

They discussed this, then said together, 'Abu Hamed.'

'Abu Hamed?'

'Yes, yes.'

'But why? Why?'

The man shrugged, shook his head. The crowd stared at this young foreign lady abandoned in the middle of the desert. It made no more sense to them than it did to her.

'Jesus.'

He had got off the train. It was true: he had left her. *Here.*

A large hand with slim fingernails holding a glass of tea roused her from a trance. The Nubian smiled, gave her the hot glass and vanished again. The black tea was sweet and soothing. Beyond the window, there were no passing lights to relieve the blackness, only her own reflection on the dirty windowpane. The train rocked her as though trying to lull her problems away. The wheels clacked, the wooden carriage creaked – sounds she loved. Richard had not fallen off or been assaulted or kidnapped. He had taken his bag and disembarked, without fuss or drama, of his own free will.

A movement in the doorway made her jump – she still expected to see Richard standing there – but it was one of the Australians.

'Hi. Just stretching my legs.'

Long and bare and covered in sun-bleached hairs, his legs didn't look like they needed much stretching. 'Hello.'

'Did you find your mate?'

'No.'

'Crikey. Wonder where he's got to?'

'He got off.'

His jaw dropped. 'Got off? Geez. Where?'

'In Abu Hamed, apparently.'

'Geez. Poor bugger. Must have gone for ciggies and missed the train, eh?' His accent was potent.

'He doesn't smoke.'

'Must have wanted something, but. There was all sorts of stuff going in that last place.'

'Are you sure you didn't see him?'

'I saw him last night and again this morning down by the dunny—'

'I mean this afternoon!'

He shook his head. 'Sorry.'

'Fuck.'

'What are you going to do?'

'I … I don't know.'

The Australian frowned. 'I wonder what *he's* going to do. I mean, there's not a lot out there.'

Frances glared at him. She needed company, yes. She needed help even. But this ill-clad, over-bronzed purveyor of the bleeding obvious somehow didn't measure up to the sustenance she had in mind.

He tried to backtrack. 'Aw, but he'll be right, don't you worry. He can always catch the next train.'

Frances sighed. She did not want this conversation, did not want to hear herself say what his bland attempt at reassurance was pumping out of her. 'The next train? That could be days, with all the usual delays, or even a week …' *A week?*

'Crikey. Hope he's got money on him.'

'He has everything he needs.'

He glanced at her, not sure what she was getting at, then sat down, issuing antipodean grunts that were either sympathetic or perplexed, she wasn't quite sure, and asked, 'Was he, eh, I mean, did you know him, or did you just meet up on the trip?'

She wanted to lie. Disowning Richard suddenly seemed an attractive way of dealing with him. She could tell the Australian that they were mere travelling acquaintances, free to move on independently at will, and he might shrug and go back to his seat muttering 'Geez'; but if he didn't, she would have to keep up the charade all the way to Wadi Halfa and maybe even beyond.

'We knew each other.'

'Aw, well, as long as he's got cash, he'll be right.'

'Yes, I'm sure he will.'

'Guess you'll have to hang about in Wadi Halfa and wait for him to show.'

As he spoke, Frances began to see beyond the train to the next stop. Wadi Halfa. The end of the line. The ends of the earth. What would she do when she got there?

'They say it used to be a real nice town before the dam was built, but all that went under Lake Nasser.'

'Yes, I know.'

'And there's not a whole lot to recommend the new place.'

'I know. I've been there.'

'Strewth, it's quiet. I know outback towns with half the population that are twice as lively. When we were coming up from Egypt, I felt like I was on Mars, you know?'

And the Nubians probably thought that's where you came from, too.

'Geez, I was glad to get outta there. Something eerie about the place. Like you're in Purgatory or somewhere. Can't say I'd fancy hanging about there too long.'

'It isn't that bad,' said Frances, knowing it was. The new Wadi Halfa was little more than a collection of flat buildings in the middle of nowhere, a waiting room on the border. Its main *raison d'être* was the ferry to Egypt. She shuddered. Waiting for Richard in Wadi Halfa would be like killing time in limbo. She had only two books with her, *The Magus* and *Slow Boats to China*, both recently read. She bit her lip. Even with the company of John Fowles and Gavin Young, she did not relish the prospect of lingering in Wadi Halfa. The loneliness, the boredom, the heat, the flies and the cockroaches would make for an intolerable concoction when mixed with the worry that when the next train eventually arrived, Richard would not be on it. After the ferry sailed, she would be the only foreigner left in the place, and what would she do, day after day, restricted to her room by the furnace beyond its walls, with such a lot to fret about?

The Australian was reading her mind. 'I suppose you'd be all right in the hotel there, would you?'

'Of course. It's not very grand, but it gets you out of the sun. And the Nubians are lovely.'

'Aw yeah, the people are good, but that's not much help if you don't speak the lingo. And what if you got appendicitis or something?'

'Oh, for God's sake, it isn't Timbuktu!'

'Too right. Timbuktu's quite a busy little town, or so I've heard.'

'So if I get appendicitis, I'll die the lonely death of a traveller. What of it?'

Her tone drove all that ghoulish fascination into silence.

Frances looked at her reflection in the window. Behind her, the compartment had become an alien place. What had happened to her lovely train, she wondered, to the ramshackle express trundling across this bleak plain – the only part of the earthly canvas, Richard had joked, which God had failed to paint on? What had happened to this compartment, which only the night before had seen some consummate loving? It added to the torture, but her mind insisted on restaging what had happened at three that morning, when the train had made one of its unscheduled, unexplained stops. While many passengers disembarked to get some horizontal sleep on the cool desert grit, Frances had sat on the carriage steps and watched Richard wander out of sight, into the darkness, as into another room. Some way from the train, he later told her, he had lain down and stared at a galaxy so busy with stars that he felt himself lift off the ground. It was like levitating far from earth, he said. When a whistle pierced the mute night and voices called out to friends to alert them, he came back quite giddy, a little ecstatic even, about his extraterrestrial experience, and as the train continued on its way, he shuffled Frances into their compartment. Kissing her as if he were drawing her into his bloodstream, he lifted her shirt over her head while closing the door with his heel. Then he hoisted her onto the top berth and joined her there. The berth was narrow. They giggled at first, about the madness of cavorting on a train in the middle of the Nubian Desert in ninety-degree heat, but the love-making that followed put them out of reach of everything else, which was exactly where Frances liked to be. When they peaked, together, they tossed one another about in a passion that almost threw them off the berth.

Making love on the Nile Valley Express was the kind of unlikely experience Frances fed on, lived on. When she woke the next morning and remembered that she was giving up this way of life, it served only to bring on melancholy again, and that insidious resentment. While Richard spent the day trying to kill the long hours, Frances attempted to draw them into infinity. She stared out, aloof and irritable, until her reproachful mood drove him into a fury.

'Would you like me to get you more tea?'

Richard vanished; the Australian picked up her glass.

'Why is everyone getting me tea?' she snapped.

'Aw, beg your pardon.'

'No, it's ... I'm sorry. I just ...'

'No worries.'

'Tea would be lovely, thanks.'

He beamed at her and left. Frances was glad to be rid of him. She didn't want tea, or pity, or anything other than to see Richard standing in the doorway, and she wanted that so badly she felt as though her body was splintering into little sharp pieces.

The Nubian gentleman wandered past, hands clasped behind his back. Frances called her thanks to him: 'Shoukran!' He smiled. She didn't want him to think that she had forsaken his quiet support for the brash company of one of her own. He moved on. She put her hands over her eyes. It was as if she had fallen asleep in one life and woken in another, and for all her experience, for all her knowledge of the world, she didn't know what to do. In no mood for small talk, she dreaded the return of the Australian, and yet knew she should be glad of it. She had long since learned that those who travel alone best survive on the impromptu friendships of people whom they might never see again, and that, it seemed, was what she was now doing – travelling alone. When he did return with her tea, she made an effort to smile.

'Where you headed?' He plonked down on the bench opposite and put one sandaled foot on the seat beside her. Scraggy dark hair fell across his unshaven face. He clearly thought he should stay with her.

'I don't know,' said Frances. She wanted to appear in control, but suspected she actually looked like a wounded animal, utterly bemused. 'We were on our way back to Cairo, but now ...'

'I can't believe he let himself get stranded like that. It's pretty bloody bleak out there, eh?'

Frances looked at him. No matter how hard he tried, he couldn't conceal his amazement that a Western tourist could be so careless as to miss his only means of escape from such a wilderness. Every time he opened his mouth, he voiced her worst thoughts.

'And it's not as if these trains are regular. Sudanese timetables have a logic all of their own!'

To block him out, Frances closed her eyes and, without really meaning to, tried to imagine herself at home. Funny that she should think of Dublin, that the home she had spent five years running from should suddenly seem like a haven. She imagined herself standing at Seapoint, looking towards Howth. It was cool there, breezy, as it would be now, in late April.

'There you are!'

Frances jumped, but when she opened her eyes all she saw was another pair of tanned legs with more sun-bleached hairs. The other Australian.

'You fell asleep,' said his pal, 'so I went for a wander.' He turned to Frances. 'This is Rod.'

She nodded. 'Hi.'

'And I'm Joel.'

'Frances Dillon.'

Rod sat down. He was marginally neater than his friend, but with blonde hair and earnest blue eyes he looked like a surfer who had wandered too far from the sea.

'Her bloke got off and missed the train,' said Joel.

'He what?'

'Missed it, looks like.'

Rod grimaced. 'You're kidding?'

Frances looked away.

'Where? The stations out here are just like big beehives.'

'Abu Hamed,' said Joel.

'Fair go?' Rod was looking at Frances.

'So I'm told. I was asleep.'

'Wasn't Abu Hamed that place where the line leaves the river?' Joel asked Rod. 'Where we took a walk?'

'Yeah.'

Frances sat up. 'You did? You got off too? But then you must have seen him!'

'Aw, the place was heaving,' said Joel.

'But he'd stand out! I mean, you must have noticed him on the platform?'

'There's the population of a small island travelling on this train,' said Rod. 'Add to that every man, woman and child in a fifty-mile radius trying to flog stuff and you've got an awful lot of people.'

'But that explains how he missed the train! He must have strolled too far and then got caught up in the crowds.'

Rod glanced at his mate. 'Guess so.'

'What?' said Frances. 'What is it?'

'Well, it's just … it's not like this is an easy train to miss.'

'Yeah,' said Joel. 'We had plenty of time to get back on, what with all the whistles going, and it gets moving real slow – gives the roofies a chance to climb aboard.'

'I know that. Don't you think I know that? But that must be what happened because someone saw him getting off in Abu Hamed!'

'Saw him get off, yeah,' said Joel, 'but maybe they didn't see him get back on again?'

'So where is he?' Rod asked his pal.

'If you ask me, he's probably up on the roof smoking something interesting.'

34

'The roof!' Frances hadn't thought about that. Hundreds of passengers travelled, were allowed to travel, on the roofs of these carriages. She stood up and paced, terrified, impatient. The people on the roof had fascinated Richard, but she hadn't let him go up there in case he fell off. If he had wanted to get away from her, that was the obvious place to go. 'I should have gone up there today. You should have said this to me earlier, made me go up to look for him! Why didn't I think of it sooner? It's too dark now; we wouldn't see a thing!'

'No need to throw a wobbly,' said Joel.

'But what if he falls off? Nobody would know. The train would carry on without him.'

'He'll be right,' said Joel.

'Yeah,' said Rod. 'I mean, if that's where he is and he knows what's good for him, he'll be down soon.'

Frances wrung her hands. Would Richard really do it? Would he climb onto the roof, his knapsack impeding him, and stay there for hours? Did he have it in him to torture her like this? Was he that nasty? No. This was like being tossed about in a tumble-dryer. Round and round in blasting hot air, suffocation and desperation tying her up like a rag into a knot.

'Why don't we keep you company while we have our dinner?' suggested Joel.

'Sorry?'

'We could eat in here, if you like, and keep you company till he comes back.'

Frances relented. If Richard didn't show up, it was going to be a long night, and in the dim, flickering light there would be little to do but talk. She certainly wouldn't sleep.

At the small table by the window, the Australians had their picnic: unleavened bread, boiled eggs, and fruit bought in Khartoum the day before. Frances asked how they had cooked the eggs.

'They boiled them for us down in the restaurant car. Want one?'

'No, thanks.' Her stomach was churning, but she nibbled on a biscuit and drank water as warm as the ambient temperature made it.

'I hope we sleep better tonight,' said Joel. 'Neither of us slept a wink last night in this heat.'

'You should try second class for size,' said Frances. 'It may be hot up here, but it's hot and crowded and noisy down there. Kids everywhere. Hard seats.'

Rod cracked an egg against the window and turned to Frances. 'So, are you going to Cairo?'

She nodded. 'Yeah, we were heading straight back, more or less. We did most of the sights on the way up, apart from Abu Simbel.'

'We did the opposite. Came straight to Sudan to get here before the real heat set in, and then we'll stop in Aswan and Luxor on the way home.'

Frances found it hard to concentrate. She wished she could just sit, saying nothing; being nothing. Instead, she struggled to make chat, knowing that the facts lay quietly, waiting their moment. Although she could not yet do it, she would ultimately have to accept that Richard had left her. It was comforting to pretend that he was lying on the roof, staring at the stars, feeling weightless, but beneath this survival tactic she had every reason to believe that he had absconded, leaving her with no recourse to him. He had gagged her, and she was choking on it.

She still had no idea what to do, but for the moment the train took care of that. It went on, squeaking and stumbling, and she went on with it. Until they pulled into Wadi Halfa the next morning there was little more for her to do, and there was some relief to be found in that. No decisions could be made, which was just as well, because before she decided what to do, she had to decide what exactly Richard had done.

'Where you from?' asked Joel.

'Ireland. Dublin.'

'We never got to Ireland when we were in Europe,' he said. 'I've heard it's a beaut place, but.'

'Yes, it's very … fresh.'

Rod sighed. 'Fresh sounds real good right now.'

There it was again. Ireland. Prodding Frances in the ribs like an invisible companion. Fresh, yes. Cool. Bright, also. 'And you're from?'

'Australia,' said Joel proudly.

'Actually, I had figured that out. I mean what part?'

'I'm from Wagga Wagga, and Rod here's from Queanbeyan. We're cousins. He's just finished uni and I've done my apprenticeship, so we decided to go overseas before getting jobs.'

'But aren't you a bit off the beaten track? The great Australian pilgrimage doesn't usually take in the Sudan, does it?'

'Not usually,' said Rod, 'but I've always wanted to see the Nile. When I was a kid, I loved reading about all those expeditions to locate the source of the Nile, and when I heard you could see the confluence of the Blue and the White in Khartoum, I just had to come this extra bit.'

'Bloody mad, if you ask me,' said Joel.

'You weren't disappointed when you got there?' asked Frances.

'Aw, it was a bit mucky, I suppose, a bit dull, but standing right between the Blue and the White Nile, that was really something.'

Frances smiled. An unreconstituted romantic, like herself.

'What about you?' Rod asked. 'What brought you down here?'

'I wanted to ride the Flying Camel.'

'The what?'

'This train. It's sometimes called the Flying Camel.'

'You like this dust bucket?' Joel asked.

'I love all trains. One day I hope to do the Indian Pacific.'

'What's that?'

'It crosses Australia, from Perth to Sydney.'

'I suppose you've even done the Trans-Siberian, have you?' Rod asked.

'Absolutely. All eight days of it.'

'Eight days. Strewth,' said Joel. 'Are you mad or something?'

'I hope so.'

'What's the big attraction to trains?'

'The seats face each other.'

'Eh?'

'The seats face each other. On every other form of transport, the seats all face in the same direction, but on most trains you sit opposite people, looking at them, being looked at by them. You can see their expressions, their taste in food, their choice of reading, and because they can't avoid one another, people talk. Even if they don't speak the same language, they somehow communicate, and there's plenty of time to get beyond pleasantries. There's always time on a train.'

'A lot too much of it, if you ask me,' Joel grumbled.

'Add to that the fact that you're constantly moving forward – well, nothing can beat it.'

'You've got it bad,' said Rod.

Frances smiled. 'People with passions live longest, you know.'

'Really?'

'So I'm told.'

'That's good,' said Joel. 'I have a few passions of my own.'

I'll bet, thought Frances. *Girls and surfboards.*

Joel pulled out his Walkman, slid in a tape and stretched out on the seat, eyes closed. He grimaced as he listened, his fingers waving with the beat.

'What's he listening to?' Frances asked. 'The Sex Pistols?'

Rod was standing by the door, looking up and down the corridor. 'Debussy probably.'

'Debussy?'

Rod grinned and sat down. 'Yeah.'

There was something in his smile, an unexpected intimacy, which made Frances feel calmer. 'What were you studying at college?'

'Oceanography.'

'You're a long way from the sea, Mr Oceanographer.'

'Na. You're never far from the sea. Just check out the fossils.' He got up and went to the door again. He looked out, and then turned to her. 'Why is it that I'm the one who's popping up and down like a jack-in-the-box? I'm not the one who's lost my boyfriend.'

Frances turned to the window.

'If you don't mind my saying so, you don't exactly look like you're expecting him. You don't really believe he's on the roof, do you?'

'No, but I hope to God he is. The alternative is too …'

'But you'd want to be crazy to get stuck in one of these desert towns. Crazy or tied up.'

'I know.'

'Maybe he *was* tied up?'

'What?'

'You know, arrested or something.'

'Don't be ridiculous. The Sudan is pro-Western. It has to be – Nimeiri has a foreign debt the size of Nubia; he needs tourists. And there are so few of us coming here, the last thing they'd do is hassle a guy as inoffensive as Richard.'

'Are you sure? The security police are a bit shady.'

'But they've no reason to arrest him. They wouldn't want an international incident on their hands.'

'Does he have any dope on him?'

'No. Look, he just got left behind, all right?'

'Maybe,' said Rod, 'but I wouldn't miss this train if my life depended on it, and you know why? Because out here my life would depend on it, which is why I wouldn't be so shit-thick as to miss it in the first place.'

'Thanks. That's very reassuring.'

'On the other hand, I wouldn't stay up on the roof for hours either.'

'You might,' said Frances, 'if you had good reason.'

'Like?'

'He … we had a bit of a fight. Well, maybe not *a bit* of a one.

Maybe *absolutely colossal* would be more accurate. I'm surprised you didn't hear us.'

'Oh.'

'Richard might need time to himself.'

'Yeah, but he'd hardly go off up to Fresh Air class and stay there without telling you, would he?'

'How would I know? Four hours ago, I was sitting here with Richard and now I'm sitting here without him. What am I supposed to make of that?'

'What's your gut telling you?' Rod sat down by the door.

'My gut is too strangled to tell me anything. He might be up on the roof, sulking. He might also have missed the train … deliberately.'

'Deliberately? Shit.' Rod took off his watch, put it on his raised knee. 'Things must have been bad.'

Frances lifted her bare foot and twisted it about. 'Things must have been … worse than I thought.'

'You been together long?' Rod was digging, gently. Offering an opening, an ear, should she want one.

Frances needed little prompting. In truth, she wanted nothing more than to talk about Richard, to tell the tale and see if a fresh set of eyes might throw light on her predicament. So she told Rod about how they had met in Germany, three summers before, and had travelled down to Greece to go island-hopping in the Aegean. 'When Richard went back to college in Dublin that autumn, I went to live in Turkey, but I moved on a few months later – there wasn't enough railway to keep me in the Near East – and ended up in India, where I put down enough railway miles to take me twice around the world. The Dehra Dun Express, the Flying Mail, the Shimla Queen … the Ganga Yamuna Express and the Jorhat Loop … the Trivadrum Kerala Express …' She smiled at Rod. 'Those are the kind of words I like to live with.'

'But what did you live *on*?'

'I got some money when Dad died, so I travelled on that, but whenever I stopped somewhere, I taught English for a living. Twice a year, during the holidays, Richard came out and toured around with me.'

'Nice life.'

'Yeah, it was. But Richard's working now, he qualified last year and got a job in London, so he only gets four weeks' leave a year and he doesn't want to spend them like this.' She waved around the dim compartment.

'Ah,' said Rod, nodding. 'Making him a bit ratty, was it?'

'I was the one who was ratty. Richard's been hassling me to go home for ages – you know, to put my rucksack away in his closet – so eventually I compromised and moved to Rome, to be closer. But that wasn't good enough, apparently. A few months ago, Richard threw down an ultimatum: him or the world.'

'And?'

'I caved in, but only on condition we'd do this trip first.'

Eyes tight shut, Joel sat forward and began playing an imaginary cello between his legs. Frances noticed that he had long, thin fingers. She looked quizzically at Rod. 'You're not going to tell me he plays the cello?'

'Double bass. Bloody good at it too.'

She shook her head. 'I had him all wrong.'

'Most people do. But when he says he's finished his apprentice-ship, he actually means scholarship.' Rod strapped his watch back onto his wrist. 'So why the fight?'

'I was getting nervous. It makes me shudder, the thought of living in London, and what on earth am I going to do there? Richard's okay – he's got a career, friends – but I'll be starting from scratch. All these years I've spent abroad might amount to nothing in England.'

'You could teach.'

'I'd be up against people with all the right qualifications. My CV isn't very impressive. It looks like a Thomas Cook timetable.'

'You'll find something.'

'Maybe, but I don't really want to. I never fancied marriage or career or any of the other bloody adhesives people like to smother themselves in, and my time isn't up yet – or wouldn't be, if it weren't for Richard, so I was making him pay.' She glanced at the door. 'The price I was exacting must have been too high.'

'I don't get it. If you'll hate it so much, why did you give in?'

'Because I love the bastard.'

Joel pulled off his Walkman, opened his eyes and became Joel again, the Aussie backpacker-musician who spoke like a trucker. He smiled. 'What's wrong with you two?'

Rod got up, checked the corridor. 'What's wrong? Mate, have you forgotten her boyfriend's gone missing?'

'Sorry.'

'You really think he might have stayed back deliberately?' Rod asked. 'He'd have to be mad.'

'He was mad. Very mad.'

'Why?' Joel asked.

'They'd had a fight.'

'And it's not as if he wanted to be here. He only came along because—'

'Because he had no choice,' said Joel, nodding wisely. 'Yeah. Like me. I know how he feels. Sitting in this thing for days without so much as a cold beer. Tell you what, it's no wonder he got shirty.'

Rod looked at Frances. 'He has a point. You'd do crazy things in this heat.'

'I know.'

The Australians invited themselves to spend the night in her compartment and slept soundly on the upper berths. Frances tried to sleep, but the oblivion she sought wouldn't come, and she spent long stretches sitting on the floor in the corridor looking through the low window at the sky. When the train drew silently to a stop sometime after midnight, her heart began to race. They were not at a station, they were not anywhere, but this halt gave her an opportunity. She went to the door and climbed down. The night was not as enrapturing as the previous one. It was blacker, if that was possible, and the stationary coaches, dormitories in the wild, stood witness to her desperation when she walked alongside them, calling out.

'Richard? Are you up there? Rich?'

Disembarked passengers, some of them lying on the ground, looked at her, but she moved on. 'Richard!'

That last call came out in such a screech that she alarmed even herself and shut up. She climbed back into her carriage, longing for the night to end, and for hours afterwards lay rigidly on her berth, unable even to rest her eyelids, which flickered with every pulse of her overwrought mind. When the train set off again she listened to the muffled clatter of the bogies, hoping that their rhythm might lull her to sleep. Instead, she heard something else. Words: Richard's voice, in the undercarriage. She tried to decipher the mantra of the wheels as they chattered and rolled along the narrow gauge, but the words remained unclear, like a whisper not quite loud enough, until finally she fell asleep. She woke to see Richard sitting opposite her. Then she woke again, properly. It was not yet dawn. Her throat hurt. She couldn't even stretch. She was too sore to move, too stunned, and her sand-ridden clothes scraped her skin. For years, she had dreamed of waking at dawn in the Nubian Desert on the Nile Valley Express, but now even the memory of the southbound trip would be tarnished and bitter to remember. There would be no separating Richard from it, and it from Richard.

'Joel, wake up!'

'Aw, what?'

'The roof,' said Frances. 'Are you game to go up? See if you can see Richard?' Strange, she thought, how hope would not be quashed by reason.

Joel stretched. 'You really think he'd spend the night up there?'

'I need to be sure he didn't.'

'Oh well, I guess the sunrise'll look pretty good.'

'Thanks.'

They woke Rod and went to the open door at the end of the carriage. It was tricky. There wasn't much light yet, and even though the train ambled along at no great speed, it shuddered unpredictably. The first shove from Rod sent Joel out instead of up and he landed spread-eagled between the two carriages, which made him laugh.

'All righty,' he said, finding a foothold, 'givez another shove.' With a push from Rod, he hauled himself onto the roof and sat on the edge. 'There's hundreds of them up here. What's he wearing?'

'Khaki trousers and a green shirt.'

Joel looked around. 'Crikey, they're saying their prayers! Oh, and wow, look at that sun.'

Frances turned to Rod. 'Get me up there.'

'No way.'

'I won't stand up; I just want to have a look.'

'Yeah, and if I drop you, you'll fall under the wheels.'

'I've got strong arms. I used to row. I can pull myself up if you'll just give me a push.' She lifted her foot.

He shook his head, but put his hands beneath her foot. The train shuddered, throwing them both sideways. Rod caught her. 'This is mad. I'm not doing it.'

Joel was standing upright on the next carriage. 'I'll head off this way,' he called, pointing towards the engine, 'see if this mad Irishman is up here.'

'Rod, please! I have nothing left to lose.'

It was precarious. She clung to the rim of the door as he lifted her, but she could not reach the roof and her hands fumbled about, trying to get a grip on something else as her toe found Joel's foothold. 'It's no good. I can't. Get me down.'

Suddenly, she was hauled upwards. One of the roof passengers had reached down, taken her wrists and hoisted her aloft. She found herself sitting on the edge of the carriage, her legs dangling above the couplings, while a great dark face, swathed in a white turban, nodded at her and grinned a huge toothy smile. 'You are up!'

'Yes, thank you. Thank you.'

He stepped past her, hands clasped behind his back, as if taking a breezy stroll along a ship's deck, and moved on.

Her fingers gripped the roof. 'Mistake. Mistake!'

'Typical,' called Rod, 'now she wants to get down again. What do you think I am, a human elevator?'

'Help!'

'Here.' He stood between the two carriages. 'Ease yourself onto my shoulders. Gimme your feet.'

'Can't. Can't move! Oh God, I'm sitting on top of an express train!'

'Express? Are you kidding? Can you see Joel?'

'No.'

'Well, of course you can't. He isn't down here, is he? You know what they say about heights – don't look down. Look up.'

'Can't.' Rod grabbed her ankle. 'Don't touch me!'

'Going to stay there all the way to Wadi Halfa, are you?'

'If I have to.'

'Mad woman.'

Frances lifted her head slowly, as if looking up would make her situation even more precarious, and as she did so, her fear drained away. The train stretched out, behind and ahead, as though she were riding on the back of a large and benevolent caterpillar. Sand flew alongside, like ribbons in a funnel; it pinched her face and made her eyes water, and the warm wind stung her arms, but exhilaration caught hold of her. The sun had already let go of the earth and its crimson shade was fading as it grew smaller, but Frances was transfixed. She had seen some sunrises in her time, many more spectacular than this, but none from the roof of a moving train.

She looked around. The morning prayer had come to an end. Some of the roof passengers were putting away their prayer mats, others were sipping tea, but most were stretched horizontally across the roof, wrapped in shroud-like sheets, showing only feet. Two carriages away, Joel moved diffidently, his arms braced, his hands stretched out, stepping over the reclined bundles, apologizing as he went. At the end of that coach he crossed paths with the tea man, who came along with a kettle and glasses, stopping to pour for customers. Both ends of the train shimmered in the early haze. It was cool there now, but when the sun moved up it would be like lying under a grill.

Still gripping the roof edge, Frances felt good. It seemed impossible, wrong even, to feel so good, to allow herself to be lifted beyond what had happened in the carriage beneath her, and yet the stress of all that was being blown away. Her heart expanded from its shrunken state to beyond normal size, and soared. 'Wo!' she called out. Some passengers uncovered their mouths and flashed their teeth at her delight. 'This is fantastic,' she cried to Rod. 'This is it!'

'Hang on, I'm coming up.'

She brought her feet up and moved away from the edge as he scrambled onto the carriage.

Joel was coming back towards them. 'I wish I had my bass. Imagine playing up here!'

Rod helped Frances to her feet. Her legs shook, but balance took over, and when Joel joined them, they stood in a circle, gripping one another's arms, their hair flying, their clothes billowing. This was an amiable beast they stood on; it had no inclination to throw them off its back, and even when it stumbled, they stayed upright.

'Unbelievable!' Frances called out.

They were smiling, her Aussies, and she was smiling, laughing, gliding, on the day after Richard had left her. There was no sense in it. They turned around, hooking their elbows together to keep them steady, and faced out to the desert, and Frances knew there would be no exceeding this. At last, she had reached the perfect pitch of living she had sought for so long. She had achieved transcendence. This culmination of pain and pleasure, of passion and sense, would validate her, and stay with her forever. It would always remind her that whatever had happened, whatever had been forsaken, there had been a moment like this. A high like this. And it would not be lost in circumstance. She would not allow Richard to steal it from her, to spike her exaltation, no matter what he had done or why he had done it.

3

They pulled into Wadi Halfa after eight. Frances was first off; she raced across the dirt in the hope of finding a vantage point from which she could watch every soul who came off that train. It was impossible. The travelling thousands swamped her, and the women's vividly coloured veils and cottons blowing in the breeze made the station look like an open-air drapery. Richard could have been swept through the crowd without her even knowing.

She despondently followed the Australians to the nearest hotel, where it took some time for rooms to be allocated. The combination of the train pulling in and the ferry arriving from Egypt made this a busy time for the hotel – a bare collection of yellow and blue corridors and courtyards – and the manager asked Frances if she would mind sharing with a Swedish student who had checked in some days before. She said no, and was shown across the courtyard to a dim room where a young woman was lying on one of two beds.

'Sorry about this,' said Frances, assuming that, like most Scandinavians, the Swede would have a good grasp of English. 'It seems we have to share. I hope you don't mind?'

'It's okay. I'm glad to see you.' The woman spoke to Frances as if she knew her, was expecting her even. Often, there was an immediate intimacy when women met, especially on the road. 'So, the train has arrived?'

Frances dumped her bag beside the second bed. 'Yeah, and the ferry's in too?'

'Yes, it leaves tomorrow.'

48

'Damn.' A delayed ferry would have kept the Australians in town. The young woman rolled onto her side. There was a sluggishness about her that seemed rather more severe than the general heat-induced languor everyone else displayed.

'You're heading to Khartoum, are you?' Frances asked, thinking her roommate didn't look fit to be travelling any deeper into Africa.

'No, I'm going the other way – north, to Cairo. With my brother and his friend. And you? You're taking the boat?'

'No.'

'Why not?'

Frances flaked out on the rickety steel bed. 'I've lost my boyfriend. Somewhere between here and Khartoum. I have to wait till he turns up.'

'Oh. That's good.'

Frances turned to look at her.

'I mean, we'll be company for each other,' said the Swede.

'How come? I thought you were going to Egypt?'

'Not yet.'

It was Frances's turn to ask, 'Why not?'

'I'm sick. Dysentery. I don't want to be sick on that boat.'

'Oh … Well, I know the loos can be fairly unpleasant, but it's hardly a good reason to miss the ferry, is it?'

'There'll be another one.'

'Not for days. A week even.' Frances sat up. This girl looked dreadful. She lay on the bed in a T-shirt, a slight thing too thin for comfort, her short blonde hair stuck to her head with sweat. 'How long have you been like this?'

'It doesn't stop. I don't eat and still it doesn't stop. For weeks now. I think I might die in Wadi Halfa.'

Frances came over and sat on the end of her bed. She tried to smile. 'I'm Frances, by the way.'

'Lena.'

They shook hands. Lena's grip was limp, but she held Frances's hand for longer than necessary. Frances squeezed her fingers. 'Lena, you can't stay here. I mean, this isn't exactly four-star accommodation, and you'll be fine on the ferry. Block yourself up with Imodium and once you get to Aswan you can find a doctor. The conditions here will just aggravate the dysentery.'

Lena looked towards the window, as if to stop herself from crying.

Frances wondered how long she had been lying here like this. 'Do you know what I mean by Imodium? It's an anti-diarrhoea pill. Works wonders.'

'I don't have any.'

'I do.'

Lena shook her head.

'Take some of mine and—'

'No.'

'Why not? They'll get you to Egypt no bother.'

'I can't.'

'Of course you can. If you want to recover, you'll have to take that boat.'

'No. I can hardly make it to the bathrooms here. On the boat it would be impossible. Two nights and two days – I can't.'

'Get a cabin and use a bucket.'

Lena's eyes widened.

Frances shrugged. 'Desperate situations require desperate remedies.'

'I'll stay here. It will stop eventually. It must. At least I can lie still. At least I don't have to move.'

Frances stared at her. She had to get through to this woman, persuade her to leave Wadi Halfa. She didn't know much about her, but in the turning of a door handle, this slight person had become her responsibility. If she didn't get her to Egypt, the consequences could be dire.

'No, you must try to get home, or to Cairo at least. If the dysentery hasn't cleared up yet, the chances are it needs something more than just lying still and starving yourself. You'll become seriously ill if you stay here.'

'I'm not getting on that boat.'

'But why? Because of a few grotty loos? You won't catch anything you haven't already got!'

'I don't care. I'm not going.'

The more determination Lena displayed, the more resolute Frances became. 'Listen to me. I know what it's like to be sick and frightened. It happened to me once in Tunisia. I became dehydrated on a bus trip and by the time we got to Tozeur, this oasis in the desert, I had double vision, a fever, and such a bad headache I thought I was dying.'

'But then you got better.'

'Yes, but I know how you feel and staying here isn't—'

'You don't know.'

'For God's sake, Lena! Why are you being so stubborn?'

'And why are you being so …'

'Bossy? Because I'd rather be bossy than stupid.'

Now they were arguing like sisters; necessity had made their friendship sudden, and sturdy.

'Bossy? What's this?'

'It means I'm telling you what to do. And I'll go on telling you until you do it. Look, you'll have to leave eventually and then you'll be even weaker. Dysentery doesn't go away on a whim. It needs treatment.'

Lena shook her head, her mouth turned down with miserable determination.

'How long have you been here?'

'A week.'

'So you've already let one ferry go?'

'Yes.'

'But what about your brother and his friend? Don't they want to get out of here? There's nothing for them to do and it's going to get much hotter. Take Imodium and—'

'I'm pregnant.'

Frances gasped.

Lena put her arm over her eyes. 'I'll lose it out on the lake. I know it.'

'Why? Why would you lose it?'

'The dysentery. Weeks of dysentery.'

'No. No, you won't miscarry. You're just worrying because you've been cooped up in here for days feeling lousy with nothing better to think about.'

'I'll lose it if I move. On that boat.'

'Don't be silly. You'll be fine.'

'I'm bleeding already.'

'Oh, God.'

'Not much, but it's the beginning; I know it is. I had a friend who lost a baby. It was horrible.'

'All the more reason to take the bloody ferry!'

'And what if it happens out there? All that time on all that water. I could bleed to death.'

'You could bleed to death here! If you take the ferry, you'll be in hospital in Aswan in two days at the latest. Otherwise it's back to Khartoum on that train, which would knock any baby off its perch. And if the train broke down, you'd be stuck out in that wilderness—'

'Lake Nasser is a wilderness.'

'Maybe, but it's smooth and it's on the way home.'

Lena shook her head.

Frances wanted to say, 'Don't be so thick!' but Lena looked so wretched, she could only take her hand. 'You won't miscarry on the boat, Lena, and you must get out of Wadi Halfa.'

Frances brought two glasses of sweet tea back to the room. She had to get Lena to drink and she didn't have much of her own bottled water left.

Lena sat up to take the tea. 'You're not English, are you?'

'No.' Frances sat on her own bed, cooling her back against the blue wall. 'Irish. How pregnant are you?'

'Eleven weeks, I think.'

'Good God. What the hell are you doing in the blinking Sahara then?'

'We were travelling overland from Cape Town to Cairo. I found out in Tanzania.'

'Look, I'd better find a doctor. There must be some kind of medic in this town.'

'No!'

'But you need help.'

'No. Per, my brother, doesn't know about the baby.'

Frances sighed. No wonder Lena had been pleased to see her. 'Why not?'

'I can't tell him and you must not either. He's so worried already, he'll be very frightened if he knows I'm pregnant. He's only nineteen. Also … he is gay, and he loves Fredrik too. He thought that was why Fredrik agreed to travel with us. Because of him.'

'But it was because of you?'

'Yes.'

'And he doesn't know about you two?'

'He does know, and he's very unhappy about it, and now with the baby …'

'But if he knew the full story, he might talk some sense into you.'

'No, please. Not yet. He will be so worried and then that is another problem for me. I can't …'

'Yeah, I see. I understand.' Lena was scarcely coping with her own fears, Frances realized, and could not be expected to carry her brother's as well. 'All right,' she said, 'so why don't I find a local mid-wife? She'd have some African treatment for threatened miscarriage, herbs and stuff, which you could take just in case.' Or, she thought, a sedative that would last long enough to get Lena on to the boat.

'There'd be … excitement. People coming, going.'

Frances raised her chin. Lena had worked herself into a state beyond reason. 'I'll make a deal with you then. I won't tell your brother about the baby, if you promise to take the ferry tomorrow.'

Lena's eyes snapped on to her. 'That's not a deal. That is …' she struggled to find the words, 'threatening!'

'If that's what it takes, then yes, I am threatening you, because I'm going to get you out of here if it's the last sensible thing I do!'

They didn't speak for a while and in the thick afternoon heat, distracted at last from her own problems, Frances slept.

When she woke, Lena was returning from another visit to the lavatories at the end of the block. She collapsed onto her bed and rolled over to face Frances. 'I was wondering when you were asleep, how did you lose your boyfriend?'

They talked. There was nothing else to do. It was too hot to move. The hotel was quiet; everyone sheltering from the mid-afternoon assault. In their dim, bare room, Lena and Frances endured a few more hours of stillness together.

Some time after five, Frances went out and found water in large ceramic pots in an alcove; she brought some back to the room, washed herself, and then helped Lena to wash and change.

Collapsing back on her pillow, Lena sighed. 'Oh, that feels very nice. Thank you.'

'Would you mind if I went for a walk?'

'Of course not.'

'I just have to work myself into the idea of staying here until the next train comes.'

'At least you know now you'll have company.'

'I don't want your company, Lena. I want you and your baby to take that boat.'

She went in search of the Australians. Their laughter drew her to their room, where they were lying on their beds, spinning yarns to pass the time.

'Have you seen a couple of Swedish lads around anywhere?' she asked.

'Strewth,' said Joel, 'she's lost another two!'

'Sorry,' said Rod.

Most of the doors were open because of the heat. Per and Fredrik were a few rooms down, also lying on their beds. It was easy to tell one from the other. Per was slight and fair and very like his sister, while Fredrik – well, Frances could see the problem. She immediately understood why both brother and sister had fallen for him. It wasn't so much his looks – a light beard, straight brown hair and dark brown eyes – as his manner. The way he held himself, looked at you. He was the kind of man who, even in the bleakest situation, would make anyone think about sex. Without knowing who she was, he welcomed Frances into the room.

'I'm sharing a room with Lena,' she explained, 'and if you don't mind my butting in—'

'I'm sorry?'

'Look, we must persuade her to leave. The ferry tomorrow could be her last chance – if she doesn't get help soon, she'll become dangerously dehydrated.'

There was clearly no need to tell them so; both men looked haggard with worry.

'She needs to drink,' Frances urged, 'to keep fluids in her system. She needs a hospital.'

'Yes, but … she won't.' Fredrik's English was not as good as Lena's, but his truncated description of her frame of mind was exact.

'It isn't her decision anymore. Per, you must take responsibility. You must insist. She needs medicine.'

Fredrik translated. They talked amongst themselves, then promised to speak to Lena again, but they seemed to have lost all hope of ever escaping the Sudan.

'Meanwhile, one of you should go to the market and buy her soft drinks. You know, fizzy drinks. They're full of sugar and the fluids will help.'

'Yes,' said Fredrik. 'I'll go.'

Frances pulled her scarf over her head and went out into the dusty, single-storeyed town. The many people who were waiting for the train or the ferry were beginning to emerge from the afternoon torpor and shuffle around the stalls buying provisions for their journeys.

Preoccupied with Lena, Frances had to force herself to concentrate on her own situation. She had to decide what to do. If Richard had simply gone back to Khartoum to fly home without her, then she should catch the ferry and allow her unexpected freedom to take her away. If, on the other hand, circumstance had come between them, then she must do whatever was necessary to reunite them. She didn't know where Richard was, but he knew where she was, so the most sensible course of action was to stay put and wait. He would probably come on the next train. At worst, it would take a week for the next one to come from Khartoum.

She looked about. There was a remoteness about Wadi Halfa that reflected her situation. Staying there could be an interesting experience, but Lena had rattled her. It was the very isolation of the place that had led Lena into that blind terror. What would it do to Frances, waiting there, stuck somewhere between expectation and heartbreak? What would the flies and the quiet and the loneliness do to her, when she knew that Richard might not come, that her future had been propelled into uncertainty, and her with it? Yet it might only be for a few days. She might sleep through it … or she might get dysentery. Had the old Wadi Halfa not disappeared beneath the waters when the Aswan High Dam was built, the prospect of staying there would have been very different – walks by the river, some swimming maybe, evenings on the balcony of the old hotel on the riverbank … But this. Frances looked back at the new hotel, all walls and dust. A mere bunker from the heat.

She wandered over to the station. The train stood abandoned, waiting to take its next overload back across the desert to Khartoum the following day. Standing by the engine, with her hands on the small of her back, she stared at the dirt on her toes and tried to concentrate her thoughts; she tried to think positively. Richard had strolled too far from the station in Abu Hamed and missed the unmissable train. He had taken his knapsack with him because he wanted to buy stuff, and he had not noticed the commotion around the departing train because ... because he just hadn't! Finding himself stranded, he would have had two options: to stay put and wait for Frances to get back to him, assuming she knew where he was, or to wait for the next train to Wadi Halfa. And there was, of course, that awful third possibility – that he would wait for the next train, not to the border, but away from her, to Khartoum. Frances had to decide which of these choices he would most likely make before she could know what to do herself. She could not imagine him twiddling his thumbs for days in Abu Hamed on the off chance that she would know to find him there. He would have to do something. It seemed most likely that he would follow her to Wadi Halfa, in which case she must sit tight and wait – here, in this suburb of the sun.

The top of her head felt as though one solitary malevolent sunbeam was burning through her scarf and zapping her brain like a laser, causing it to melt in disarray. And yet out of this quagmire came one clear and sweet revelation: whatever Richard decided to do, he would have to wait for this train to do it. It was improbable that he would attempt to get to the border without the railway, since such a trip would take days by bus or truck, even if he could organize one. As it was a single-line track between Wadi Halfa and Abu Hamed, he would have to wait for this train to return there before he could come down on the next one. Therefore this very train – Frances reached out to touch it – was her salvation, because when it returned to Abu Hamed, she would be on it.

This allowed for every contingency. Should Richard be planning to return to Khartoum, he would be standing on the platform at Abu Hamed waiting for the southbound train to pull in, and when it did, he would see Frances hanging out of the window whether he wanted to or not. If, on the other hand, he had already made his way back to Khartoum by some other means, she could stay on the train and follow him there. It should be easy to find him in the capital. He would almost certainly return to the hotel they had stayed in, the Acropole, so she would be able to track him down without much difficulty – unless he had taken the first available flight out of the country. The variables were endless, and exhausting.

She walked beside the express, past the peeling wooden carriages built in grander times, and wondered how she could encase herself in it for the third time in two weeks. She loved trains, but even she had her limits. Could she survive the suffocation? The infamous halts in the middle of nowhere, due to breakdowns or whimsy, with the worry of being stuck for days? Would her system stand up to more tinned beef for breakfast? And to the toilets, the awful, awful toilets? *Yes.* She would think of Richard, not Abu Hamed or Khartoum, as her true destination and that would make every trial worth enduring. All she had to do was survive this train – about which she had held such romantic notions – for another few days.

The last of the thirteen carriages took her some way from the evening hubbub in the town. The sun was dipping, but the landscape still shimmered like an all too solid mirage, and there was no sound. At such a point of silence and nullity, Frances thought, there must be some answer as to why Richard had done this.

There was. As she stood there, leaning her forehead against the burning wooden slats of the last coach, she heard again the mumbled words that had tried to reach her at dawn, but this time she heard them clearly. And then she remembered, and she knew.

That was her answer, as clear as the bleak line that ran across the horizon. There was no need to suffer again the stifling discomfort of the Nile Valley Express; no reason to go searching in the heart of the Sudan for someone who did not wish to be found. She could take the ferry and be with Lena, who needed her, and go on into the familiarities of Egypt where she would not feel so desolate. Remembering the last words Richard had spoken before storming out of their compartment spared her all those difficulties, and she must not allow herself to forget what he had said, or allow hope to block it out.

Her life had been changed in the Sudan; all she could do now was go on.

Camp beds had been erected all over the hotel compound and there were people everywhere, but Frances skipped between beds and bodies until she found the Australians sitting in the shade in the courtyard drinking karkaday.

'Guess what,' said Fran. 'I'm going back!' Her resolve had lasted all of five minutes; she had already changed her mind. She could not possibly go on without Richard, no matter what he had said.

Rod's jaw dropped. 'You're kidding? Back on that train?'

'Why not? I love that train. Besides, we know Richard is in Abu Hamed, so I might as well go to him there as wait for him here.'

'But he might be on his way here,' said Joel.

'Not before our train gets back to Abu Hamed,' said Frances triumphantly. 'It's a single-line track!'

'Aw, right.'

'It leaves tomorrow evening, and I'll be on it.'

'Why didn't you think of this before?' asked Joel.

'She didn't think of it,' said Rod, eyeing her carefully, 'because she reckoned he'd done a runner.'

Frances scowled. 'I wasn't thinking straight, and nor would you be if you woke up and found Joel had disappeared!'

'And if he isn't in Abu Hamed when you get there?'

'I'll carry on to Khartoum.'

'*What?*'

'Geez,' said Joel, 'you'd better get out there then and stock up on water. We could only find five litres. The town's been bought out.'

'I'll use purifiers.'

Rod stood up, brushing dust off his clothes. 'And if you don't find him in Khartoum?'

'I will.'

'What if you *don't?* You'll end up stuck there. You'll have to come all the way back here again to get home.'

'I'll fly out of Khartoum. I won't come back this way.'

'That's fine, if you can afford it. Can you?'

Frances bit her lip. 'That's a risk I'll have to take.'

'So you're nearly broke as well. Good one!'

Joel held up his glass and looked at his pink drink. 'What's this stuff made from?'

'Hibiscus,' said Frances, relieved to escape Rod's glare.

Joel's face screwed up. 'I'm drinking pansy juice?'

'Did you purify that?' Frances asked.

'They said it was made with bottled water.'

'Did you see the bottle?'

Both men looked apprehensively at their drinks.

'I'm taking that train, Rod. At least I'll be doing something, getting somewhere, instead of sitting around in this dustpan. Why stay here when I could be going to where Richard is?'

'To where you *think* he is. Listen, I don't happen to think you should hang around here either, on the off chance he comes back this way. If you want my opinion, you should come to Egypt with us.'

'Egypt? I can't go looking for someone in Egypt who's gone missing in Sudan!'

'You could wait for him there. In Aswan or Cairo. This isn't the kind of country a woman wants to go walkabout, Frances. You don't know for sure where Richard is, or why he's there, or where he's going, but either way, I don't know any bloke who'd want his chick going up and down the Nubian Desert looking for him! Anything could go wrong, and if that train breaks down, you could end up like the Swedish girl. Far better to take the ferry and track Richard down in Cairo, or even back in London if you have to.'

'No! I can't – I *won't* – leave the Sudan without him.'

They had dinner with Per and Fredrik. Joel alone competed with the flies for appetite; the others fiddled with their food, taking occasional mouthfuls. Afterwards, when Rod asked Frances if she fancied a walk, she readily accepted; anything was better than facing the walls of her bare room and the fears that inhabited it. They strolled away from the hotel, along a sandy track with low, mud houses on either side.

'It's very brave of you to go off looking for him,' said Rod. 'And bloody stupid, if you ask me.'

'I'm not asking you.'

'Hope he's worth the hassle.'

'He is.'

'Yeah? Any guy who ups and leaves his chick in the middle of nowhere's got some answering to do.'

'Something must have happened. You said so yourself.'

'Took his bag.'

Frances glowered at him in the darkness.

He turned to her. 'Are you sure you want to swelter away in the desert for another three days just to ask him why? And then find yourself in a big town with your cash running out?'

'Yes,' she said. 'I am.'

He sighed. 'Promise me, then, that if you can't find him, you'll go straight to your embassy to get help.'

'I can't.'

'Why not?'

'Because there *is* no Irish Embassy in Khartoum. The nearest one is in Cairo.'

He threw up his hands. 'Aw, marvellous! This gets better! So who's going to look out for you?'

'I don't need looking out for!'

'But this is all the more reason to come to Egypt. I mean, assuming Richard is looking for you, what's to say he won't get help from the obvious place? The nearest Irish Embassy: Cairo.'

Frances's throat tightened. She ran this over in her mind. What would Richard do? She put her hands over her ears. 'Oh God, I can't think straight anymore. All these whys and ifs and maybes – they're driving me mad!'

'Cairo's your best bet,' Rod repeated earnestly. 'That's where your embassy is. They're the people to deal with this, not you. If anything has happened to Richard, they'll take care of it, and if not, at least you'll know where you stand and you can move on.'

He made it sound so uncomplicated; he was weeks ahead of her.

'Move on? Just like that? I've been with him for three years, and I'll have you know he isn't the shit you seem to think he is!'

'Look, it isn't that I have it in for the guy,' said Rod, 'it's that you're here and he isn't. I can't do anything about him, but I can do something about you and I hate to think of you dragging upriver again without knowing where you'll end up.'

'But that's *my* business, *my* decision.'

'You reckon? You know, you've shrunk since I first saw you at Khartoum Central. You're drying up like a starfish on a hot rock and if you head back alone, only to find Richard's left you high and dry, you'll shrivel up even more, and by then you'll be running out of options. Going back isn't the thing to do. Staying with the pack is always a safer bet when the chips are down, and Richard would say exactly the same thing if he was here, you mark my words. But he isn't here, so I'm saying it for him. He'll track you down if he wants to. All you have to do is not get lost as well.'

Frances looked up at the sky. The constellations glistened so energetically that she felt weary. The walls of her belly seemed to collapse, leaving a void inside her that asked to be addressed. All this was meant to be so different. Had Richard been with her, the stillness would have been peaceful; the cool would have given relief after the dry day; the desert would have been an ally instead of a great black hole that had ingested the man she loved.

Rod nudged her. 'You'd be right in Cairo. Halfway home.'

'Home? Now there's an alien word.'

'How d'you mean?'

'I haven't got one. I told you, I left home years ago.'

'It's still there, though. Everyone has a home.'

'Not everybody needs one.'

'Oh yes they do.' He looked up at the sky, his hands deep in the pockets of his shorts. 'No Southern Cross. A place like this would make a man think of home all right.'

Back in their room, Lena remained resolute.

'Change your mind,' Frances urged.

'Only if you will. You must be mad searching for someone out there. It's almost a thousand kilometres to Khartoum; he could be anywhere. You should wait for him here or leave a message saying you'll meet him in Cairo. Besides, I'll need you on the ferry if I go.'

'No, you won't. At best, it'll take twenty-four hours to get to Aswan.' This, Frances knew, was optimistic. Actual sailing time was no more than eighteen to twenty hours, but some of the boats did not run at night so, depending on which vessel they got and what time it left the port, it could be tied up to the shore for one night or two. *Two nights*, she thought. *Such a long time for a thirsty foetus.* 'You can't pin this on me, Lena. That's not fair. When I walked in here this morning, I thought things were as bad as they could get. Now I know otherwise, but that doesn't mean I can wipe away what has happened to me. If Richard has left me, I have nowhere to go. I've used up my savings, I have no job, no base, no friends. I left all that behind ages ago and the only way back was with Richard, so I can't afford to take a chance on this. If he hasn't left me then I bloody well have to find him, and that means staying in the Sudan. But all I'm trying to save is a relationship – you're dealing with a baby. You have to get the two of you out of here.'

Lena's eyes filled. 'I want to, I do, but I'm frightened of leaving this room. I'll miscarry on that boat – I know it.'

'But even if you do, Fredrik and Per will be with you.'

'What good are they? How would they know what to do?'

'They'll know the same way anyone does when babies come: instinct.'

Nits, heat and an unfamiliar terror kept Frances awake all night. Lena slept fitfully and made several trips along the corridor with her diminishing roll of toilet paper. When she returned to the room just after three and realized Frances was awake, she said, 'Tell me about this Richard. What's he like?'

'Ooh, careful, Lena. I might go on all night.'

'Good. So much better than the silence.'

Frances bunched her pillow up under her elbow and lay facing her friend. 'Right. Well. He's tall, broad. Light brown eyes, dark brown hair, good teeth, and he has a cleft in his chin.'

'What is he, a piece of meat?'

'Hmm. Fillet steak, actually.'

'But what kind of person is he?'

'He's okay. Nice.'

'Nice.'

'Yeah, you know, one of these caring types. Big on social conscience. A member of Greenpeace and Amnesty International, and not averse to the odd sit-in protest if the cause is right. Politically, he's left of centre and—'

'This sounds like a résumé,' said Lena dryly.

'I'm trying to be objective.'

'But it's so boring! Tell me why you're with him, what attracted you.'

'What attracted me was that he's a fine thing.'

'I'm sorry?'

'An FT. You know, a Fine Thing – good-looking. Gorgeous, actually. And he's good company, easygoing, most of the time, thoughtful, kind, perceptive, generous—'

'Okay. Okay. I think I get it.'

'He has these really intense eyes that never look away. He tells me everything I need to know without saying a word, whether in anger or otherwise. One of those steady glances and I get the message every time.'

'Go on.'

'You should get some sleep.'

'I can't sleep. I've been lying here for a week with no one to talk to. Tell me more about Richard and then I'll work out what has happened to him.'

'Well, he's twenty-five, loves the Police and Neil Young, and he's big into Monty Python.'

'So he has a good sense of humour.'

'Of course.'

'I think I like this man.'

'Yeah, well, he isn't perfect. He's very stubborn. You know, determined. If he wants something badly enough, he goes after it until he gets it, but in a very calm way. He just keeps moving forward. I can fluctuate, change my direction, my point of view, and he'll simply nod and wait for me to stabilize.'

'Is he a student?'

'No, an architect. A good one. He has a great future, and great vision about what he wants to achieve, whereas I'm just along for the ride. Ambition wouldn't be one of my outstanding personal traits, but Richard is focused. While I have dreams, he has talent – solid, appreciable talent – which seriously interferes with my life plan.'

'Which is what, your plan?'

'My plan is to have no plan. To be rootless, homeless, and still survive. Richard travels only to be with me. He doesn't need it, like I do, although sometimes it does get to him. Like the other night, he got off the train to look at the sky and it really moved him to find that he could be somewhere and nowhere at the same time, but that's exactly where I've been for years. It's where I always want to be.'

'Ah, you are a dreamer, Frances. Just wait until something nasty happens, and then you'll wake up and be glad to go home.'

'But something nasty has happened and I haven't woken up. I only wish I could,' she sighed, 'because I'm beginning to feel like Winnie.'

'Who's Winnie?'

'A character in *Happy Days*. A play by Beckett. She's buried in sand. Up to her waist in the first act, and up to her neck in the second. But she chatters on regardless, whereas I'm finding it hard to breathe already and the sand is only up to my thighs.' She got up and stood by the window. 'Richard's out there somewhere, Lena. And he thinks I don't love him enough. I love him too much. So much that loving him has curdled me, because there's no love without fear, and fear sours. I tried to outpace it, running all over India as if there were some risk-free destination to be reached, but I couldn't shake it off. No matter where I went, *I still loved Richard* ... And so to the consequences. I kid myself that I dread the settled life back home, but the truth is that I dread losing him. It's so easy for him to love me like this, on the move, in a whirl, but would he feel so enchanted, day by day, with the same four walls around us? The same stained coffee mugs in the sink every morning? If I were no longer tanned, no longer flitting about in sandals and light cotton, if I were pale instead, and wearing vests and woolly socks, would he still love me then? Or would he wonder where Frantic Fran had gone?'

'Any love affair can end, for any reason.'

Frances pulled up the only chair in the room and sat down, grasping from beyond the window what fresh night air she could find. 'You know, when I was in France a few years ago, I visited a medieval castle – somewhere in the Jura – and they brought us into this room, on the edge of which was a ... cavity. A small, enclosed space between the inner and outer wall. And this was where, hundreds of years ago, the Lord had locked up his Lady when he discovered she was having an affair. There was a narrow slit in the outer wall from which she could see woodland on the hill beyond, but her husband had her lover hanged from a tree at the edge of the wood and left his body there for all the time she was imprisoned. Eleven years. I stood in that space where she lived for eleven years. The breadth of maybe four coffins lying side by side. It had a high ceiling, so she had loads of space over her head, which was useless to her.'

'She survived?'

'Yeah. I can't remember if her husband died or freed her, but I do know she got out. So if she could survive being encased in a stone cupboard for eleven years, you and I can presumably survive this.'

'Is this story supposed to make me feel good?'

'It just came to mind.' Frances went back to her bed and lay down. 'I have no idea where Richard's parents are, you know. They've gone out to Australia to see his two sisters – they live out there, but I don't know where exactly – and his brother lives in a houseboat in Ireland, so if something has happened to him, I have no idea how to contact any of them.'

'*Skitsnack*. Nothing has happened to him. He missed a train, that's all.'

'Yeah, so I have to go get him.'

'Not when it requires that you should go off into the desert. He would not expect that. In Egypt, your embassy will find him for you.'

'No. You're all ganging up on me about Cairo, but you're wrong. It's too far. It'd be like abandoning him. I mean, put yourself in my place. What would you do?'

Lena thought about this for a moment, then said, 'Is Richard a good lover?'

Frances chuckled. 'What's that got to do with anything?'

'Even I would go a long way for a man who loved me well,' Lena giggled.

'A man like Fredrik perhaps?'

Lena sighed. 'Oh, yes, like Fredrik.'

'Go on, then. Tell me all about it. Your turn.'

'The first time he made love to me, he was in another room.'

'My, he is gifted! How'd he manage that?'

'I was sitting on the verandah of a safari lodge in Botswana. He was inside at the bar. He could see me through the doorway, and I felt him looking at me, so I turned. I knew then. After that, all that mattered was finding the opportunity.'

'Which can't have been easy.'

'No. We were with a group, so I was always sharing a room or a tent. I met him one night in the bush when everyone was asleep, but I was afraid of insects and snakes.'

'So much for passion.'

'Finally, it happened in the shower tent. I went to have a shower and he came in behind me, and *voilà*.'

'Voilà indeed. You got pregnant. It didn't occur to you to use contraception?'

'Ya, and where were we to get it? We hadn't planned this. I have a boyfriend in Sweden. I wasn't expecting to betray him.'

'You have a boyfriend? Jayzus! This isn't complicated enough already?'

Lena giggled again. 'Yes, and his sister is in love with Per.'

'And how will the boyfriend take it when you tell him about Fredrik?'

'Not at all well!'

They laughed, loudly this time.

'And when his sister hears that Per is also in love with Fredrik,' Frances snorted, 'she'll take it even worse!'

They tried to keep quiet, but both needed the release too much to let it pass. 'So your boyfriend's sister is in love with a man who is in love with the man who's having it off with his sister! God, and I thought my life was a mess.'

'How did you and Richard get together?'

'It was very similar, actually. We were mad for each other, but we were on this crowded train, chugging through Yugoslavia and then Greece. Interminably. In Athens we stayed in a hostel, me in the girls' room, him in the boys', so by the time we got out to the islands we were panting for it.'

'*Men herregud!* Again!' Lena jumped up and stumbled to the door, leaving Frances at the mercy of the empty darkness. With so little to see – a bit of sky beyond the building beyond the rectangular hole in the wall that made up her window – it was too easy to remember that night on the beach, when she and Richard first made love. Her chest tightened. Would they ever do so again?

Ten minutes later Lena returned.

'You okay?'

'Yes.' She lay down.

'What do you do, back home?'

'I'm studying English in Uppsala.'

'You hardly need to. You speak it so well.'

'Yes, but I want to be a journalist, so I need to have a very good command of it.'

'What about the other two?'

'Fredrik works in his family business – they make window glass – and Per is starting university in the autumn.'

'Have you other brothers or sisters?'

'No, we are only two.'

'Parents?'

'Two, also.'

Frances smiled. 'Do you get on with them?'

'Oh yes, very much.'

'Richard gets on really well with his parents too.'

'And do you?'

'I've never met them. I've only been home twice in three years, but we were always too busy with each other in Dublin to bother going to Galway to see his folks.'

'I was asking about *your* parents.'

'Oh. Yeah, well. Therein lies a tale. I got on okay with Dad, he was great, but he died when I was seventeen and Mum, well, she's a basket case. She's a sculptor, the creative type, which apparently excuses anything. When I was growing up, she was always so distracted by her work that she never knew where I was or what I was doing, but if I got angry about it, she'd say that her artistic sensibilities meant her mind was busy elsewhere, and I was expected to put up with it. Motherhood never made any impact on her, so far as we could see. My sister and I used to joke that the pregnancy hormones must have failed to find her brain, because her mind remained completely untouched by the concept of nurturing.'

Lena winced.

'No, honestly. I'm telling it like it is. Dad used to compensate, but after he died, Mother never noticed whether I was even there or not, so I decided not to be there. I was trying to punish her when I went away, but it made no difference. In fact, it suited her, so I didn't bother going back. Eventually I got into the swing of being on the move; hence my rambling existence. Nobody misses me. I go home only to see my sister.'

'What's she like?'

'She's okay, but she got married at twenty, had three kids, and can't see beyond the end of her cul-de-sac. She lectures me about my wayward life. She thinks Richard is wonderful because he's persuaded me to settle down, while Mother simply fancies him.'

'My mother will like Fredrik, I think.'

'Bloody right. Any woman in her right mind would fancy Fredrik.'

They lay without speaking for a while. Then Frances said, 'What would your mother say if she were here now?'

That was a mistake: Lena started crying. 'Oh, I wish she was! She would know what to do!'

'*You* know what to do.' Frances got up and went to Lena's bed, tearful herself. 'Lena, don't do this to your family. Your parents would beg you to leave if they could, so I am begging you in their place. Please. I know you have the courage. Take that ferry and get the hell out of here before it's too late!'

Lena lay still, sniffling. Finally she whispered, 'All right. I'll go.'

4

It was a relief when the muezzin finally announced the arrival of morning. A general stir grew outside the rooms as those on camp beds began to rise for prayer. From the window beside her bed, Frances could see dawn sneaking into the night sky. Voices echoed in the streets. The muezzin's call resounded across the town, then lost itself in the emptiness beyond.

Weary with lack of sleep and stiff with anxiety, Frances got up. Her head humming with the likely and the unlikely, the probable and the improbable, what Richard did, might have done, could not have done, she left the hotel and sat beside a tree near the entrance. The short spell of fresh morning air was invigorating, but it wouldn't be long before her friends boarded the ferry, and the prospect of staying behind in a place as bleak as her thoughts and then facing out into the desert again made her stomach burn with apprehension.

Lena, too, was so smitten with apprehension that she could hardly speak as she lay on her bed, terrified.

The morning passed, a belt of gloom hanging over it. Only the Australians were cheerful. They had *fuul,* a fava bean purée, with eggs on top, bread, jam, and tea for breakfast, talking all the while about Abu Simbel, Queen Hatshepsut's Temple and every other wonder they were planning to see in Upper Egypt. Frances sat with them, worrying. She worried not only about the ferry, but about the journey to the ferry – undertaken on a rickety old bus over rough ground at inappropriate speed – because the slightest bump could dislodge a baby that must be clinging on against the odds of Lena's dehydration.

The sight of rucksacks stacked in the lobby made Frances swallow hard. Was she doing the right thing? This was the life she loved: boats, trucks, the romance of leaving, moving on, never staying – all the things she had given up for Richard. She envied the Australians their Abu Simbel and toyed with the idea that if she went with them, she could reclaim her right to roam and be a drifter again, instead of a forsaken lover.

When the bus that was to take them to the lake was ready to leave, Per carried Lena from their room, lifted her in and sat with her in his arms. Frances took a seat across the aisle, unable to look at either of them. She didn't want to see the fear in Lena's eyes, or any suggestion of abandonment, however groundless. Other passengers piled in, shoving, pressing. Fredrik tried to make space around Lena, his jaw set, his eyes flitting from passenger to passenger, window to driver, but, like Frances, never stopping on Lena or Per. Unabashed by the tension, the Australians did what Australians do best, chatting to the locals in sign language, cracking jokes, disarming them of their distaste for two men who walked about in no more than underwear – singlets and shorts.

The bus set off across the bumpy track. On the horizon, the lake spread out, a great, blue reminder to Frances of the freedom she could no longer enjoy, and she wished for a great hole of quicksand to swallow her up.

The port was buzzing, a welter of people queuing, shouting, insisting: women draped in multi-coloured veils, grasping babies; men hanging about in gallabiyas or grubby Western clothes; *bokasi* – pick-up trucks – tearing across the dirt, going to and from the town. Frances waited with Lena on the bus while the men went to deal with Customs; they didn't speak, just as they would not have spoken had they been sitting inside a hot stove. Frances waved languidly to keep flies from Lena's face. *Don't die*, she was thinking, her eyes turned away, *don't die on that boat*. And yet if Lena did die, or simply miscarried, Frances would never know about it. Once this tragedy had passed on to its next stage, away from her, she could concentrate again on her own little drama. And how little it seemed, truly, as she glanced at her companion.

The Australians got back onto the bus to say goodbye, and at that moment they seemed like the best friends Frances had ever had. Rod asked her again to change her mind. Reluctantly, she shook her head. Richard already seemed to belong to some previous life, which she could scarcely remember. This was actuality – Joel and Rod and Lena. People who wanted her to be with them.

They sat for nearly an hour in their oven. Frances dabbed Lena's face with a cloth, warm but wet. Lena had taken two Imodium tablets to try and ensure that she wouldn't be caught out on the way to the ferry. The pills could be fatal for the baby, Frances and Fredrik knew that, but they had agreed that Lena's life came first – and this had shocked them, for it was a decision neither had ever expected to have to make about anyone. So far, the Imodium was working, but at a price. Sharp stabs of abdominal pain regularly jolted Lena, and Frances felt it too, for Lena squeezed her wrist so sharply that it hurt. Finally, Per and Fredrik came across the dust, surrounded by a swarm of officials who clambered onto the bus and had a good look at the sick girl. There was much discussion before they nodded at Per, indicating that they could take her onto the ferry.

Frances squeezed Lena's hand. 'I'm sorry to let you down, but you're almost there. Before you know it, you'll be in Aswan. And the baby will be all right,' she added, with as much certainty as her voice could muster.

With equal certainty, Lena shook her head.

On the way back to the town, for a short moment, Frances felt a familiar stirring. She was alone, with the Nubian Desert stretching about her and a hot wind scorching her face as she bounced about in the empty bus. This was what she had always wanted – to be absorbed into the unlikely.

Before returning to the hotel, and the grim perspective of her room, she wandered through the town looking for provisions for a journey of indeterminate duration to an uncertain destination. Wadi Halfa reminded her of the village she had once made with shoeboxes as a child – every building low, windowless; shady within, scrappy without. This was a place taken away from its namesake – the wadi, the valley (the Nile Valley, no less) – and dumped somewhere else, where it had been left without landscape, without any determining factor to call its own. The only reason people came to Wadi Halfa was to leave it. This endeared it to Frances, but not enough for her to stay.

She strolled past open stalls, their cotton canopies flapping about, and looked for appetizing non-perishables. She could not, she knew, swallow another morsel of cold tinned stew, and bread had already been sold out, but she found some tins of fruit, biscuits and dates, and haggled with the shopkeepers in an attempt to stimulate the excitement she usually enjoyed before departure. It was no good; the adventure had already lost its zest.

It was lonely, back in her room, and a weariness set into her at the prospect of spending the following days in a rail carriage in stupefying temperatures. When she was packing her rucksack, one of Richard's T-shirts fell out. She held it to her face, expecting to cry, but nothing came. The heat had dried what tears there might have been.

She slept, lightly. Lena haunted her dreams. The eyes, betrayed, beseeched her. A baby's cries, muffled, as though crying inside the womb. Thirst. Frances dreamt that she was thirsty and Lena was thirsty and a sad, dusty kitten was thirsty. She woke, fretting. Where were her water-purifying tablets? Did she have enough for the journey? She grabbed the rucksack and shoved her hand into one of the side pockets, then into the other, then the front pocket, and inside, and under, and through the whole rucksack all over again. She turned it upside down, emptying the contents onto the floor. No tablets.

They were in Richard's knapsack.

He, at least, would not die of water poisoning.

'Fuck!' Frances fell back on Lena's poorly sprung bed.

She felt frightened, and she had never before been frightened. Often alone, in far-flung places, she had always been brave. Why not now?

Because Richard had weakened her, had made her less gutsy by dismembering the soloist in her. Or perhaps it was not Richard who had done it, but love. Capitulation. The tumble into coupledom, and irrevocable need.

Raised voices drifted over from the reception area. Frances went to investigate. People bound for Khartoum were gathered around the desk, arguing amongst themselves. The manager sat behind the counter, expressionless, tapping his pen.

Frances pushed through the crowd. 'What's happened?'

'The train is not going.'

'What? Why not?'

He shrugged. 'Problem. Not going today.'

'When then?'

Another shrug. 'You must ask at the station.'

At the station a similar mêlée had gathered around the shabby office, but there was no way through the bodies glued together, so Frances accosted a passing engineer, who confirmed that the express had an engine problem and would not be leaving for Khartoum until it was fixed. He was cheerful about it, smiling and saying, 'Ma'lesh.'

Half an hour later, Frances was no wiser. At the Nile Hotel, passengers were already resigned. Nobody knew how long the delay would be and no one cared anymore; Allah would provide transport in His own good time. They went back to their camp beds, where they lay about smoking and talking, but Frances was trembling when she returned to her room. Where did this leave her? And Richard? Would he, likewise, be stuck in Abu Hamed? She was trapped. Trapped in a torrid transit lounge. Why, she wondered, did this have to happen in one of the hottest and loneliest places on the planet?

The train could leave in two days, or in eight. She had no drinking water. Not for now, and not for the train. The hotel might boil some for her, but would they mind her standing over them in the kitchen to make sure that it did, actually, come to the boil? The cheap fizzy drinks available at stalls in the market would make her ill if she drank nothing else, and tea would dry her out. A desert thirst demands water. And she had nothing to do. Two books, both read. She could write letters, if she could find paper, but that would be a chore in the heat, and to whom would she write and what would she say? She could walk, in the morning and evening, but not at night and not by day. The walls of her room were blue, the floor bare, the furniture sparse. In this basic cell, there was nothing to absorb the sound of her anxieties, to blunt the squeal in her head. There was only solitude, and simmering panic. She could be there for a week, worrying, worrying, until she would end up fried to a frazzle not by the heat but by the fear that while she remained there, Richard was slipping farther and farther away from her.

For a long time, she sat on the edge of Lena's bed, not moving, defeated by the sheer relentlessness of rotten luck.

The boat.

She wasn't quite sure how it came into her head that the ferry might not have left yet, but when it did, she darted from the room as if it were on fire and ran about the town looking for a pick-up to take her to the lake. People were still milling around, resigning themselves with amazing alacrity to their non-departure, while Frances hurried around asking people for a lift to a ferry that should have left at least an hour before – if it had kept to its schedule.

But what are timetables out here? she thought. *Who the hell cares about time?*

Certainly not the Nile Valley River Transport Corporation. Every time she asked for help, people shook their heads, but just as she was becoming frantic, a young man offered to take her to the port in his *boksi*. Never in her life had she checked out of a hotel so quickly, asking the manager to tell Richard that she would wait for him in Cairo. She jumped into the truck. The driver tore across the dirt, his haste an aberration in such an aimless day. He called out in excitement when he saw the ferry still at the port, and although it seemed to Frances that it was pulling away, she was determined to swim the difference. *To hell with Richard*, she thought. *To hell with us!*

The Australians, on the crowded deck, saw her coming. They cheered when she leapt from the truck, and when, finally, she had fought her way through the wall of paper anarchy necessary to release her from the Sudan and boarded that squat little ferry, Rod lifted her into the air with an enormous hug. She sank onto the deck beside them, relief gushing from her pores in a sweaty flush.

She need not have hurried. The ferry did not leave for another three hours. No one knew why. No one cared.

Lena had taken a first-class cabin and was sharing with a young Egyptian woman and her small child. When Frances went in, Lena was too weak to be surprised. She held out her hand. 'Thank you.'

'Don't. I didn't come because of you. I'm here because the Express isn't running. I wish I could say otherwise, but I'm just not that selfless.'

'Do you think I care about that? I am not selfless either.'

The cabin was stultifying. The Egyptian lady's luggage took up two full berths and she gesticulated at Frances, talking at her in Arabic but making it clear that her presence was more than the small space could stand. She showed Frances her own ticket and seemed to be asking to see hers. Frances showed her the ticket, with no berth reserved. The woman opened the door. Her message was clear: out.

'But she's ill. I must stay with her.'

The woman shrugged, spoke loudly.

Frances pointed at the woman's daughter and then at her own stomach, with a glance towards Lena. Pointing again at her belly, she shook her head, hoping the woman would understand that the pregnancy was in danger.

The woman frowned, talked, gesticulated. They were trying to communicate without understanding one another, while also striving to make sure that Lena wouldn't understand them either. The Egyptian seemed to be asking if the baby was falling out; Frances nodded. The woman's jaw dropped in sympathy. She spoke to Lena, and then tried to make room for Frances. Her name was Afaf. She had a round face, arched eyebrows and wide eyes, and she wore her blue scarf pulled over her forehead and tucked under her chin, Egyptian-style. It was a relief when she was hustled out of the cabin by her daughter, Jameela.

Finally, the engines groaning as though the ferry itself were giving birth, they dragged away from the shore. Lena was dozing, so Frances went up on deck, desperate for air, and looked out as the boat pulled away from the bleak outlines of the Sudan. Behind them, their boat was tugging not one but two old hulks, which looked rusty and porous, and which were dangerously low in the water, such were the crowds travelling on them. Families with radios and mattresses and aluminium pots were settling in for the journey to Egypt, and Frances wondered why these floating platforms, like leaves on water, didn't sink under the weight of their cargo. Around her, the lake was blue and sterile in the evening light. She had finally got there, had finally taken the Nile Valley Express to Khartoum, had seen the confluence of the two Niles and the Mahdi's tomb in Omdurman, and yet everything that had brought her to the Sudan had been outplayed by everything that had happened there. She thought about Richard, and prayed that he was all right, and she wished beyond wishing that this was just a hump, an unfortunate incident they would somehow overcome.

At sunset, the ferry pulled into the bank and cut its engines. It was one of those that did not sail by night. This stop had been a novelty, an atmospheric interlude on the way into the Sudan, but on the way out it was trying. The delayed departure meant they would probably not reach Aswan the next day.

After the evening prayers had been said, Frances took a walk through the multitude thronging the decks. The riverbank was coarse and uninhabited, but on the two platforms tied up behind the ferry, people were cooking and talking, apparently enjoying this dreadful trip. Babies cried, children shrieked, women laughed. All aspects of life on a raft floating on a man-made lake far from everywhere. *And where is death?* Frances wondered.

The hours of darkness were hard. For Frances and Fredrik, every minute was like a day; for Lena, much longer. It was a sleepless, airless night, and even the warm, sunny morning offered little relief from their anxieties.

Frances smiled at Lena. 'One more day, and you're home free.'

'One more night also.'

It was still early when the Australians summoned Frances on deck to see the monument of Abu Simbel on the shore. Three statues of the seated Ramses II stared back at them, unmoved.

'What happened to the fourth guy?' Joel asked, clicking his camera. 'He's lost everything but his knees.'

'He cracked up,' Rod chuckled.

'Too right. The boredom must have got to him. Four thousand years sitting out in the desert without the footie results – that'd be enough to make any man fall apart!'

Frances rued her impatience to reach the Sudan. She had promised Richard they would make the detour to Abu Simbel on the way back to Cairo; now this unsatisfactory view from the river might be the best she would ever have of these extraordinary temples.

That afternoon, she went with Fredrik and Per to ask the captain if he would please sail through the coming night, but he told them kindly that this would be impossible, against regulations. It would be too dangerous to pull the hulks in the dark.

'But our friend is seriously ill.'

'I understand, but I have many hundred people to think about, and we will be in El Sadd el Ali early tomorrow.'

Despondent, Fredrik and Per walked away.

'She's expecting a baby,' Frances said. 'Two people could be at risk, not just one. We must get to Aswan as soon as possible.'

'Look, look.' The captain, a rotund little man, led her to the railings and pointed at the barges and their dangerously exaggerated populations. 'I cannot pull those in the dark. I'm sorry, but it would be very crazy.'

Very crazy indeed. Only weeks later, out on Lake Nasser, that same ferry would go on fire and sink, with hundreds of souls lost. Frances often wondered, afterwards, if her gentle captain had gone down with his plucky little ship.

Lena had been right: she miscarried that night on the lake and it was horrible. When it started, some time after midnight, they were moored to the shore. Not for the first time Frances felt snared, and she wondered how much deeper she could tumble into this unlikely abyss.

She had been trying to sleep when she heard little gasps from the lower berth. 'God, no,' she whispered. She tried to ignore Lena's groans, to block them out, but there was no denying it. The contractions had started. Afaf switched on the light and looked grimly at Frances.

They were inexperienced and frightened. They called the ship's medical officer to the cabin, but he was no help. He was not a doctor and had no idea what to do, or no will to do it. This was women's business. He offered only towels and painkillers and went looking for professional assistance. The public address system was broken, so he had to rely on sailors wandering around the decks calling for a doctor, but amongst all these hundreds of passengers there was not one trained medic.

Frances kept hearing her own voice making all those false promises in Wadi Halfa. 'You won't miscarry,' 'You'll be fine.' Oh, it had been easy then to make promises when she thought she wouldn't be around should those promises not hold! And where was the instinct which she had glibly assured Lena would fall upon Per and Fredrik should they need it? There was no instinct; only fear.

Her stomach in a clutch of terror, she vigorously wiped Lena's forehead as if determination alone could stop this happening. How would it go? What would an eleven-week-old foetus look like? Would she have to see it? Would she know when it was over?

It was Afaf's idea to take Lena to the toilets, and it was probably a good one. They struggled with her to the lavatories, just after three, and held her over the hole in the floor while her insides came out. Frances's head tingled with dizziness and she wanted to retch, but she managed to stay upright.

After the baby had been flushed to its grave in Lake Nasser, they dragged Lena back to her berth where she became delirious, hot, cold, and finally grey. Everything she had dreaded came to pass – she was losing so much blood that Frances thought she would die, but she had promised Lena that she would get her out of this hell and she was more determined than ever to carry that through.

Per and Fredrik stood outside in the dim passageway. Every time one of them tried to gain access to the cabin, Afaf yelled at them in Arabic and pushed them out. She was running the show now, for she at least had given birth and had some notion of what should be done. With a stomach of steel and character to match, she ordered people about, demanding water and more towels, and sent Per and Fredrik on errands to keep them busy. In spite of all the fuss going on – the captain coming from his bed, the medical officer huffing and puffing – Per never worked it out. He assumed it all had to do with the dysentery and was too stricken with shock to think otherwise.

By five, the worst was over. The haemorrhaging was no longer so violent; Lena lay still and pale. Frances sat at her feet, silently urging the captain to start up his godforsaken tub, as he promised he would at first light, and get it to Aswan before Lena died. Afaf dozed in the corner, snoring lightly, while Jameela continued to sleep on the top bunk as she had done right through. Frances went outside; Fredrik and Per were crouched on the floor in the corridor. Fredrik followed her without speaking. It was still dark and they had to feel their way between the slumbering bodies on deck until they found a quiet spot by the railings. When Frances took a deep breath, her head went light and she fell sideways. Fredrik caught her. Billions of stars did nothing to relieve the claustrophobic impression that they were caught in a night that would never end. It had started when she had woken and found herself alone on the train, and it had continued relentlessly since then. Now a baby was lost. How much worse could things get? Leaning on the railing, she felt the earth turning beneath her and wished she might fall off the edge. She was stuck on a steamer in the middle of a huge reservoir and nobody knew she was there.

'My baby is gone, yes?' Fredrik asked.

'Yes.'

On the horizon, a hint of colour pushed into the black sky. Light came tentatively from beyond the earth's rim, until Frances could see the water spread around them. Voices crept into the quiet, bodies began to shift, to stretch and push, and the sounds of morning unravelled themselves like a cat unfurling, echoing against the dawn.

Fredrik wept. Frances had no comfort for him. She hadn't slept for four nights. Richard was gone. And now this. She couldn't cry. That would have been too easy.

5

Arriving at Aswan was like coming home after a very bad term at school. The night that had pursued Frances finally turned around and tiptoed away from the light. As they berthed at Sadd el Ali, she held Lena's hand and smiled. 'You see. We're here. Wadi Halfa is a long way away. You made it.'

'Only half of me made it.'

'Lena, listen. Fredrik told Per about the baby. I made him.'

'Fan också.'

'It wasn't right to keep him in the dark any longer.'

'He must be so angry.'

'Yes, he's furious. Furious that you nearly killed yourself to protect him.'

'I took the man he wanted. I have been punished for that.'

'Don't think that way. You're so lucky, you three. You've gone through all this together. You'll come out of it together.'

Lena nodded.

'And I tell you what,' Frances teased, 'I would never have been able to turn Fredrik down in a canvas shower or anywhere else either!'

A weak forbearing smile crossed Lena's face. 'You'd better go now.'

'Don't be silly. I'm coming to the hospital.'

'No, I'll be okay. You must go to Cairo to find that man.'

'Hmm, do you think he wants to be found?'

'I don't know.' The apprehension that had weighed down Lena's every movement in Wadi Halfa had been replaced by an even heavier resignation. 'But you must find him. If you don't, this journey will never end for you.'

'Maybe that's why he did it; because he knew I never wanted the journey to end.' She started packing her things. 'All right, look, if you really don't mind, I'll go and check into my hotel. I'll have a shower and some breakfast, then I'll come to see you at the hospital.'

'No, don't do that, Frances.'

'Why not?'

'There is no point. We'll never meet again.'

'Of course we will. We must. After everything we've been through together—'

'Exactly. Let's leave it like that.'

'But these last three days—'

'Ya. These last three days. This is something I want to put away, and never go back to again.'

'Lena, that's ... that's not fair.'

'Thank you, Frances, for saving my life.'

'Don't be silly, you saved yourself. But what about, well, us?'

'All we have between us is this disaster.'

'There could be more. Much more.' Frances smiled wanly. 'I mean, don't you even want to know if I find Richard?'

'I know already that if you don't find him, you'll meet someone else. Someone to reward you for what you have done for me.'

Frances stared at her. 'You really don't want any further contact?'

Lena shook her head. Afaf came in, jolly and loud. She took Lena's hand, speaking to her all the while in reassuring tones of Arabic, and then, with a wave, she was gone, the accidental midwife, like a genie going back into a bottle.

'That's the way,' said Lena quietly.

Frances stood with her toilet bag in one hand, but she was beginning to understand. What they had been through may have been grounds for a lifelong friendship in her eyes, but what mattered to Lena was not what Frances had done for her, but what they had all failed to do: save her baby. Frances had unwittingly strayed into someone else's calamity and would always be a reminder of it. She had to stay there, in it, rather than force herself into the life beyond it.

Per knocked and came in, looking a lot older than he had three days before, and spoke to his sister.

'The ambulance is here,' Lena explained. 'They're coming for me.' She reached out to Frances. 'I'll never forget you,' she whispered. 'Never.'

Unable to speak, Frances hugged her quickly, pulled her rucksack onto her back and stepped towards the door. Per stopped her. His eyes full, he squeezed her arm and nodded.

For the first time in six days, Frances was alone. Her room at the Abu Simbel Hotel had an air-conditioner that didn't work and a temperamental shower, but it was cool, dark and still. After showering and putting on a fresh kaftan, she had breakfast on the balcony and ate well for the first time in days. From the moment she had stepped off the ferry, Egypt had begun its work. It soothed her, made her feel as if she were sitting in a favourite armchair in familiar surroundings. It looked right to her. Perhaps it was the colour – the greenery on Elephantine Island, the river, properly blue here, the white sails of the feluccas and the great golden sand-dune on the bank opposite, or perhaps it was the air, no longer laden with grit, and the hum of the town behind her which helped to ease away the strain. Her muscles unclenched, tentatively at first, as if sensing a danger pass, then relaxed, allowing her spirits to rise.

The Nile flowed by without meaning to; feluccas drifted; the hotel ferry went back and forth to the island. There weren't many tourists about, but the Corniche was busy with local women scurrying along the pavement, their black *abbayahs* pulled around them as they rushed past the cruise ships resting on the quayside. In the garden below, people sat beneath the trees having coffees, ice creams and soft drinks. Life in Upper Egypt went on as Frances sat alone on her balcony, untangling the knots in her life and in her hair. At last, her hair was clean and her body had been released from a prison of ingrained grime, but above all, she relished the privacy. Nobody was talking to her, looking at her. Nobody could even see her. She was alone, perfectly alone, and for that moment Richard's absence mattered not a lot. She would almost have forsaken him herself just to have escaped the turmoil, the shunting of her emotions, the crowds that had jostled and sweated alongside her since she had left Khartoum. She had slept with them, eaten with them, queued outside lavatories with them; she had bared her desolation to them. Now, in spite of the click of horses' hooves along the Corniche and cars passing, she had solitude. The river held her gaze, sucked her in, cooled her.

Too exhausted to take the train to Cairo that night, she remained in her room all day. This was a holiday, a respite in between the harsh isolation of Wadi Halfa and the dizzying metropolis of Cairo, and she wanted to stay. She had been happy in Aswan, with Richard.

After sleeping for several hours, she woke with a heavy head and no energy, and glanced in despair at Richard's clothes that she had pulled from their joint rucksack after retrieving it from storage. It seemed unfathomable that she had finally found the courage to draw out from her rootless soul that one crucial decision, to spend her life with someone, only to have him vanish, as if the very force of her decision had snuffed him out. She lay on for another hour, immobilized by longing. She had often longed for Richard during their separations, but then at least she could look forward to their reunion, whereas now there was only yearning with no certain respite at the end of it. Her eyes clasped shut, she imagined him in the room, coming from the shower, ready for her.

She spent her last night in Aswan wandering in the souq with Rod and Joel. There was no shortage of romance to captivate her, but it left her unmoved.

'Aw! A hubble-bubble pipe!' said Joel. 'Gotta try that.'

At a café, they took a table that wobbled on the uneven pavement, and ordered tea and a hookah. Joel was wide-eyed with glee when the waiter showed him how to use the pipe. 'Get outta my head on this for sure!'

'You won't, you know,' said Frances.

'You've done the right thing,' said Rod.

'Hmm?'

'Coming to Egypt. If the embassy can't help, you can take your flight to London. Richard will find you there if—'

'If he wants to? It isn't that simple. My mother has recently moved. I haven't seen her new house myself. Richard doesn't even know where it is.'

'So go see his family.'

'I can't. They're away. In Australia, as it happens.'

'Mutual friends?'

Frances shook her head. 'Our friends were the people we travelled with. That's the only life we had together.'

'Well, what about his office?' Rod asked, exasperated.

'… I could go to his office, I suppose.'

'Yuck. What's that stuff?' Joel pointed at a man feeding sugar cane through an old-style presser.

'If you're so keen to try the pipe,' said Frances, 'you should try the cane.'

'No, thanks.'

'So, if you don't make contact before you get to London,' Rod insisted, 'you'll go to Richard's office when you get there, right?'

Frances turned to him. This rough-looking oceanographer had been guiding her since all this began. Without meaning to, she had followed his lead so far. She would go to the embassy in Cairo, yes, and if that yielded nothing, she might even take that flight to London. But if she didn't find Richard before then, she would certainly not turn up at his office and beg to be taken back.

That night, she went to bed early, acutely aware of the empty space beside her, where Richard should have been.

The next morning, the Australians descended on her when she was having breakfast in the restaurant. A huge fan whirred behind her and a great black cloth had been pulled across the windows, shutting out the sun, and the view.

'When do you leave for Cairo?' Rod asked.

'I'm taking the sleeper this evening.'

'Great. We can spend the day together.'

'Thanks, but I've already seen the sights.'

'Right-o, so we'll take out a felucca instead.'

'Can't afford it.'

'Our treat. With the season winding up, we should be able to bargain them down to something affordable.'

'What is this?' she scowled. 'Be Good to Frances Week?'

On Naguib al-Moneim's felucca, memories came.

In a light breeze, they drifted behind Elephantine Island, and Frances recognized a pathway below the hotel gardens where she had walked one evening with Richard. Farther on, amongst reeds on the shore, women from the village were washing tin pans and children ran about in clusters, just as they had been doing when she had settled between Richard's knees on a rocky outcrop. His arms resting on her shoulders, they had watched the river change colour at sunset. It was a moment of acquiescence. Both had what they wanted. Frances was enjoying the fusion of the exotic with love, while Richard had everything he had so long yearned for: Frances. In perpetuity.

They had started kidding about. When he prodded her in the ribs and she had turned to wrestle with him, they slid off the rock. Their hands clasped, they had pushed and laughed until Richard fell backwards into the river.

'Nothing like exposing me to bilharzia!' he had grumbled, stumbling out. 'Do you want me blinded?'

'I thought you already were?'

'By you? Oh no, I have x-ray vision where you're concerned!'

She had put her arms around his neck and kissed him then, because in spite of herself, this most settled of men made her happy. While they stood in the river kissing, the children nearby had giggled and teased. Yes, things had been good in Aswan.

'Strewth!' Joel, in baggy T-shirt and a baseball cap, was stretched across the cushions on the felucca. 'I need a bloody swim!'

Rod fingered Frances's ringlets. 'Amazing hair.'

The sun scorched her skin through the fabric of her shirt. 'I want to get off.'

'Relax.' Rod grinned. 'I'm not making a pass. I would, if you weren't pining for someone else, but I'm not.'

'It isn't that. I just want to get off.' She pointed to the bank. 'Over there. Is that possible?' she asked the boatman.

Naguib shook his head.

'I'll swim then.'

'River not good for swimming,' said Naguib.

'I don't care.'

'You can't be serious,' said Rod.

'I am. I want to walk on the island. I'll get the ferry back.'

'But—'

'Mind my bag, would you? I'll see you at the hotel.'

Naguib, unfazed by the peculiar antics of tourists, manoeuvred the felucca as close to the shore as he could, and Joel took photographs as Frances put her legs over the edge and dropped into the river. She swam until she could stand, then stumbled through the shallow waters that harboured the bilharzia parasites, sludge seeping between her toes, only to find that setting foot on the island did not bring Richard back. For a moment she had almost believed that she could swim through time, that the Nile would carry her into the past and she would find herself standing on Elephantine Island with Richard's arms around her. Instead, she emerged from the river as solitary, wretched and wet as she had ever been.

Rod stood on the felucca, hands on hips, cursing, while Joel's camera clicked. Frances wondered vaguely what the photos would show. Would they show a woman in a wet skirt standing on a shore with little Egyptian girls dancing all around her, or would they show the abandon, the broken heart?

The Australians sailed on. The children stared at the woman who had jumped off a boat to swim to the edge of their village; the women looked up from their washing, and Frances wondered how some things could stay so much the same and others alter so drastically? She squeezed water from the hem of her skirt and tried to cry. A large sob came from her chest, but it was dry, empty, and nothing followed behind it. She would feel better if she cried, for Lena and her baby if not for herself, but it wouldn't happen. The tears stood fast behind her eyes, the thumping in her heart receded, and the feeling that she must weep and weep for some relief dissipated, as if out of spite. Her isolation, even from herself, was absolute.

That evening, the Australians walked her to the station. On the Corniche, calèche drivers hounded them, interfering with Frances's attempts to make a private farewell to the river and the desert beyond it, because the first roots of reality were beginning to take hold. Something within, which she couldn't yet acknowledge, knew that this was it. With or without Richard, she had come to the threshold again, no longer stepping in, but stepping out and going home; ending her travels in the bustle of the Aswan evening.

And yet when she stood in the languid confusion at Aswan station watching the train slide in to platform three, ready to shunt her down to Cairo, the sound and the sight of it accelerated the beat of her heart, as the uncharted miles tugged on her sleeve.

The Australians boarded with her. The carriage was luxurious compared to the Sudanese sleeper, and Frances had a compartment to herself.

'That's good,' Rod said. 'At least you'll get a good night's sleep.'

'The last for a while,' said Joel.

'Thanks, Joel.'

'Aw, Cairo's gotta be the noisiest city on earth. It's bursting at the seams. One of these days it's going to implode and disappear down the river.'

'As long as it doesn't do so tomorrow,' said Frances.

Joel threw her rucksacks onto the high bunk. 'There ya go.'

There was a moment's awkwardness. 'Well,' said Frances, 'have a great trip.'

Rod nodded. 'Can we have an address?'

'I ... I don't have one. I'll write to you, if you like.'

'You do that.' Rod scribbled an address on her map of Egypt. 'And be sure to let us know ...'

'I will. Promise. Thanks so much for everything. I'd probably still be on the Nile Valley Express if it weren't for you.'

Rod hugged her. She held on for longer than she should have. So far, these lads had carried her forward; now she would be entirely on her own and it was an unpalatable prospect.

Joel kissed her wetly on both cheeks. 'See ya in Australia, eh? You haven't seen *our* blinking desert yet.'

'I'm done with deserts, thanks.'

'Yeah, I guess being deserted in a desert is a bit much for anyone.'

Rod and Frances groaned. At the carriage door, Rod kissed her not so swiftly on the lips and got off. They stood on the platform, waiting, and Frances wondered if she would ever see this pair again.

Whistles blew, the carriages struggled into motion; Frances said thanks a dozen times, Joel cracked poor jokes, and Rod smiled. 'You'll be right,' he said.

Her final glimpse was of two pairs of long, tanned legs standing on the platform. Losing three excellent friends and a boyfriend in the space of a few days had to be some kind of record, Frances thought.

She settled in for the seventeen-hour journey ahead. On one side of the track, the desert asserted itself in huge rocky hills which stood out of the sand in the pink light, but looking out at the other side was like watching a running documentary about the evening life of the fellaheen, seeing the progression of daily routine towards night as the train passed through each village at a different stage. The villages were drier than those near Luxor, made of sandstone bricks rather than mud and reeds. Frances stood in the corridor, watching but removed, as though she were looking at slides of a long-forgotten holiday. There were untethered donkeys relaxing after their day's labour, camels grazing, and bullocks dragging around wells, supervised by children. The women, hidden in their black garb, went to and fro fetching water, often from taps in the middle of stagnant, muddy pools, and there were children everywhere, in multi-coloured clothes, playing familiar games: a lad being pushed onto the school wall by his pals, boys playing football, and, in one village, a little girl turning around and around on a sandy path. *That's me*, thought Frances, *spinning and spinning on the same spot.*

6

Ramses Station was like an ants' nest, busy with bodies going somewhere, doing something: workers, soldiers, peasants, mothers, kids. Frances had to brace herself before leaving her cabin and joining the rush, and when she did, it dragged her into a stream of perpetual motion. Cairo was an ogre, but it was a familiar ogre and that helped.

When she came out of the station, the drivers and touts hanging around the taxi rank made for her like bees.

'You want limousine?'

'No, taxi.'

'Taximeter?'

Before she could reply, an argument erupted between those who wanted to put her in a taximeter and those who wanted her in a limousine. She was an insignificant part of the transaction, a mere spur to an apparently vital release of aggression, and when she was finally shoved into Car Three, which had already been occupied by another passenger, the driver went wild. He leapt out of his car, yelling in a virtual detonation of the Arabic language, while the other passenger, an impeccably dressed businessman, was spirited from Frances's side and dumped into another car by the limousine brigade. Her nerves were in shreds. All she wanted was a taxi. As the driver's outburst continued, his unhelpful colleagues negotiated an agreeable price with Frances. The driver then slammed the passenger door, jumped into his seat and drove away at speed. Cowering in the back, Frances wondered would she live or die. The din of the city attacked her every sense. After the tranquillity of the south, it was like being caught in an explosion. This was Cairo in its truest form and there was little point in wishing it any different. With Richard, weeks before, the city's extravagant disorder had been invigorating, not intimidating, as now.

In the quieter suburb of Zamalek, she humped her two ruck-sacks into the lift of the Longchamps Hotel and went up to the lobby on the second floor. The receptionist, a young man with thick glasses, recognized her and asked if her trip to the Sudan had been pleasant.

'Has my friend been here?' she blurted. If Richard had flown back to Cairo, he might have arrived ahead of her.

He blinked, perplexed, and said, 'I'm sorry, no.'

'Is there a message for me?'

The man checked the cubby holes. 'No message.'

'Damn.'

'You would like the same room as before?'

'Oh, em,' Frances did some swift calculations. It was all very well falling into the Longchamps with a view to waiting for Richard in this pleasant, family-run establishment, but at seventeen pounds a night it was rather expensive, now that she could no longer fall back on Richard's credit card. And yet, where else could he find her? She could not risk being anywhere else.

'Madame?'

She had, in truth, no option. Her purse was making the deci-sions, and it decreed that the humble Longchamps was beyond her means. The Australians had talked about a hotel near the station that had a swimming-pool on the roof and cost only eight pounds a night. 'Em, I'm sorry, I won't be staying. But if Richard Keane comes, would you please tell him to contact me through the Irish Embassy?'

She pretended to be carelessly confident when she was deposited back in Ramses Square, and walked along with her head held high as if she knew exactly where she was going. She didn't. All she knew from the Australians was that this hotel – she didn't even know its name – was in a street off the square, right opposite the station, but Ramses Square was a vast octopus of a place, jammed with vehicles and streets flailing out in every direction. The overhead footbridge offered the best vantage point. Frances struggled up the steps, weighed down by the rucksacks. Since she was no longer in the high, dry temperatures of the Sudan, damp heat slid around her body in great wads of perspiration. Beneath her, the square was busy with commuters hurrying to work, while cars pressed across the junction like passengers forcing their way into an overcrowded bus. On the footbridge, which crossed the square like strands of wayward hair, people came at Frances with intent. Men rushed past, clutching their caps against the wind; women laden with shopping bags hurried along, talking at such a rate that it seemed they were being reeled by on fast-forward, teeth flashing, lips racing, and a shrill uninterrupted gabble permeating the dusty air.

Frances leaned against the railing and looked about for some sign of this elusive hotel. She could see nothing opposite the station that looked as obvious as a hotel with a swimming-pool on the roof, but she cast her eyes around the blackened, hapless confusion of decrepit buildings until she saw the name of a hotel peeking out from behind another building. The Commodore. That rang a bell. She made her way towards it, struggling down the steep steps and onto cracked pavements. Honing in on the building like a bat, she found the side street in which it stood and stumbled towards the entrance.

The lobby was grisly, the lift probably fatal, but the rooms were clean, if basic, and the bathrooms cool. The hub of the hotel was not in the dark lobby but on the roof, where there was a restaurant (in which almost everything was red), the famous swimming-pool (the size of a large bath, and empty), and a shabby terrace from which you could see Ramses Square. Not much of a view, but it was cool out there in the evenings and there was always music playing in the background.

*

In this ramshackle place, Frances spent ten extraordinary days, days that weren't like days at all, more like a succession of events that led her steadily downwards. The traffic always woke her at dawn, and then there was no let-up from the din until three the following morning, so she lay, restless, going over every word, every glance that had passed between her and Richard during those last days, searching for some clue that he had become genuinely unhappy, some evidence that he had been close to the brink. After a few dawns spent like this, she no longer knew what had really been said and what had been reconstructed in the grim loneliness of her room, but the one moment that kept coming back to her, more vividly every time, was waking up on that train and finding Richard, and every trace of him, gone. Even when she was crossing the deadliest street in Cairo that moment would revisit her, set her back, and what struck her as most extraordinary was that, over a week later, he was still gone and she was still without explanation. She tried to persuade herself that a natural disintegration had been skulking about their relationship for longer than she cared to admit, but even the slightest backwards glance – at the day they spent on the White Nile or the morning they went riding at Saqqara – suggested otherwise, and she could not make herself believe that their troubles in the Sudan had been terminal.

Her every instinct insisted that Richard would not have left her like that, but logic told her that he had. She tried to crush that logic, to dismiss the doubts that slipped over her like an incoming tide, because she had to have hope. Without it, she would never have stayed in Cairo, would never have trudged around looking for him, waiting for him. She had to find some plausible reason for being there and so spent her time trying to create plausible reasons for his actions.

The day after she arrived, she made a list of what had to be done. She would check the Longchamps every day to see if Richard had turned up or phoned; she would ask the Irish Embassy if they could help locate him; she would go to British Airways to see if he had changed his return flight allowing him to leave from Khartoum instead of Cairo. To begin with, however, she had one vital call to make.

She was lucky. It took only an hour to get an international line to the Sudan, and when she got through to the Nile Hotel in Wadi Halfa, her heart was racing. She spoke to the manager, Ibrahim, and asked if another Khartoum train had come in. It had. Was Richard on it? No. There were no tourists on that train, he said.

Frances was not surprised, only diminished. It was like being in a compression chamber; with every additional blow the air grew thinner and the walls came in closer. There was some comfort, though: she had been right not to linger on the border – Richard had obviously gone back to Khartoum – and yet this had to be filed at the back of her mind, like certain other details, well away from the hope that kept her going. There could still be explanations. She must not condemn him yet.

Too embarrassed to go to the embassy, she started with British Airways. They had an office on Kasr-el-Nil Street, which was quite a hike on foot, but economy made a taxi too extravagant. She walked and walked. Men hassled her, called out, followed her even, for several blocks, but she kept her head down until the chaos ebbed, the crowds thinned, and Mediterranean-style buildings graced the sidewalks. Reaching Kasr-el-Nil Street was like strolling into Europe. In the British Airways office, the woman who dealt with her was English.

'Hi.' Frances placed her ticket on the counter. 'I'm travelling with my boyfriend, Richard Keane, and we're booked onto the London flight on Sunday—'

The woman took the ticket, checked it, nodded as Frances spoke.

'—and I was wondering if you could tell me if Richard has changed his reservation?'

The lady looked up.

Frances smiled, feeling like an imbecile.

'I'm sorry, I … ' She waited for Frances to clarify.

'Has Mr Keane changed his flight? From Sunday to some other day, or from some other departure point perhaps?'

'I'm not at liberty to give out that information,' the woman replied, bemused.

'But he's my boyfriend.'

The woman opened her mouth and closed it again. It was too obvious – *If he's your boyfriend, why don't you ask him?* 'I'm afraid we're not allowed to divulge details about passenger lists.'

'Well, can you tell me if … if the ticket is still valid? Or has he used it already?'

'I'm sorry, but there are strict regulations about passenger information.' She handed back the ticket.

'But, look, the thing is, Richard and I got split up and I don't want to get stranded here on my own. I need to know if he's left the country.'

'I see.' The woman looked at her with interest. 'Has he left your hotel?'

'We didn't have one at the time. Anyway, the point is that if he's gone home, I might as well go too. Can't you just take a little peek?'

'I'm afraid not. I could confirm your own reservation if you like?'

'No, thanks.' Frances stuffed her ticket into her money-belt. 'Not yet.'

With nothing better to do, she went along to Groppi's, a famous Cairo coffee shop, to plan her next move. It was like stepping back in time, fans whirring overhead, wooden tables and chairs, and old-fashioned cakes on display. A bit like Bewley's, Frances thought, though Groppi's was cool and subdued, not warm and steamy. She stayed there for hours, drinking tea and nibbling expensive pastries, before walking back to the hotel. Her first foray had not gone well.

The next day, she braved the embassy. When the taxi pulled up outside the tall green building by the river in which the Irish Embassy had its offices, Frances was fantasizing that Richard would be inside, waiting for her. She made her way to the seventh floor and, stepping into a cool, neat foyer, felt immediately at home. This was Ireland after all, not Egypt.

Two Egyptian women in dark suits sat behind a glass partition, one of them attending to two people at the counter, the other typing at a desk. Frances took a seat and picked up a glossy coffee-table book about Ireland. Turning the pages with clammy hands, she glanced mindlessly at shiny pictures of the Cliffs of Moher, the Rock of Cashel, the Ha'penny Bridge. Her heart pounded, her gut moved. This was worse than waiting at the dentist. These people had the potential, the means, to locate Richard. He was an Irish citizen gone AWOL. It was their responsibility to track him down.

When the secretary called her to the counter, Frances came to the partition, her jaw adrift. The woman smiled. 'Can I help you?'

'Em, I was wondering …'

The smile held. 'Yes?'

'I was wondering if you could … that is, I've just come back from the Sudan and while I was there I lost …'

'You lost something?' Eager, helpful. Big, eastern eyes.

'In the Sudan, yes, and I thought you might be able to find him.'

The smile faltered. 'Him?'

'Yes.'

The secretary, a voluptuous woman with dark wavy hair, stuck out her chin, then pulled it back in. 'I'm sorry, you have lost something in the Sudan?'

'Yes. No. Not something. Someone. A friend.'

'And how exactly did you, ah, lose him?'

'We got separated after we left Khartoum.'

'Ah.'

'And we were travelling at the time, you know, so it's not like we could meet back at the hotel. But he should be back in Khartoum by now and I need to let him know I'm in Cairo.'

Of all the questions that were flashing past the secretary's eyes, Frances could read the most prominent: why was she in Egypt if her friend was in the Sudan? So she answered before she was asked. 'My friends persuaded me that it would be better to come to Egypt, because we've no embassy in the Sudan.'

The woman looked nonplussed. 'And your friend – the lost one – he is in Khartoum, you think?'

'Yes. He must have gone back.'

'Have you telephoned your hotel there?'

'In Khartoum? No, I don't have the number.'

'Ah, well, I can send a message, if you like. Where were you staying?'

'The Acropole.'

'And your friend's name?'

'Richard Keane. And I'm Frances Dillon.'

'So you would like me to ask them to let Mr Keane know that you are fine and in Cairo?'

'Just get them to confirm that he's there. We can worry about niceties later.'

The woman scribbled down their names. 'Okay, I'll see if I can find a telex number for the Acropole, but it could take some time to get through.'

'I don't care. I'll wait.' Frances returned to her seat, relief flooding through her. Richard had to be at the Acropole – it was the only hotel he knew in Khartoum – which meant she might soon be speaking to him!

It was an interminable morning. She had brought nothing to distract herself, nothing to eat, but after an hour spent reading Irish tourist brochures, she was becalmed. She no longer jumped every time the phone rang, but instead stared at the walls with a numbed and vacant mind. There was no sign of diplomats rushing to and fro, only the two secretaries, and Frances was glad of it. Her situation was humiliating enough without looking ridiculous in front of curious officials.

Interrupted by phone calls and other work, it took the secretary almost two hours to find a telex number for the Acropole Hotel and then get a telex through to the Sudan. At one o'clock, she came out from behind the partition and introduced herself as Sabah. 'We are closing for lunch now, but I will contact you at your hotel when I hear from Khartoum.'

Frances's whole body slumped. They couldn't make her leave. She would go mad, pacing her empty room, the city screaming beyond the windows. It was quiet here, safe, and only by sitting right under Sabah's nose could she be sure of keeping her on the case. 'I'll come back this afternoon,' she said, getting up reluctantly.

Outside, she sat on a low wall by the river. There was no sky, just a dirty, colourless atmosphere which allowed only the more singular buildings, like Cairo Tower, some definition in the murky haze. The river was brown. Frances wondered if these were the same waters that had been with her in Khartoum. Had their journey to Cairo been simpler than hers?

After a long walk, she resumed her vigil. It wasn't very busy in the office; there were phone calls, but no visitors that afternoon.

At four, Sabah brought her a cup of tea and sat on the low table in front of her. 'When did this happen with your boyfriend?'

'Over a week ago.'

Her jaw dropped. 'So long! Have you phoned his family to see if they've heard from him?'

'I can't. They're in Australia.'

'Well, maybe the telex will bring some news, but I can call you at your hotel.'

'I'd rather wait here. I've got to find out where he's gone.'

Sabah smiled. 'Everything will be fine. Communications are not so good between Cairo and Khartoum, but we will find him, insh'allah.'

At the end of the day, Frances was about to leave when Sabah came out of the back room and called her to the window. 'Here,' she said, holding a telex. 'A reply from Khartoum. I am sorry, but your friend is not at the Acropole.'

Frances read the telex. It should have been enough for her; she should have walked out of that office and gone straight to book herself onto the next flight to anywhere, but she could not accept it.

'Perhaps he is on his way to Cairo?' Sabah suggested.

'Yeah, and maybe he's back in London.'

'You think he would go home?'

'He might, but the airlines won't tell me if he has or not.'

Sabah glanced at her colleague. Frances wished she hadn't spoken. She had to maintain caution, for if these women were to suspect the truth they might withdraw their assistance, believing that Richard had absconded by choice, and so she was forced to conceal the bewilderment that sat like a brick in her heart.

Numbed, she returned to the hotel.

That evening, when her bedroom grew oppressively lonely, Frances went up to the roof and stood by the railings looking out across Ramses Square. Standing on that rooftop was like perching on the fringes of hell and looking into one of its great pits. Humanity stirred there, moving about in great waves, harassed by volumes of dust and dirt, and almost drowned from sight by sheer noise. The masses moved swiftly, urgently; there was nothing languid about them, nor was there even that comfortable rush-hour feeling of commuters going to nice, cool homes, for this was a desperate movement and a desperate place. And every day Frances became part of the drive, hurrying across that feverish junction to get to the other side, and out of it, but sometimes she feared she would get stuck there forever, indefinitely condemned to the chaos of Ramses Square.

The next day, she lay about thinking. It had been nine days since Richard had vanished. Plenty of time for him to get to Khartoum. Time to get to Cairo even. To go to the Longchamps and ask for her. That was all he had to do. As for herself, she had pinned too much hope on the embassy. If Richard had become seriously ill or had fallen into the hands of the Sudanese authorities, his embassy would have been notified by now; if he was looking for her, he would have contacted the embassy himself, or the Acropole or the Longchamps; but if he had taken the first flight home, there was nothing anyone could do about it. Frances wasn't even sure what to do herself, and so an empty day passed, and it was like being drawn across time, slowly stretched, as over a rack.

Another omelette for supper, another pot of tea at a small table on the terrace, and another pointless conversation with the sympathetic waiter about what a wonderful time she was having in Egypt. The waiter knew better. He knew better than to go beyond the deep distraction on her face, to comment on the half-eaten food that always went back to the kitchen; instead, he spoke enthusiastically about his country in the hope that a little warmth would stop this lady from turning to stone on his terrace. Her movements grew more rigid every day; unlike the floppy-bodied tourists who slouched at the tables exhausted by the city's extremes, Frances walked and moved like someone whose limbs had stiffened. Her mind, likewise, was stiff. She registered the waiter's unspoken concern, and promised herself that when she had found Richard, she would explain to the Egyptian why she had always been so muted when he brought her tea on the top floor.

Dunking one end of a chip into the small pile of salt on the side of her plate, she watched the backs of a young English couple, new to the hotel, who were standing at the railing and gazing through a veil of pollution at one of Cairo's least attractive districts. The woman was clearly enthralled by the minarets, the wail of the muezzins, and the shrill cacophony of car horns, and when she came to sit at a table next to Frances, she smiled at her wide-eyed, shrugged her shoulders and said, 'I simply can't believe I'm here!'

Frances smiled back.

The girl leaned towards her. 'Ooh, that looks nice. What is it?'

Glancing at her plate, Frances replied, 'An omelette.'

'That's what I'll have, Sam,' the young lady said to her partner.

'We should keep it simple and save the tummy bugs for later. Won't be much of a honeymoon if we're both stuck in the loo.'

'You're just married?' Frances asked.

The dark eyes widened. '*Just* being the operative word!' She proffered her hand. 'Hi. I'm Lucy, and this is my husband, Sam. Ooh. Haven't said that yet.'

'Never thought you would,' said Sam, ruefully.

'We almost didn't make it to the altar,' Lucy began.

Frances felt as if she was being sucked into a whirlwind, but it proved a soothing place to be. Lucy was bubbling over with giddiness after their extraordinary wedding in Henley and was clearly bursting to tell someone – anyone – all about it. Although she had little choice in the matter, Frances was happy to oblige. Indeed, she welcomed this refreshing contrast to Lena's dreadful predicament.

Lucy was stunning, in looks and character; she had short black hair, almost black eyes, and was so ebullient that even Sam seemed a little exhausted after only two days of marriage. Frances sipped her tea, listening, and often laughing, as Lucy entertained her with tales of their multi-racial nuptials. She came from a well-to-do professional background and had been educated at Cheltenham Ladies' College, while Sam, who was of West Indian origin, had been brought up in Wandsworth. Both families had found their relationship difficult, and their wedding a nightmare. 'It was Notting Hill Carnival meets Chelsea Flower Show!' Lucy giggled. She insisted that Frances join them at their table, unaware that they were rescuing her from another evening as awful as the one before, and the one before that.

The next morning, Frances turned up at the embassy as soon as it opened. Hanging around in her hotel room was simply too excruciating; she had to do something.

Sabah was on the phone. The other lady, the angular Gina, came to the counter, her glasses perched on the end of her nose.

'I was just wondering,' said Frances, 'if we could maybe try

Khartoum again?'

'You have had no word from your friend?'

'No.'

'You must speak to Sabah.'

Sabah came to the counter, frowning. 'Still nothing?'

'No. You haven't heard anything, have you? I mean, if he had some kind of accident …'

'I'll have to speak to the ambassador when he gets in.'

'Oh, God, is that really necessary?'

'I think so, yes.'

An hour passed. Frances doodled in a notebook, drawing maps of Egypt and the Sudan and the railway that linked them, with two little stick people at either end. As she was doing so, a small dark man marched in, greeted the secretaries breezily and went through to another office. The ambassador. Sabah followed on his heels and came out again ten minutes later.

'Ambassador Doyle would like to see you.'

Frances hesitated.

Sabah smiled. 'He might be able to help.'

In his large, bright office, the ambassador greeted Frances with a warm smile and a reassuring handshake. He looked to be in his late fifties and had so much the appearance of a gentle father figure that she had to stop herself from bursting into tears and telling him the whole sorry tale. He waved her into a seat beside his desk. She sat down, twisting her fingers.

'I understand you've lost your companion.'

Although unwilling to come across like a silly tourist who didn't know east from west, Frances was too miserable to appear otherwise. She nodded.

'I see. And where were you exactly when you last saw him?'

She didn't answer for a moment, thrown back to that dusty rail carriage, creaking in the heat. 'I … We were on a train. The Nile Valley Express. Coming back to Egypt.'

'Yes, Sabah told me as much, but was your friend,' the ambassador glanced at his notes, 'Richard Keane, isn't it?'

She nodded.

'Was he in the compartment, or in the corridor perhaps, when you last—'

'He was sitting by the door. Then I fell asleep and when I woke up he was gone.' There. She'd said it.

'Good Lord.'

'I think he got off somewhere.'

'You think?'

'No, he *did* get off, according to another passenger. In Abu Hamed.'

'I see. He wanted to stretch his legs, I suppose, and missed the train?'

'Probably.' The office had huge windows. Frances looked out across the river; so grand, the Nile, and yet so dull and slovenly.

'When did this happen?'

'The Monday before last.'

'Does he have his passport on him?'

'Yes.'

'Money?'

She nodded.

'Good. So he's carrying his documents. That's something, anyway.'

'He has one of these.' She held up her knapsack.

'I see.'

There was a pause.

'Perhaps some tea?' the ambassador suggested.

'Thank you, but I really don't want to take up your time—'

'Not at all. This is what we're here for.' He buzzed through to the office, and then said, 'How long have you been in Africa?'

'About a month.'

'You're from Dublin?'

'Sort of. I've been away for years.'

'Where are you based now?'

106

'Nowhere. I've been living in Rome, but I'm moving to London after this trip. Richard works there. Look, I'm sure he'll turn up. If we could just phone around some hotels in Khartoum—'

'I think we need to be a little more proactive than that. Having one of our citizens going missing in the Sudan is no small matter.'

This was exactly what Frances did not wish to hear. She bit her lip. Should she come clean? Before this turned into an international incident should she admit that she might have driven her boyfriend right off that train herself? No. She needed whatever help came her way.

'What do you think he would have done, left behind in this Abu Hamed place?' asked the ambassador. 'How often does that train run?'

'Twice a week in theory, but it's very unreliable. When you get on it, you can never be sure when you'll get off. It even broke down in Wadi Halfa when I was there.'

'But I take it you waited for the next one to come through?'

'No, I … I didn't.'

'Oh? Why not? Surely the obvious thing would have been for him to catch the next train?'

'Yes, but when our train broke down, I thought all the others would be delayed, and I had no water left and there was this girl having a miscarriage and …' Frances stopped herself. 'I made a mistake. I should have waited.'

'You didn't consider going back to Abu Hamed?'

'I did, but I was afraid to get on the train without enough water.'

'Quite right. That wouldn't have been very wise.' He moved some telexes around his desk. 'Did you leave a message for him?'

'I left a note saying I'd meet him in Cairo, but I've spoken to the hotel in Wadi Halfa and they say he hasn't shown up, so he must have gone back to Khartoum.'

'But why would he go back instead of forward?'

'I don't know.'

The tea was brought in – nice china cups with Lipton's tea bags and milk, not the usual glasses of *shay bil na'na'*, sweet mint tea. Even though Frances loved the Arab brew, something akin to homesickness rumbled in her stomach.

The ambassador looked almost suspicious as he took three large gulps from his cup. 'Hmm. I'll have to get on to the British Embassy in Khartoum. They take care of our interests there, so we'll see if they can throw any light on this. I don't much like the idea of one of our nationals disappearing in that part of the world.'

'You don't think he's been abducted?'

'Oh, I doubt anything sinister has happened, but we don't like to lose sight of our tourists all the same. Richard wasn't ill, as far as you know?'

'No.'

'Could something have happened while you were asleep?'

'I hope so, but I can't think what.'

'You hope so?'

'I mean, I hope not.'

'Did the passenger who saw him disembark mention any commotion or trouble?'

'No, he made very little of it.'

The ambassador mused over this for a moment. 'All right. We'll start with the British Embassy and we'll try the Acropole again. Meanwhile, if he comes to Cairo, he's likely to go straight to your hotel, wouldn't you say?'

'Yes, I go over every day to see if they've heard from him.'

'You're not staying there?'

'No. We were at the Longchamps in Zamalek, but I can't afford it now. I'm staying near Ramses Station.'

'Then we must make sure the Longchamps people understand how vital it is that they let us know if he turns up.'

Frances put her cup on his desk. 'Thank you.'

'Not at all. We'll track him down for you. After all, there isn't much to detain a man in the Nubian Desert.'

Sabah immediately telexed the British Embassy in Khartoum

and then tried to telephone the Acropole. While she dialled, over and over, Frances paced. Back and forth along the coarse green carpet she strode, her stomach churning. For the first time in ten days, something solid was about to happen.

'Frances, I'm through,' Sabah called.

She jumped towards the counter. Sabah asked for Mr Richard Keane, and glanced at Frances. A conversation in Arabic ensued, which had Frances crawling over the desk in anticipation, but when the phone call ended, her knees buckled. She gripped the counter. 'What? He still isn't there?'

Sabah came over to her. 'There is nobody of that name staying there now. He was there some weeks ago, they said.'

'Yes – with me. Did you—'

'I asked them to check very carefully.'

'Oh, God. Where *is* he?'

'In another hotel, perhaps? I'll try the Sheraton and the Hilton, places like that.'

'He can't afford those. Jesus, what if he fell off the train and died in the desert?'

'You must not think like that. He's all right, I'm very sure.'

There was no immediate response from the Khartoum embassy. It was as if there was no one and nothing at the end of the line. For most of the day, Frances sat quietly, listening to every call that came into the office, even though she didn't understand most of them, but nothing related to her. And yet her heart leapt whenever the phone buzzed; and whenever the telex machine clicked into action in the back room, she held her breath until Sabah or Gina went to get the incoming message. Coming out again, telex in hand, they would look over at her and say, 'Sorry. It's only Dublin.'

And Frances would think, *Dublin*. It's only Dublin. The place she came from. That place where the 46A bus operates at whim, where yachts bob about at their moorings in Dún Laoghaire Harbour and Howth twinkles on the horizon like an island floating past, yet never leaving. Stuck rudderless in Cairo, Frances suddenly thought of Dublin as a nice town to come from, maybe even a nice town to be. Hills on one side, sea on the other. Wide, uncluttered pavements. Butter. Scones. Ice creams from Teddy's … Dublin toyed with her in her boredom, and she knew suddenly that Rod was right, that her home town would have her back, if she would go, even though in five years she had not once wanted to be there.

It was mid-afternoon when a telex came in from the British Embassy in the Sudan stating that no Richard Keane had come to their attention, but that they would make enquiries and get back to Cairo on Saturday.

'Saturday?' said Frances. 'Why can't they get back to us tomorrow?'

'Because we're closed tomorrow. It's Friday. Nothing can be done now until Saturday.'

'But I'll go mad before then!'

Gina looked at her as if she were already mad.

Friday was long and tedious. Frances crossed Ramses Square to meet the overnight train from Aswan, as she did every day, then went to the Longchamps, but found herself back at the hotel, back in the red restaurant, by noon. Muzak and tea. There was nobody there. Lucy and Sam had gone to the pyramids. They had invited Frances to join them but, quite apart from intruding on their honeymoon, it seemed inappropriate to take part in such an excursion when her life was on hold. Whether Richard's loss was accidental or otherwise, Frances felt like a person bereaved, and she had little inclination to retrace steps she had taken with him. But she longed for Sam and Lucy to return. She had become a parasite, hooking herself onto whoever happened to be floating by and travelling with them until they shrugged her off, as Lena had done. Amusing, really. All those years spent revelling in her hobo ways – the loner, the asteroid in space on its own unshakeable trajectory – only to discover now she was nothing of the sort.

7

Sabah came to the counter when Frances arrived early on Saturday morning.

'Anything from Khartoum?'

'I'm afraid not,' said Sabah. 'Perhaps you should contact his parents, Frances, and see if they have heard from him?'

'I don't have their number. They're in Australia.'

'I'm sure we could find them.'

'Can't they be left out of it for now? They'll only worry.'

'That's up to Ambassador Doyle. He'll be here shortly.'

Frances sank into one of the armchairs and closed her eyes. She felt less isolated here, less aimless. It was like hiding in a little piece of Ireland, away from all the frenzy and fury of Cairo, which had no respect for her predicament, and it gave her an uncertain sense of belonging. Being Irish had never meant much to her – it was simply a characteristic tagged on at birth – but here in Egypt it was acquiring new meaning. It meant that she was no longer adrift or alone, that she could come to this office and expect help, and as long as she sat here, she would not be forgotten. And nor would Richard.

The ambassador breezed in. 'Oh. Still no news?'

Frances shook her head.

'Dear, dear, dear, this is turning into quite a mystery. The hotels in Khartoum have drawn a blank, and he's had plenty of time to get to Cairo. Have you tried your hotel in Aswan?'

'Yes, and Wadi Halfa, when I can get through.'

'Hmm. Come along into my office.'

'This is all becoming a little peculiar,' he said as they sat down. 'We really ought to make more concrete enquiries. At this point, the embassy in Khartoum needs to do rather more than we have asked of it thus far.'

Frances didn't know what to say. If she gave any hint that Richard might be in some kind of trouble, his parents would be contacted and all hell would break loose. It might even become a newsworthy story: *Irish tourist missing in the Sudan*. Is that what she wanted? Was she prepared to draw British and Irish diplomatic attention upon them, terrifying his parents and friends, only to end up suffering humiliation when Richard turned up, saying all he'd done was to give his girlfriend the slip?

'I am quite as befuddled as you,' the ambassador went on, when she had not replied. 'It amazes me that a backpacker would allow himself to miss his train and become so stranded. And the fact that he hasn't turned up anywhere is very curious. If he got into trouble with the law, the Sudanese police would notify the British Embassy immediately, and if he had some other difficulty one would expect him to seek help. Trouble always rises to the surface, you know. So one could assume that he must be all right, which is encouraging, of course, but the question remains: where the divil is he?'

Frances fiddled with her money-belt.

'I am inclined, at this point, to contact his parents.'

'No, don't do that!'

'Why not?'

'Because, well, he might have flown home. To London.'

'London? But surely discovering *your* whereabouts would be his first priority?'

Frances's mouth was dry. She was running out of pretence. The ambassador was wheedling his way past the barriers behind which she had concealed certain facts.

The ambassador sat back and rocked his chair. Then he leaned forward. 'Is there any possibility, Frances, that we're dealing here with something … more personal, perhaps, than a missed train?'

'Of course not. We were very close.'

'But he took his belongings.'

Just like that, he said it. When had he seen through her? When had he guessed that there was more to this job than reuniting two careless tourists? 'He missed the train,' she insisted. 'We were going back. We were going to be together. It was all over, this roaming. I'd given it up. Why would he walk out when he had what he wanted? And why would he get off like that, and leave me asleep in a railway carriage not knowing what had happened to him? He wouldn't. Not Richard. He isn't that cruel. I wish I could tell you where he is, but I can't. I can't!'

The ambassador came around his desk to sit beside her. After a moment, he said, 'I take it then, that there is a possibility that he missed that train because he meant to?'

She shook her head, but as she did so, it began nodding of its own accord.

'I see. Curious way to go about it.'

Frances looked at the wall, blinked, bit her lip.

'You'd better tell me what happened – exactly.'

The whole truth divulged, he went to the window. 'I see your dilemma. Even taking into account the argument you'd had, we're not much wiser. It seems such an extraordinary reaction to make himself disappear in the Nubian Desert. Is he usually subject to extreme behaviour?'

'No, he's very sensible and steady, but I had been horrible all week. Who knows what I drove him to?'

'Have you tried phoning him in London?'

'I can't. He gave up his bedsit last month. We were going to get a new place when we got back.'

'Where were you going to stay in the interim?'

'With friends of his, but I don't have their number; I've never met them.'

'When is he due back at work?'

'The day after tomorrow. Our flight leaves tomorrow morning.'

'Then I suggest we give it another couple of days. We'll try his office before tracking down his parents. I don't want to alarm them unnecessarily, especially when they are so far away and ...'

And there is probably nothing to worry about.

'I have his office telex number,' said Frances.

'Grand. Give it to Sabah.'

'Ambassador, what do you think is the worst thing that—'

'You mustn't think like that. With a bit of luck, he'll turn up soon.'

Frances returned to her seat in reception and hardly moved for the rest of the morning. But the ambassador had uncorked a plug, and when Sabah brought Frances a cup of tea, the full story was unleashed upon her with all the vigour of a flushed lavatory.

Sabah was enthralled. 'You really think he stayed in Abu Hamed because he believed you no longer loved him?'

'Something like that. And because he'd lost his temper. My bet is he got off to spite me, then stood in Abu Hamed wondering what the hell he'd done.'

'If this is what has happened, why are you still in Cairo?'

'Because he might have a change of heart. He might come, or call. However angry he is, he must want to know that I'm okay.'

'But you left the Sudan because you believed it was over between you, and now you won't leave Egypt because you think it might not be over. This is a little confusing.'

'Sabah, when I left Wadi Halfa, I had somewhere else to go – some chance of finding him – but if I leave Cairo, where would I go then?'

In her hotel bedroom, Frances lay on her bed staring at the ceiling, thinking, thinking, until it seemed her head would spin off her shoulders and fly out the window. To prevent it from doing so, she went up to the restaurant, where she was driving a teaspoon around the red tablecloth when Lucy found her.

'There you are!'

'Hi. Nice day?'

'Fantastic.' Lucy sat down. 'We went around the museum. Amazing place, but my feet are aching. Sam's asleep. What have you been up to?'

'Oh, this and that.'

'I see.' Lucy's eyes narrowed. 'And was "this and that" as much fun as the museum?'

'Probably not.'

'Frances, can I ask you something?'

'Yeah.'

'What are you doing here?'

'Same as you. Seeing the sights.'

'Except you're not. You've seen the sights already. You've been upriver, and downriver, so what are you hanging about for?'

Frances sighed. 'It's a long story and one you don't want to hear on your honeymoon.'

'I knew it! I told Sam there was more to you than you were letting on. Come on, tell all.'

Now that her subterfuge had been tumbled by the embassy, there was no reason to prevaricate, but if she expected sympathy from Lucy, she didn't get it.

'My God,' she said, 'this is unbelievable. Losing your lover in the Sudan! Waiting for him to come and find you in Cairo!'

'Completely bloody ridiculous, isn't it?'

Lucy glanced at her coyly. 'Romantic, though. Far more romantic than my Henley-upon-Thames wedding.'

'It might seem romantic, but it isn't much fun!'

'Well, no, of course it isn't now, but once you get back together, you'll look back and think, golly, what an adventure that was! And just imagine your reunion – rushing into one another's arms in a crowded Cairo street, taxis hooting, dust blowing—'

'Jesus, what kind of books do you read?'

'Well, you have to admit, it is rather dramatic.'

'It doesn't feel in the least dramatic. It feels dull, Lucy; deathly dull. And long. I feel as if I've been in Cairo forever. Stuck in slow motion in a disaster zone.'

'Just you wait till he turns up.'

'And if he doesn't?'

'But that would spoil my honeymoon!'

Frances smiled. 'You're incorrigible.'

'And you worry too much. The embassies will find him – that's their job. This kind of thing happens all the time, you know. Tourists get lost. So, come on, let's go shopping. You need some retail therapy, and I want to check out Khan el Khalili.'

'Thanks, but I can't keep intruding on your honeymoon.'

'Why ever not?'

'It just isn't on,' Frances insisted, but she went shopping anyway, because Lucy had become her prop, the crutch that held her up. And it was in the busy alleyways of the vast Cairo souq, where even the oppressive evening air could not slacken Lucy's enthusiasm, that an unexpected shift took place.

They were in an Aladdin's cave of a shop, dim and smelling of spices, and while scarves, tablecloths and kaftans were spread across the counter for Lucy's consideration, Frances sat by the door on a carved wooden stool watching tourists ambling, and locals rushing, by. Her fingers were beating against the seat of the stool. Something was bothering her. She was worn out and unhappy, but that wasn't it. She was, she realized, bored. In Khan el Khalili, the greatest of all bazaars, she was bored. There had been a time when the very words *Khan el Khalili* would have seduced her, but now, sitting plonked in the middle of the biggest souq in Egypt, with its stolid heat, the whiff of pipes and spices, and the roar of Egyptian street life in the air – her fingers were beating against her seat.

She had been there before, of course. She had visited those brown, over-hung passageways with Richard, and countless other bazaars too, from Istanbul to Calcutta, all of them frenetic, aromatic, captivating … And yet one unacceptable thought hovered over her: *just another souq*. For so long she had believed she would never arrive at *just another souq*.

This was the first indisputable sign that she could tire of travel, that all the emotions it awoke in her could yet exhaust themselves. Novelty was no longer available to her, as it was to Lucy, and without it, her surroundings were losing their impact. She had always been certain the wonder and awe would never wear thin, and she had told Richard, often, that she would never tire of diversity or take it for granted. The shock that she might have been wrong made her tremble – expatriation had been her haven for years, had saved her from complacency. That her escape route should be barred to her now, when she most needed it, terrified her, for to drift about these places without the passion to sustain her would make for a questionable lifestyle.

And yet her fingers continued to pound against the stool. There was no denying it: wanderlust had taken its toll. That evening in the souq, her capacity for fascination stood weakened by the ravages of familiarity.

Richard came that night, as he did most nights when the thundering traffic made sleep impossible. She let the fantasy run its course. If she was destined to lose him, she would eventually forget the gestures and traits that had made him her lover, so she allowed herself to wallow in his details while she still could, even though the pain of seeing but not seeing, feeling but not feeling, loving and not loving, was akin to self-mutilation.

The following morning, she went to the airport to see her own flight leaving. She thought she might see Richard there, sneaking on to it. He was due back at work the next day. Not yet ready to give up on their future, she had cancelled her own seat on the plane, because if she failed to find Richard, she had yet to decide where to go. Without him, a different life lay ahead of her, so empty she could see right through it.

She had him paged. His name echoed around the terminal, unacknowledged. Cats sloped about the concourse, and one miserable kitten took to walking around with Frances. Lonely, like her; a beggar for company. When the flight finally took off, she still didn't know if Richard was on it or not, but seeing the tail-wing soaring off into the sky made her feel lower than any time she had seen him off in the past.

She spent the rest of the day in her room.

At five, Lucy came looking for her. 'Any word?'

Frances shook her head.

'Oh, poor you. Why don't you come and have tea with us?'

'No, thanks.'

'Frances—'

'I can't move, Lucy. Don't you see? I can't move. And even if I could, what would I do? I have nowhere to go, and no will to go there. I look at you and Sam and I think: that's what Richard wanted, that's all he asked – that we should be together – but I punished him for wanting me and now I see you two together and I *envy* you. I had what you have at my fingertips, and I blew it away.'

'I'm sure that's the purpose of all this, you know,' said Lucy. 'You'll get back with Richard, and when you do, you won't spurn what he has to offer.'

On the Monday that Richard was due back at work, Frances went again to the embassy. She didn't want to go, to face the truth, but she could no longer afford to stay in Cairo without income or purpose. It was past midday when she finally arrived in the office, and as soon as she did, Sabah stood up.

'The ambassador wants to see you.'

'There's news?'

'I think so,' she smiled as she held the door open.

'Ah.' Ambassador Doyle stood up. 'Miss Dillon, come in, come in.' He waved her towards a seat.

She clasped her hands so that he wouldn't see them shaking.

'I have good news at last. You can relax. Your friend is in one piece.'

Her chest caved in, every ounce of breath expelled by relief, and she slumped in the seat, fighting back tears. Good news, yes. He wasn't dead. Bad news, also.

'We telexed his office this morning. They came back to us a short while ago. Mr Keane hasn't returned to work yet—'

'What?'

'—but he does appear to be all right, thank God. He telephoned from Khartoum to say he's been delayed.' He handed her the telex.

Her hands shook. Her heart hammered. It said that Richard had been held up in Khartoum and would not be back for another week. 'But they give no reason!'

The ambassador tilted his head. 'No, and they don't say where he's staying either, but the fact that he hasn't contacted either embassy is a good sign. He clearly isn't in any difficulty.'

'But he might be sick.'

'Yes, possibly, but if it were serious, they wouldn't be expecting him back at work next week. All in all, I take this as very reassuring.'

Frances sat stunned, not reassured. Richard had had two weeks. He had contacted London, but not the Longchamps or the embassies or the Acropole or any other obvious point of contact. He was in Khartoum without her; would make his way home without her. All the questions that had been pounding about in her brain like wild horses had been answered.

The ambassador said, 'It seems likely you were right: he missed the train and returned to Khartoum.'

'I should have gone back,' she mumbled.

'I'm sure you made the right decision at the time. Travelling in such a harsh environment on your own is not to be recommended when the temperatures are beginning to soar. You might have fallen ill along the way and become very debilitated. It can happen so easily.'

Frances thought of Lena.

'And then I would have been looking for you instead.' He smiled. 'In my view, you took a very sensible course of action.'

'But now I'm here and he's there and I still have no way of reaching him.'

'You can catch up with him in London, surely?'

'No, I … I won't be going to London. I have no reason to.'

'You don't wish to see him?'

'It's apparent he doesn't wish to see me.'

'Perhaps,' said the ambassador gently, 'but London is, at least, on the way to Dublin.'

She caught his eye. Dublin. What was Dublin doing in her life all of a sudden? It kept peeking around the door like someone waiting to come in.

Beyond the window, Cairo had grown dim. A brown cloud had descended on it. As if in defiance of the grim, featureless horizon, she said, 'I'll stay here. I could get a job teaching English.'

'You could, but you've been through something of an ordeal. If you want my opinion, Frances, you should go home for a while.'

She stood up. 'Thank you so much for everything. I suppose it's been a very odd case for you.'

'Not the oddest by a long shot. Let me know what you decide to do.'

'Yes.' She held out her hand.

'You've drunk the water of the Nile at least. That means that one day you will return to Egypt.'

When Frances stepped out of the office block that housed the embassy, a gust of *khamseen* hit her. It was not a cloud that had descended on Cairo, but a notorious seasonal wind that was sweeping across it, bringing half the Libyan desert for company. Every crease in Frances's skin was colonized by sand – dirty sand at that, hard and grimy – which stuck to her scalp like a skin disease. Blinded, she fell back into the lobby, gasping. She and Richard had planned their trip to avoid this wretched wind, but here she was, still in Cairo, caught in the midst of it on her own. Her taxi drove up. When she ventured towards it, she was blasted again. Through emptying streets, they made their way to the hotel, and by the time they got there, the wind was blowing so hard that even with a scarf over her mouth, Frances couldn't breathe when she got out of the car. The city had shut down. It was a sudden affair, the khamseen, and the Cairenes' response was rapid. Ramses Square was already deserted, taxis had vanished, shutters were closed. Cairo was ducking.

Frances went to her room. In a matter of seconds, her ears and eyes had been filled with dirt and there was a revolting sensation of grit all over her teeth. Her hair felt as if it had been dead for years. After a long shower, she went up to the dining-room in the hope of finding Sam and Lucy. They were there, sitting in a corner, grounded by the wind.

'Nothing for it but to stay in until it passes,' Sam said, 'that's what the waiter says.'

'More tea then,' said Lucy.

'I'm going for a kip,' said Sam. 'Leave you two to do what women do best.'

'What's that?'

'Talk your way through time without noticing.'

When he had gone, Frances turned to Lucy. 'He's in Khartoum.'

'What?'

'Richard. The embassy telexed his office this morning. Apparently he rang last Friday. He's still in Khartoum.'

Lucy's eyes lit up. 'Fran! He's waiting for you!'

This startled her. 'No. No, of course he isn't. Lucy, he may be in Khartoum, but he has made no attempt whatsoever to locate me.'

'How do you know?'

'Because it's bloody obvious! He hasn't tried any of the likely places, but he had no problem phoning his boss to say he won't be back to work on time.'

'So why is he still there?'

'The flights are probably booked out. God, I don't know! Maybe he met someone else?'

'And maybe he's waiting for you to come back from the border.'

'No, Lucy, no. Look, he isn't even staying at the Acropole, the hotel we stayed in. I mean, why would he go anywhere else except to avoid me?'

'Damn. If only you'd turned back.'

'I'll never live that down, will I? Coming to Egypt. But at the time, if you'd been in my place, you wouldn't have stopped in the Sudan either.'

'I would, you know, if Sam had missed our train.'

'Richard didn't miss it!'

'How can you be so sure?'

'Because I can feel it in my gut. I know that man, and I know what he said to me that day, and now he's in Khartoum and he's done feck-all to locate me! I think I should get the message and move on, don't you?'

'But so many different things might have happened.'

'Oh, take off those rose-tinted glasses, would you? You'll be no help to me until you do!'

'All right. But you can't give up on the basis of one telex. You should phone his office yourself and find out what's delaying him.'

'I can't afford to phone London.'

'Ask the embassy to do it.'

'I can't ask the embassy to do any more. Their brief was to establish that Richard is okay. They've done that.'

'All right then, I'll do it. Give me the number. I'll pay for the call. Let's find out exactly what's going on with that man.'

'I can't expect you to—'

'Come on. We'll call from your room. What time is it at home?'

'About twelve.'

Frances stood by the window while Lucy patiently tried to get through to London. Over and over, she dialled the number, and when her call was finally answered, she spoke at her officious best. 'Could I speak to Mr Keane, please?'

Frances didn't breathe.

'... Oh. But I understood he'd be back by now? ... I see. And have you any idea why he's been delayed?'

The answer to that question was short. 'Well, can you tell me where I might contact him? It's important I speak with him.' Her accent was becoming more arch with every word. 'But you must know where he's staying? I'm an old family friend—' She shook her head at Frances. 'Very well. But when you hear from him, please tell him—'

Frances swung around. 'No!'

'—I called. Lucy Welder. Thank you.' She hung up. 'If they knew it was you phoning, they might tell us where he is! He might have left a message for you.'

'Why should he leave a message there, when he hasn't left one anywhere else? What did they say?'

'"Unavoidably detained overseas." That's their line. They won't even say where he is. You'll have to meet up with him in London, Fran. Forget Khartoum. Forget Cairo. Get this sorted out at home.'

Frances looked out of the window. Dilapidated buildings with peeling orange walls; blue shutters clattering against the wind; a carpet hanging out of a closed window flapping madly. Strange, she thought, how Ramses Square and its district didn't seem such a hellhole anymore. It was where she lived, and she liked it.

'Fran, you know we're leaving for Luxor tomorrow?'

She nodded.

'It's just ... I'll be worried about you. What are you going to do?'

'Stay here. Get a job.'

'A job? Here? Why?'

'What option do I have?'

'You could go to London and see Richard.'

'If I go to London, I'll get trapped. If Richard has dumped me, I'll get stuck in England, penniless. I'd rather be here. If I can't have him, can I at least have the life I would have had without him? The life I know best?'

Lucy was sitting cross-legged on Frances's bed in a long black dress, her black hair greyed by deposits of dust, her eyes dark and earnest. 'I'm worried about what will happen to you if you stay, because this isn't Cairo anymore, Frances. This is limbo you're living in, and I wish you'd get out of it.'

Frances sat down, squeezed Lucy's hand, and nodded.

The idea came to her not long after Lucy had left her, and the decision followed in a flash: she would turn around and go back to Khartoum. It was the only thing to do. She had to retrace her steps and return to the point where she had lost him, because she could live with herself only if she finally did the one thing she should have done at the start: turned around. Lucy was right: he was waiting for her in Khartoum. He was holding tight, expecting her, knowing that she would keep on moving until she found him. Therefore, he had to remain still or they would go on forever, circling one another like planets and never colliding.

The trip would be long and lonely. Pacing her room, Frances asked herself over and over if she could do it all again? Yes. She had to do it, had to cast the widest net to find him, even if it meant facing that wretched steamer again, with its awful memories, enduring temperatures ever more demanding, and maybe even getting stuck in Wadi Halfa. It would take a week or more to reach Khartoum, and when she got there, her funds would be virtually non-existent, but she wouldn't have to worry about money once she found Richard. She grabbed her bag, determined to brave the khamseen as far as the taxi rank outside the station. Time to cash in her British Airways ticket and get another visa for the Sudan.

The wind had dropped quite a bit when she came out of the hotel and made her way around the corner towards the footbridge. The shifting ground moved beneath her feet as the desert raced across it like Ramses Square commuters rushing to get home. That crumbling sidepath knew her well. Two shopkeepers – one sold fruit and vegetables, the other soft drinks – were opening their shutters as she passed. Frances smiled, knowing that she would trundle past their doors no more on her way to meet the trains. To reach the footbridge, she had to negotiate her way across some dangerously disintegrated pavement and walk through a pile of sand that had accumulated at the foot of the steps. A few people had emerged in the lull and were braving the tail end of the wind, but Frances had never seen the square so empty. Cairo: The Last Day. All sand and dust and a few straggling inhabitants. And an Irish woman.

On the steps, a couple of children huddled under a thin piece of torn, striped cotton. They begged as she passed. It was dull. No sky, even, only a sandy-coloured gloom. Frances pulled her scarf over her face and made her way up, holding the railing, and nearly tripped over the old legless beggar, citizen of the bridge, who hadn't moved from his spot in spite of the khamseen. Three young boys came towards her, gadding about, their gallabiyas blowing around them, and others emerged, stepping out tenuously to resume their day. Cars started up again. Buses honked. And yet, for all the familiarity, for all the things she had grown used to, even particular characters known to her, Frances began to feel peculiar. She sensed, suddenly, that she was horribly out of place, and the more the Cairenes came at her, the more desperate and separate she seemed to become. But it wasn't them at all, or even her.

On that footbridge, it all burst. Frances burst, and it was no mild display. She never even felt it coming; she simply found herself leaning over the railing, crying as she never had. She sobbed and sobbed. For Richard, for herself, for Lena's baby even. The tears poured from her and dropped towards the dusty cars as they passed below, but she couldn't hear the relentless beeping, the drone of the city as it stood up in the aftermath of the khamseen. All she could hear was the heaving in her chest, the raspy desperation, the great sobs queuing up to escape her. All she thought about was Richard. Not Cairo, nor the Sudan, nor their pathetic disagreements. Only Richard. Every time she caught her breath, she cried his name. She missed him. She missed him so thoroughly she thought she had died.

No one came near her. The walkers of the walkway had seen worse, probably, than this woman draped over the railings. It was not accumulated stress that had overcome her, it was a simple fact. She and Richard were finished. She hadn't really understood it until then, and so her insides came out.

The tears retreated, but for a long time she didn't take her eyes from the traffic, as cars zoomed about beneath her, pushing through haphazardly, filling every tiny gap with their bulk. She might have stayed there in a trance forever, but her eyes were stinging, her face gathering grime, and her ribs ached. She pulled herself up and turned back towards the hotel. It was quite simple, the easiest thing she had done in weeks. After trudging about with lead in her soles, this was like walking for the first time. She went back across that bridge, looking into the faces, and came down those steps and off that footbridge, and everything was clear. She may have been stranded in Cairo, but she and Richard had seen the last of their time together and all she could do now was step into the void that lay beyond him.

Two days later, she flew to London.

two

8

Richard watched Frances sleeping. He wondered how she did it. Curled up like a foetus on the bench, her head near the window, she was out for the count. In this heat. In spite of what had been said. He would have liked to sleep, but was too cross, too seriously pissed off. His mind boiled over. He sat by the door, hunched up like an angry gnome, his bare feet on the seat opposite, and looked at her with unkind eyes. When would she stop flogging him for wanting to be with her? Would she ever stop? Or would their lives in London decompose in time, infected by bitterness, because she failed to settle and he failed to be worth it? He glanced at her slender feet, the blonde curls bunched up behind her head. Everything he loved about her made her difficult to love. The abjuration of responsibility; the hatred of convention; the crazy embrace of the unexpected. It turned him on, and drove him wild, but he could not spend the rest of his life chasing her from platform to platform.

He looked up. Outside, the desert was flat. So flat, and still. Telegraph poles followed one another in single file across the plain. Little heaps of sand and occasional piles of rubble pockmarked the bare land. *The beautiful, desperate, desert*, Richard thought. Frances was right. There *was* beauty in its unadorned, uncompromising emptiness.

His feet rocked of their own accord, keeping time with the gentle sway of the carriage. The creaking of the old wooden coach was regular, monotonous, like somebody sawing manually through a large tree trunk, and beyond it, he could hear the low purr of the engine. The brakes hissed then, and the train shuddered as it slowed. They were coming into Abu Hamed.

Richard closed his eyes. Tried to stop thinking. He had been reasonable, more than reasonable. He had played it her way from the start, and yet she resented him now for wanting to secure their future. He had said awful things. She had said awful things. It was wearying, and he really had to wonder if taming her would not also break her. And if it did, could he take the consequences? The train came gently to a standstill. Voices called out. Did he *want* the consequences? This thought in mind, he fell into a light sleep.

A sudden movement in the compartment woke him. His knapsack was snatched from his side. He leapt to his feet, dazed, and momentarily lost his balance when he leaned out the door. A young boy was darting down the passageway. Cursing, Richard pulled on his sandals and ran after him.

He fell into a sea of bodies milling around the platform, but the boy had vanished into the crowd and since Richard had only seen his back, he wouldn't have known the kid if he came up and asked him the time. That didn't stop him rushing about looking for him, pushing his way through the crush, certain that he would recognize the brat if he could only find him. He shouted, 'My bag! My bag has been stolen!' No one seemed interested.

He went too far from the railway. Unaware that they had already been in Abu Hamed for a while, he ran down to the river, a few hundred yards from the station, and waded from boat to boat, seeking out every face.

When he heard the whistles, he thought he still had time. He thought getting his passport back was the only thing that mattered, and he was knee-deep in the water when he looked up and noticed through the haze that the people on top of the train seemed to be moving. It was like a mirage. He couldn't hear the engine above the sound of the outboard motors and the chatter of people around him, so he just had this shimmering impression of bodies sitting upright, gliding through the air. He made a dash for it, but he hadn't a chance. The Nile Valley Express was no bullet train, but it wasn't the locomotive he was racing against, it was the heat. It was like running towards a giant blowtorch. The air held him back. The rush of sand particles burned his eyes and scorched his throat, his trousers stuck to his legs, and when he reached the tracks and came in behind the last carriage, he lost his footing and tumbled. He got up, took another sprint down the line, but in that heat couldn't run at even half his normal speed – he'd whacked his knee pretty badly and it was hard to breathe. He couldn't make it.

When the crowd at the station dispersed, Richard realized he was categorically in the middle of nowhere and absolutely banjaxed. He was stranded in a desert town with *no* passport, *no* money and *no* Arabic. Not even a bleeding hat. Looking along the track at the shimmer in the distance which was all that was left of her, he had the oddest feeling that he'd never see Frances again.

He searched the platform, the station, every nook and cranny, hoping the boy might have taken the money and dropped the bag, but there was no sign of a knapsack. There was a great flurry of sand and traffic as pick-up trucks and vans left town in the wake of the train, and Richard supposed the young thief was amongst them. Some Sudanese men sat against a wall, watching him, so he approached them and tried to explain – boy, so big, snatched bag, ran ... They stared at him, expressionless.

'Look, my bag has been stolen! I was on the train and this boy came along and took it.' They frowned, and it occurred to him that accusing one of their own of theft was probably not the way to go about gaining their sympathy. As a small crowd gathered around him, Richard's story evolved into a pragmatic moulding of the truth. 'A boy ... so big ... we were talking, you know. And I missed the train. Do you know this boy? He might be able to help me because now the train's gone and I'm stuck.' He motioned towards the tracks. 'It's bloody gone without me!'

They talked amongst themselves, gesticulating, arguing, looking with consternation and some concern at this foreigner, who kept raving at them about the train leaving as if it was a personal affront. Richard felt as if he was standing inside a glass bottle – everyone could see him, but no one knew why he was there – and soon, with a few of them muttering that there would be another train, that he would be all right, the little gathering broke up. The show was over, as far as they were concerned. Some stupid foreigner had missed the train. Not much anyone could do about that, except tell him to wait for the next one.

In the station building, Richard found a couple of men sitting behind old mahogany desks in a bare office. 'I need help,' he said. *A boy stole my bag. He took my money.* 'I ... I missed the train.'

They could see he had missed the train, and in that gentle, patient, African way, looked at him as though he were more foolish than unfortunate.

'You did not hear whistles?' one of them asked.

'I was down by the river.'

The other man shrugged. 'Next train two, maybe three days.'

'But I can't wait that long. I have no money! Some rotten kid ... I mean, everything's on the train. I have nothing.'

The same one raised his chin towards the door. 'You go lacunda.'

Lacundas were the far from salubrious local hotels, but Richard couldn't go to any hotel, not without his passport, since hotels were requested by law to ask for identification, and register the details, of every guest who checked in.

What he needed was to think, but every molecule in his body resisted any notion of coherent thought. He went outside again. Out, into air so hot that just breathing made him burn inside. There were trucks parked in front of the station and boats were still motoring back and forth across the river, but nothing within Richard's line of vision gave him any clue about what to do next, and his powerlessness irked him.

'Talk about being absolutely fucking stranded,' he said to nobody at all.

With what energy he could muster, he ran about again, down to the river and around the station, looking for the boy and his knapsack; he spoke to lingering travellers, paced beside the track, then went back into the station, leaned against a wall, and slid to the ground, exhausted. One of the stationmasters came to him. The other brought the inevitable glass of tea. They were sympathetic, but not big on suggestions.

Richard waved a squadron of flies from his face. 'What should I do?' he asked the quieter man, when the corpulent one had gone back to his desk.

'Wait next train.'

'But I have no cash, nothing to live on. And my girlfriend will be wondering what the hell's happened to me. I have to get out of here. I have to—' he leapt to his feet and pointed at the desks '—telephone! Of course. I have to call somebody! Can I use your phone?'

'Yes, yes.' He led Richard to his desk and held the heavy black receiver out to him.

But who to phone? Even if there had been some semblance of a telephone directory within a two-hundred-mile radius, Richard would have been unable to read it. As for Directory Enquiries ...

'I call police?' asked the man helpfully.

'Jesus, no! I mean, I'm sorry, thank you, but they might not understand. They might think—' He waved his hand around meaninglessly, because he didn't know what they might think and he didn't want to find out. The traffic police in Khartoum had been all affability with tourists, but Richard had heard mention of a secret police and, way out here, he didn't wish to make their acquaintance, even as the victim of a robbery, unless he absolutely had to. He looked hard at the man, waiting for his reaction.

The stationmaster lifted his chin, but did not nod in collusion. Nor did he press the point.

'What I need to do is call the British Embassy. They'll tell me what to do. Could you call them? In Khartoum?'

'You have number?'

'No, but it must be in a telephone book. You know, in the directory.'

The man shook his head and replaced the receiver. He was a gentle, handsome man, tall, like most Nubians, with exceptionally bright, long teeth, and a shirt to match. Richard could see in his eyes that he wanted to be helpful, but even if they could get through to the embassy, what could the diplomats do? Tell him to sit fast in this sandpit for two days until they came to fetch him? No, if he was going to get out of here, he would have to do it on his wits alone.

'What's the best way to Wadi Halfa?'

'Train.'

'Besides the train. Is there a bus?'

The man wobbled his head. 'Sometimes.'

'Could I get a pick-up truck?'

'Boksi?'

'Yes, boksi. I could pay when we get to Wadi.'

'Wadi Halfa not so easy. El Khartoum maybe.'

Richard didn't need to be told that Wadi Halfa was the wrong way to go. Even if he got there, he couldn't get across the border. Their trip was done for. There was little point in going after Frances just to tell her he had to go back to the capital to get another passport. He could forget about Abu Simbel.

'I only have one option,' he told his puzzled friend, 'I'll have to hitch – you know, get a lift – to Khartoum.'

'El Khartoum,' the man repeated, flashing those extraordinary teeth.

'But to hitch, I need a road. There is a road, isn't there?'

'A bit. Train better.'

'I understand that, but we've already established that without any money, I can't buy a ticket, so a train isn't much good to me – even if there was one, which there isn't!' He slammed his fist onto the desk. 'Fuck it!'

The two men jumped.

'Sorry!' Richard raised his hands. 'I'm sorry. I just … I just …'

Eyeing him warily, the second man gathered his belongings, shook Richard courteously by the hand and bade him good evening.

Richard turned in alarm to the other one. 'The station isn't closing, is it? You're not leaving too?'

Another wobbly nod was his only reply. Two men came in then and for some time absorbed the attention of the stationmaster, leaving Richard to wander out into the town again, in search of that lift to Khartoum. Not far from the station, a young man was leaning against a pick-up truck, smoking a cigarette; Richard approached him, pointed at the truck and said, 'El Khartoum?'

The man looked him over, considering this potential business opportunity, and smoked thoughtfully. When he spoke, in Arabic, Richard was well able to understand he was talking money. He shook his head and pulled out his pockets to show he had nothing. The sun scorched the back of his neck, blurring his bargaining power. Flies explored his lips. The owner of the truck shrugged and walked away.

Back at the station, Richard stood on the platform, looking down the tracks, then kicked a wall. He paced, dust swirling around his feet. 'What's wrong with a nice holiday motoring in France, eh? A few weeks on a beach in Spain?' he said out loud. 'Oh no, that's far too common for our Miss Dillon. We're much too alternative to holiday with the masses! Much better to have killer heat, an intimate relationship with fine dust, and get stranded in the fucking desert!'

Exhausted by his outburst, he stumbled into the shade and slumped to the ground. There was no escape. It seemed absurd that an average human being of adequate intelligence and resourcefulness was apparently unable to get himself out of this predicament, but every idea that came to him was quashed by the fact that he had no money with which to make it happen. With the right notes in his pocket, he could have been out of there in a matter of hours.

There was a terrible stillness about the place, now that the fuss of the train had died down, and Richard was as far from anywhere as he had ever been. Nothing was familiar, and the alienation was crushing. Anything common or recognizable had vanished. He could hardly grasp it: one minute he had been asleep on a train, trundling along on his holidays, and the next – in a blink – he was in a desert town, removed from anything he knew, and penniless to boot. Frances was the only person within two thousand miles who knew him, and it would take her days to get back from Wadi Halfa. He couldn't wait that long. Apart from the fact that he would go hungry waiting for her, he didn't fancy sitting in a station for several days. The police would almost certainly take exception to this *hawajah*, this foreigner, hanging about their jurisdiction without identification. They could pick him up. If they did, they might notify the embassy, but then again they might not, and Richard wasn't inclined to chance it. His head whirled. He blamed Frances and her wanderlust, blamed himself, cursed everything. It was particularly infuriating that all this stemmed from one moment, one lousy moment of poor judgment, which had utterly changed his circumstances and thrown him way off course. He was out of control, and lost.

The stationmaster was sitting alone when Richard went back in to him. He extended his hand. 'I'm Richard. Richard Keane.'

'Suleiman.'

'Pleased to meet you, Suleiman, and I'm sorry to cause you trouble, but I wonder if you could get a message to Wadi Halfa to let my girlfriend know what's happened?'

This course of action required a lengthy discussion, at the end of which Suleiman finally picked up the receiver. He leaned into it, frowning, then called out to one of the engineers hanging around the platform.

'What's wrong?'

'Not working.' Suleiman, tapping the cradle, continued his conversation with the engineer.

'What do you mean?' Suleiman held out the receiver. Richard

took it. No dial tone. No line. Like the electricity supply, communications were intermittent in this country. 'For how long? When will it be fixed?'

'Soon,' said Suleiman helpfully. 'Maybe tomorrow.'

Richard suppressed a yowl. He was truly cut off now. 'Look,' he said, 'I have to get to Khartoum. I need to get to the city.'

Suleiman looked at him at length, not smiling this time, but genuinely absorbing his plight, and it concerned Richard that he might still notify the police. Instead, after great deliberation, he repeated 'El Khartoum' several times, and put away the great ledger he was working on. Indicating that Richard should wait there for him, he strode out of the building.

Richard walked, inside and outside, and even along a stretch of track, his stomach knotting when he realized he would have slid away along these very tracks aboard that train if he had only stopped to think. Old locomotives and coaches were hibernating on the sidings, shunted off the main line, as he had been.

Driven indoors by the sun, although it was now evening, he allowed every conceivable course of action to run through his head, but as time moved on he grew nervous. Where had the bloke gone? Would he come back? He paced around the station. This was like being locked out of his home – the house was there, the car was there, but he couldn't get into either – except that in this case there was a bloody awful heat wave going on and the neighbours didn't understand that he needed a ladder.

It was almost dark by the time Suleiman returned. Richard was sitting on the floor, leaning against the wall, mentally and physically exhausted. The Nubian had another man with him, a small, spindly individual, wearing a white shirt, an old pair of brown pinstriped trousers, and a pair of spectacles.

'This man go to El Khartoum,' Suleiman said. 'You go with him.'

Richard stood up, unable to believe his ears. 'Go with him? …

Are you sure?' He turned to the driver. 'I have no money, nothing to offer you.'

Suleiman tutted and vigorously shook his head, as if he had insulted them both.

'Thank you,' said Richard, shaking the driver's hand. 'Thank you so much. This is wonderful. You've no idea—'

'I am sorry, he does not speak English. He is Madgid.'

They led Richard outside to where a truck, stacked high with sacks, was parked. It seemed Madgid was going to Khartoum anyway. His knees weak with relief, Richard kept saying 'Shoukran! Shoukran!' as if they had opened the very gates of Paradise, not organized a lift out of their own home town. 'You are so kind,' he said. 'I'm eternally grateful for your help.'

Madgid spoke to Suleiman, then called 'Assalam aleikum' and walked away. 'Aleikum assalam,' Suleiman replied.

'Eh? Where's he off to? I thought we were going to Khartoum?'

'Yes, yes,' said Suleiman. 'But not yet.'

'Not yet? When then?'

He shrugged.

'But—'

'Come. You come with me.' Suleiman went back to the station.

Richard's elation collapsed. He could be there for days. The truck was loaded – with dates, probably – but that didn't mean anything. Time was dispensable in this part of the world.

Suleiman led him some way along the platform to a tiny hovel of a room with a mattress on the floor. It was probably where he slept himself when trains were due to stop during the night; or maybe he lived there. Richard looked into this bare cement cell. Suleiman seemed delighted that he had, against all odds, managed to sort out the crazy foreigner who had missed his train, and while Richard tried to rise to this generosity, he failed to shake off the disappointment that they couldn't just jump into the van and go. Still, he appreciated the bed, however rank, and the privacy.

Suleiman said, 'You okay here. No one come.'

This confirmed that Richard was at risk travelling without documents, and if Suleiman understood this, then Madgid must know it too. With a warm handshake, Suleiman disappeared into the great unknown of Abu Hamed, leaving Richard alone.

He lay down on the mattress. It was cooler now, and it had grown very dark very quickly. There was no bulb on the wire that dangled from the ceiling, so he left the door open to hang his eyes on the light of the stars. The mattress stank and he was soon scratching, but the luxury of being horizontal after rushing about all evening made him pass out almost immediately.

He woke within a few hours, flea-bitten, stiff and hungry – and that was the easier part of the night. Too tense and thirsty to sleep any more, he wondered how and when he would next get food, how long he would be there, and then, when he thought he had exhausted his stack of things to worry about, he remembered scorpions. The thought propelled him off the mattress and left him standing in the middle of the room, his eyes darting about redundantly in darkness. If a hungry scorpion was about to make a move on him, there was not a lot he could do about it, so he comforted himself that it would be best not to see it coming and lay down again. They might find him dead in the morning; if they didn't, he hoped they wouldn't let him die of thirst.

It was so quiet he imagined he could hear the wildlife that inhabited his mattress going about its nocturnal routines. This was the real silence of the desert, and he was sure even Frances had not experienced it. He had to suppress the desire to call out, to shatter the quiet and blot out the sound of blood sliding about his veins. So far beyond any point of recognizable reference, it was as if he had been absorbed into the night.

He got up again and went outside. At least it was cooler now. 'Okay,' he said, 'so this is awkward and uncomfortable and a pain in the arse, but it'll be okay. Once we get to Khartoum, it'll be fine. Pop over to the embassy, get another passport, and swoosh. First plane home.'

He felt his way back into his cave and lay down again. Mosquitoes. Malaria. Rats. Hepatitis. Crotch rot. All the things he had so far avoided on his travels with Frances would now come at once. In this eerie blackout, it was hard to believe otherwise. Without taking daily prophylaxis, he would surely contract malaria at the very least. His knee throbbed from the fall he had taken, and would probably become infected. He scratched. He could feel the bed lice and head lice and fleas feeding off him. Could imagine them sucking. The next day he would be covered in bites, and he'd probably have diarrhoea too, in spite of the fact that he hadn't eaten anything. Dehydration was his greatest concern. Even if they gave him an endless supply of tea, it would only dehydrate him further, since tea is a diuretic. He would have no choice, in the morning, but to drink whatever water he could find and take the consequences.

'This is great craic,' he said out loud, 'great craic altogether.'

He spent another day at Abu Hamed, hostage to his own impetuousness. When morning came, dry and scorching, he woke suddenly and thought he was suffocating. He dived towards the door, but the air was equally tight outside, and an accumulation of dust lodged in his throat made it difficult to swallow. He longed for a drink, but would have to wait for Suleiman to arrive if he was to get some tea, so he went for a walk to kill time – down to the Nile, of course, which, in an unassuming, timeless way, demanded veneration.

The river bank was quite lush. Beneath a couple of palm trees, Richard rested on his hunkers and stared at the water. He could drink it and risk hepatitis, bathe in it and invite bilharzia. Instead, using every ounce of self-restraint available to him, he turned away from its deceptive enticements and strolled on. There was some life about. A few goats and a donkey. He even heard an unseen camel protest loudly at some injustice being done to it.

Abu Hamed station was quite impressive, given its location. Frances would have loved its broad platforms and neglected colonial buildings, the untidy sidings littered with under-used locomotives. She would have loved the anachronism, the very dereliction of the place. The town, too, was bigger than the dot on their map had indicated, but Richard was afraid to explore it. He couldn't risk missing his lift. He drew comfort from the sight of Madgid's truck, still parked in the street, waiting to leave for Khartoum. Every twenty minutes, he checked it had not moved.

Hunger was becoming increasingly difficult, but he had to make slight of it, because all he really needed was a drink. As long as he could drink, and as long as Madgid left that day, everything would be all right. But how he longed for money. Cash. Without it, he was nothing. He could not even feed himself, water himself. Without it, he had no meaning in this landscape, for he was neither tourist nor aid worker nor anything of any value to anyone, even himself. It was a curious place to be: no identity without papers, no hope without Madgid. He had freedom, of course; he was not shackled to a wall or locked into a cell, although that is what Suleiman's humble bunker felt like. But his freedom was of no use to him without money. The only asset he had was the charity of those who had so little.

Suleiman arrived at last, bringing with him a chunk of bread for Richard's breakfast, and set about making tea. Richard stuffed the dry bread into his parched mouth, and when he had swallowed it all, longed for more. Oh, to reach into his pocket and summon a waiter to ask for the same again!

Suleiman handed him a glass of steaming tea. They drank, sitting in the office, where the phones still weren't working, and when Richard asked when Madgid would be leaving, Suleiman was noncommittal. A shrug and reassurance that he would not be left behind was all Richard had to go on. He must wait, then, until fortune moved him on, and so he must drink. With one eye on the kettle, he asked Suleiman if he could boil some water.

'You like more?' He held up his own glass.

'No, no, thanks. I'd just like to drink some water.'

Suleiman motioned him outside and led him to another dank, dark room, where there was a tap dripping into an old enamel sink.

'Yes, but I must boil it first. It's better for me that way.'

Suleiman shrugged, but made no fuss when Richard took the kettle to the tap and filled it. Out in the sun, he poured some water onto the platform. As expected, it was cloudy, an unappetising shade of brown – Nile water, no doubt, with all its rich, bacterial components – so he boiled it again and again, and when eventually it cooled, he drank it with his eyes closed. It could do no more damage than the tea, he told himself, and he had the presence of mind to ask Suleiman if he would kindly bring him some empty bottles, so that he could prepare a supply for the journey to Khartoum.

Even though he spent the whole day waiting to leave, the hours passed quickly. His mind was preoccupied at every minute. He might have been stuck in a railway station where nothing happened, but the very unfamiliarity of his whereabouts kept him stimulated. He talked to Suleiman and some engineers, climbed around the redundant coaches in the sidings, and at one point stood out on the narrow track thinking about the men – Kitchener's men – who had laid this line in brutal conditions. Richard had read about Kitchener before the trip. It had been his idea to take the line straight across the desert, from Wadi Halfa to Abu Hamed, instead of following the great curve in the Nile. He was mocked for imagining it could be done, but he and his men had succeeded in the 1890s. How had they done it, Richard wondered now, when he was beaten back into the shade after only minutes?

Exhaustion also played its part in shortening the day, allowing him to doze through the hottest hours, but when he woke and found that Suleiman had left the station, he became jittery. It was the isolation that unsettled him most. The nullity; his own nullity.

Horrible thoughts tormented him. What would become of him if he couldn't get away from here? How would he live? Would he become a tramp, a vagrant, attached to the station? Would tourists come through here when the weather cooled again, months later, and find him bearded and mad, like the Monty Python hermit, ranting and raving about getting to Khartoum?

As evening crept in, Suleiman returned with a banana and more bread, but, instead of bottles, he brought water in a rusty tin flask. Richard thanked him profusely, swallowing the banana in three bites, but he could not risk drinking the water, even though he was already drying out. His lips were splitting, he had an unrelenting headache, and he wasn't urinating much, but he could not invite illness on the road to Khartoum so he emptied the flask and replenished it with water from the kettle.

A few hours later, Suleiman closed up the station and went home. Richard hoped he might come back with more food, but he never saw him again.

At dusk, he sat on the platform, wondering.

That night, he slept.

'Go to it, boys and girls,' he said to his busy bedmates as he crashed out on his mattress, exhausted from doing nothing in torrid temperatures all day. 'No point in all of us going hungry.'

A creak in the door woke him from a deep slumber. He lifted off the mattress in fright when he saw a figure standing in the doorway, shining a torch in his face.

'Who's that? Who are you?'

It was not Suleiman – too small and the voice too raspy – but he indicated with the torch that Richard should follow him. He thought, *This is it. They're taking me away to murder me in the night and dump me in the desert.* The voice, however, was courteous, so Richard followed the beam on to the platform, keeping well behind his guide, whom he soon recognized as his saviour, the little man who would take him to Khartoum. They were leaving! It was 5 a.m. and they were hitting the road! He hopped into the pick-up with nothing short of euphoria. Madgid smiled a toothless grin, the engine hit out at the silence, and within minutes they were on the dusty road out of Abu Hamed – on their way to Khartoum.

It was a long, tough journey. Richard's delight lasted only a couple of hours. Initially smug – *clever me, to have got myself out of that one* – he soon realized he was not yet out of anything. This was merely a continuation of the ordeal. He had only a small flask of water and no food. He had thought Suleiman would give him warning, might bring those empty bottles and even a few bananas or bread for the trip, but of course that had not happened. Suleiman was not a travel rep.

They dipped and leapt over a track which disappeared so often that Richard wondered how Madgid could conceivably know which way to go. Something sharp dug into his shoulder blade and his head hit the roof with such regularity that it had to be compromising his sanity. Every time they took particularly daring plunges across the crevasses in the surface, he ducked, and Madgid chuckled.

At sunrise, Madgid stopped the truck and got out to pray. Richard moved away, into the grey morning, to allow Madgid some privacy, but he couldn't help turning to watch. The little man spread out his prayer mat and prostrated himself, bowing over his knees in that vast empty setting, then sat back on his heels, with the light of a half-risen sun yellowing his face. The rhythmical words he recited made a strange music, and Richard was moved.

Daylight came quickly, along with its pitiless heat. They had left the river and the railway line behind at Abu Hamed. All signs of habitation too. There was nothing, anywhere, except a sizzling white plain stretching in every direction. Richard did not allow himself to think about what would happen if the truck broke down. Instead, he tried to 'do a Fran' and relish the experience of being lost in the unfamiliar, but it was more a question of endurance than experience. His animal instincts stomped out any refined aspirations of adventure and left him yearning only for more water and cool air. He couldn't help it – he had drunk every drop from his flask by midday. Madgid shared some of his own water then, but not enough to ease the throbbing in Richard's head, caused by dehydration and the relentless battering. His vision was blurred by heat

– it was well over one hundred and ten degrees for most of the day – and when he saw a shimmering inland sea on the horizon, he allowed himself to believe it was real.

He had no idea how long it would take to get to Khartoum. Two days at least, he calculated, because progress was slow. They stopped a lot: Madgid had to eat, sleep, say his prayers. During the hottest part of the day, they took refuge in the shade of an abandoned building and rested, and whenever they chanced upon any paltry cluster of civilization, Madgid stopped for tea and a chat with his countrymen. He always invited Richard to join them, but it was never clear if he understood his passenger's state of penury and was therefore offering to buy him tea, in spite of his own restricted circumstances, so Richard thought it best to decline. At one such stop, however, he was desperate enough to risk drinking the stewed tea proffered to him in a dirty glass, and begged his body to withstand the bugs. Dehydration, hunger and exhaustion were bearable; loose bowels on top of all that would be intolerable.

In the late afternoon, they met up with the Nile again, and later, just as evening was taking the glare off the sun, they came into the small town of Berber, where Richard was relieved to see people going about their evening perambulations. It was comforting to know that there was life going on somewhere, even if he had been suspended from it.

Beyond Berber, when they stopped beside the river, he flung himself into the brown, sludgy water, unable to resist it any longer, and splashed around, moving too fast, he hoped, to allow any parasites to latch on. He had to keep himself cool, stop his body temperature soaring out of control. When he clambered out, Madgid was praying beside his truck. Once again, the sight touched Richard. He thought there might even be a God if a man like this, hungry and tired after a long day's work, would stop and prostrate himself to pray.

They shared Madgid's picnic afterwards. Richard ate sparingly; Madgid had very little food for the long journey, and yet he kept offering his hitchhiker more and more. Richard hoped Madgid understood that he declined out of concern and did not mean to insult his deeply ingrained generosity. Besides, he had already drunk too much of Madgid's water. After eating, Madgid climbed onto the sacks on the back of his truck, pulled a bit of jute over him and went to sleep; his passenger sat on the bonnet and stared at the sky. Lying against the windscreen, he too fell asleep.

In Richard's dream, Madgid drove off without him and left him standing in a scorched wasteland. He woke with a jolt, thirsty and dry, and got into the cab, where he succeeded only in dozing fitfully. It was another long night, but easier to endure because he was less fretful than he had been. He had company, and he had wheels. Moreover, he knew with certainty that this was the last such night. The next day they would arrive in the capital.

They reached Atbara, a large uninspiring town about halfway between Wadi Halfa and Khartoum, around mid-morning. It seemed full of possibilities from a distance, but as they drew into the centre Richard sensed again that he was sitting in a bottle. No matter that there were shops, traffic, civilization. He still had no money and no identification, and without either, he was better off sticking with Madgid instead of looking for some other form of help. They stopped for breakfast in a travellers' rest, where Richard declined the offer of eggs and fuul and took just enough bread to keep him from passing out. By now, his appetite had been blunted by neglect and he had to force the bread down his dry throat, but he could not resist a tall glass of karkaday. Not caring who would pay for it, he slugged it back in one go. It eased his headache and cleared his vision.

'Shoukran,' he said to Madgid.

The little man smiled. 'Afwan.'

'I'll repay you for all this in Khartoum. As soon as we get to the British Embassy, I'll sort this out with you. How long now? How long to Khartoum?'

His spirits improved with every mile they put behind them, and

Madgid too was refreshed and less retiring than the previous day, so they chatted to pass time. When Madgid first started talking, Richard thought he was talking to himself, whereas in fact he was telling a story, and it was mesmerizing. Richard had never *listened* to Arabic before, had only blurted against it in English, but it was a lovely language and, even though the words made no sense to him, it was like enjoying Latin hymns without knowing what they meant. Occasionally a funny little cackle came from Madgid's throat which made Richard laugh, and thus they communicated without either understanding a word of what was being said. The story told, Madgid urged Richard to do likewise. It didn't come easily, but in the end he found himself speaking about this crazy girl he knew, who had spun him around and ripped off his blindfold and taken him through territories he had never thought of crossing. 'And in one such terrain', he said, 'I lost her.'

Every now and then they made contact on one word, its meaning clear to both. Madgid would say it in Arabic, Richard would repeat it, and then he would say it in English and Madgid would repeat it; if only for a word here and there, their conversation merged. They taught one another the words for sun, sky, desert, truck and road, but since there was nothing else to point at, their language lesson soon ended. Exhausted from the effort of learning five Arabic words, Richard fell asleep.

This day was the longest. Confident that they would reach Khartoum that night, he found the hours interminable, and even a view of the Nile, the pyramids at Meroe, and the bustling town of Shendi could not alleviate an ordeal that grew worse with every hour. He had been drinking suspect water for four days, albeit in minimal quantities, and could not hope to escape without some reaction to the unfamiliar microbes he was ingesting. How long would his stomach hold out? How much worse could this headache get? When, when, *when* would they reach Khartoum?

Not that day. A blown tyre impeded their progress. There was a remould in the truck, but Madgid's tools were old and it took him over an hour to change the tyre. Richard held an umbrella over him to shade him while he worked, then they had a long rest. Too long; it was after five when they woke, and since Madgid never drove very far in the dark, there was no hope of reaching Khartoum that night. By seven, they were camped out yet again. Richard could not sleep. He was weak, tired and stupefied, but the moon was shining on the river and it was incredible, unlikely, that he should be there at all, spending the night on a deserted bank of the Nile. Moon river.

9

The smooth run of tarmacadam beneath the wheels woke Richard the next morning. They were on a surfaced road at last. There was traffic. He drew a sigh of relief. Soon he would have the security of money in his pocket. He felt undressed without it, for cash, he had discovered, could cross a language barrier faster than any Linguaphone course. Too impatient to notice what ran past them, he glanced at his watch every few minutes.

By the time Khartoum North started to weave its tentacles about them on the outskirts of the capital, Richard was in a sweaty daze, but the grim sight of the city's outlying shanty towns revived him. In the few days since he had left it, Khartoum had acquired cult-status, and it crept around him like a mother reaching out to embrace him. The proverbial oasis in his desert. But then Madgid turned off the main road and headed in the direction of Omdurman. Richard didn't know the area at all, but after weaving in and out of dusty streets, Madgid stopped his pick-up beside a heap of rubble and managed to explain that this was where Richard got out.

It was a quarter past eleven. Richard had no idea where they were, but he knew that in the midday heat it would be a long walk into Khartoum proper. Madgid waved his hands about, in no clear direction, confident that he was indicating which way Richard should go. Relieved to be there, it seemed to Richard that the main road couldn't be hard to find, so he leapt out of the infernal truck, and sincerely thanked Madgid for saving his life.

Madgid drove off in the dust, waving happily. Richard tried to find his bearings. He was miles from any part of the city that would have been familiar to him – he and Frances had not set foot in Khartoum North, which is a town in its own right – but all he had to do was find his way to the main artery into the city centre, follow it, cross the bridge, and he'd be home free ... Except that he was in a state of acute torpor and getting out of the airless truck offered no relief. It was as breathless out as in. There was nothing for it but to start walking, and he was, at least, in Khartoum. Sort of. There was no longer an insurmountable desert between him and the blessed embassy, and, confident that he would soon see something vaguely indicative of which direction to take, he set off. But he wasn't feeling too good. His head suffered the worst of the high sun, his eyesight quivered, and his cut knee throbbed. Hunger had long since stood aside, leaving only intolerable thirst, but he kept himself going by day-dreaming of the long drink of cold water he would have within the hour, for he had little doubt that he would find his way to the embassy quite easily.

He would change his mind about that, however, some three hours later.

It was difficult to make any headway. Having started out in a state of fuzzy disorientation, his senses blurred, he seemed to take the wrong direction every time he turned. The streets were quiet, dusty, baking, and the grid layout, one crossroads after another, was more of a hindrance than a help, because Richard went on getting nowhere. There were no signs and few street names, only row upon row of featureless, identical streets. With the sun almost directly overhead, the only thing he knew about his whereabouts was that he was somewhere in the northern quadrant of Khartoum North. For all he knew, he might have been walking around the four sides of a square.

When he wandered into a particularly abject district, he tried not to see as he stumbled along the unpaved streets. This was like a guided tour through all the horrors of existence which were usually boxed into a television set. Although he knew he should look, that he owed it to these people to face up to their circumstances, he resented them for being there, just then, when he was exhausted and thirsty and more wretched than he had ever been. His problems were bad enough without adding remorse, without taking on the guilt of the Western World, and yet what he saw presented a vile comparison to his idea of hardship. It ridiculed him, and his insides shrivelled with a singular mixture of shame, disgust and relief. He didn't want to know. Not then. He needed a commercial break, and a swimming-pool.

Out of nowhere, a dozen children descended on him like an army of colonizing ants. They pulled at his arms, his shirt, his trousers. They begged and joked, made fun of him. It was maddening. They were so paradoxically happy that they ruined the one comfort he still had – self-pity. Their shrill laughter pierced his pounding head. They wanted something, anything, but when they didn't get it, they still ran about him, shrieking and unbegrudging. The violent sun that was burning him to the core didn't seem to bother them at all, nor did the flies or the smell of the place, and if Richard could have harnessed a fraction of their energy and put it in the soles of his shoes, he would have been out of there in a flash.

He considered enlisting the children's help to find his way, but apart from the language problem, something inside him didn't want to bridge the gap, to reach out and acknowledge that their existence had encroached on his. He promised himself that he would think about them some other time. He would account for this later, he would even sacrifice his comforts, but not now. *Get me out of here first*, he thought.

Eventually the children fell away, bored by his relentless forward motion and the dreariness of his stride. No doubt they thought him mad, this foreigner without a four-wheel drive, trudging lost amongst their hovels, and he nearly was mad, because all but a trickle of coherence had been smelted in his brain.

Water. Waterwaterwaterwaterwater. Now he understood about water. It was the juice of life. The only drink. Guinness? Pah, potable tar. Whiskey? Potable fire. Milk? Baby food. But water was the vintage of heaven. Bubble-free Champagne. *Cool – clear – water!*

Over and over, these words played in his head, resounding off his skull in a distinctive voice that was not his own. He tried to change the tune, but it pursued him until he recognized the voice – it was John Lennon's – and when Richard struggled to remember the song, it became a game, following those three words through to their source. Eventually, more came to him – something to do with there being no more weather on the old dirt road … 'Old Dirt Road.' That was it. That was the song that tormented him, and Lennon's voice went on teasing him: *You know the only thing we need is water. Coo-ool – cleeeeeah – wadder!* Cool. Clear. Water.

He stopped people to ask for directions into Khartoum city. Some shook their heads, unable to explain themselves in English, while others did direct him, but he kept forgetting where they had pointed, confusing left with right, five blocks with four, keeping straight with turning off. It didn't help that the town was quiet, with few people on the streets. When a Land Rover belonging to an aid agency drove past, Richard ran after it, almost dropping into an unmarked open manhole in the process, but it disappeared around a corner.

He was coming closer to being that crazed and hirsute Monty Python character, and it crossed his mind again that he might be found, years later, wandering around the city asking for directions. He might even become part of Khartoum folklore, the weird Irishman who didn't know where he was going. Perhaps a friendly dog warden would throw a net over him and put him to sleep a few days later when no one claimed him. Except that there were no dog pounds in Khartoum, only thousands of stray dogs wandering as aimlessly as Richard. They sniffed around his ankles, meagre and mean-looking, and as thirsty and burned-out as he was.

After almost three hours, he finally hit a wide and busy main road and knew that his marathon was nearly over. By then, however, he was ill. His bowels held steady, and that was an incalculable blessing, but to be out in that blast furnace without so much as a rag on his head was nothing short of insanity and his body revolted. His lungs were like burning bellows, his lips bled, and every time his heels hit the ground, his temples thumped in protest. He suffered severe cramps in his legs, and stopped himself from passing out a couple of times by leaning against cool, shaded walls until his head cleared a little, and when, at last, he saw the Blue Nile up ahead, the sight of it revived him as much as if he had drunk it down whole. Reaching the bridge, he saw Khartoum city twinkling on the other side of it, and his pace quickened. He was out of the woods. All he had to do now was to go straight to the British Embassy and put himself in their care.

On the other side of the bridge, he turned into Gamma Avenue, certain that he would soon find the embassy, even though he had no idea where it was. Nor could he find out. Businesses were closed for the afternoon break, and many of the pedestrians whom he asked for directions did not understand him, which led him to wonder was he doomed to wander forever, lost in Arabic, unable to find his way back to English. Exasperated, he turned off Gamma Avenue at the first roundabout, and walked south.

He had covered several blocks when he reached another roundabout and realized that he was heading away from the centre. He wondered if he had ever really been in Khartoum before, because it was as unfamiliar to him as Nairobi would have been. Finally, he found a policeman who told him he must turn back towards the commercial centre of the city, since many embassies were in that sector. Richard did so, heading north-west, until he came to Gamhuriya Avenue, unaware that he had already crossed it. This area was vaguely familiar. The Acropole Hotel, where he had stayed with Frances, was south of Gamhuriya Avenue and if he could get there, they might remember him and give him a drink before directing him to the embassy.

But could he find it? No. He and Frances had taken taxis everywhere and now all he could remember of the hotel's whereabouts was that it was on a street parallel to Gamhuriya Avenue ... he thought. He came to the first left turn off Gamhuriya and considered it. It didn't look like the street the taxis had taken to get to the main road, so he walked on to the next left turn. This, also, was unfamiliar in every respect, so he walked on until he came to a perpendicular main road that he definitely recognized. One block from the British Embassy compound, he turned south, and walked away from it.

Cramps assaulted his toes, his calves. Yellow taxis cruised by, a temptation Richard could not avail of, but he hailed two of them anyway and asked for directions to the embassy or the Acropole. As soon as one of the drivers realized he wouldn't be a paying passenger, he drove off. That was the worst moment; when the wheels spat dust in his face and he was left standing on the street. But when he said, 'Can you tell me the way to the Acropole Hotel?' to another driver, the man nodded enthusiastically and began explaining how to get there. This was at least the tenth time Richard had been given directions and they became less clear every time, because he kept imagining swimming-pools and cocktails, kept seeing himself passing over a credit card at reception. Besides, the taxi looked so tempting, such a simple conduit to where he wanted to be, that he almost stepped in. He could explain at the hotel what had happened and they would maybe pay his fare ... but the Acropole Hotel had no responsibility for Richard Keane, just because he was a Westerner who had stayed there for a couple of nights, and they might as easily call the police when he rolled up in a taxi unable to pay for it. It wasn't worth the risk. He let the taxi go.

He was coming closer to collapse. So close that he almost stepped into another open manhole and disappeared into the sewerage of Khartoum. *At least it would be wet*, he thought.

He found another traffic policeman and again asked for the embassy.

The policeman blinked. 'Yes, but—'

'You know it? You can tell me where it is?'

'Yes, but—'

'Oh, great.'

'But it is closed today. Today is holy day. Friday.'

Richard stared, mouth hanging open. *Friday?* No wonder the

city was so quiet! Too stunned to say any more, he wandered away and walked on, past the street on which the Acropole stood, too dazed to care where he was heading.

He had to find a drink, any drink. He had to find a hotel, where he could drink the tap water in the Gents. This would mean drinking yet more suspect water, the consequences of which would be dire for someone wandering city streets, but without a drink he could go no farther anyway. His head spun, his throat felt like sandpaper with sores on it, and his eyesight had become so blurred that he felt as if he was walking inside a mirage. It all appeared to be ten steps ahead of him, and he never got there. Everything shimmered. Worse than that, his thoughts were blurring. He heard himself speak aloud without meaning to, and he was missing bits of time, absenting himself without notice. Sunstroke.

But this wandering couldn't go on much longer; he would either arrive somewhere or pass out. The afternoon was waning. He had to rest, so he moved into the shade of a building and leaned against the wall near an old man who was sitting by a doorway on a box. Richard slid to the ground and decided to stay there forever and die of thirst. The simplest thing to do.

'You sick?'

Richard opened his eyes.

'You sick?' the old man asked again.

'Lost. I'm lost. I'm looking for the Acropole Hotel.'

'Acropole? That way.' He pointed in the direction Richard had come from.

'Oh. Great.' He tried to focus. 'Back that way. And then?'

The man thought for moment. 'Then like this,' he waved his right hand.

Right. Go right.

'Then this way.'

Go left.

'And again like this.'

Right again.

'And then you must—'

155

'Oh God, isn't there somewhere else? Some other hotel, easy to find? The Hilton maybe? The Hilton would be nice.'

'Hilton? You need taxi.'

'Can't I walk?'

'A long walk. Out by river.' His eyes seemed to say, 'A very, very long walk in your condition.' And then he added, 'Meridien just here.'

'What?'

'Meridien Hotel.' He pointed down the road. 'That way.'

'Really? Easy to find?'

'Yes, yes, that way. Straight, straight.'

He had only to walk in a straight line until he came to a cross-roads. The Meridien was on the corner. He thanked the man profusely, but when he tried to stand up, he stumbled.

'You like drink?'

'God, yes. Please. Water. A glass of water would be fantastic.'

The man disappeared through the door and up a staircase. He was gone for some time. Richard sat on the pavement and realized the day was beginning to cool. It was after four; all diplomats were off duty for the day, but the Meridien would surely be able to track someone down for him. His feet throbbed. His skin stung, for he had no sweat left, and that worried him, because now his body had no cooling system.

When the man reappeared carrying a tray with a large kettle on it, Richard stared.

'You like tea, yes? All English like tea.'

Richard couldn't speak. The man put the tin tray on the pavement beside him and there was no need to thank him, to say anything, because the old man's eyes said it all. Richard looked at the battered kettle, the small glass, some sugar. His hand was shaking so much that he spattered tea when he poured it and for a moment, he couldn't even drink. The man went back inside, leaving him sitting on the ground in a Khartoum street, taking tea. There was traffic about, doing familiar manoeuvres, making soothing sounds, and Richard felt, suddenly, quite safe. The sugar was sweet, the tea hot. As he sipped it slowly, the dryness in his throat eased and he believed that his insignificant little adventure was over, because for the first time since he had been snoozing on the train, his situation was no longer desperate. Constant physical and mental concentration were no longer necessary. He had almost arrived somewhere. And yet he so badly wanted to collapse, to give up, just when he was nearly there.

He swallowed two spoonfuls of sugar and got up. His feet stepped reluctantly ahead of him – they hadn't expected to be put back into commission quite so soon – and his head felt like a dead weight hanging off his neck. His eyes struggled to stay open, his skin began burning after its midday scorching, but before he knew it, the Meridien Hotel was looming up in front of him like a great Western Mecca. He dragged his heels up the drive and trundled into the cool lobby.

He stood just inside the entrance, disoriented and confused. The air-conditioning fed into his system like a transfusion of cold blood, and he would have remained there, wallowing in it, had the opulence of his surroundings not reminded him of his status as *persona non grata*. He still had no money, and now he also looked like someone with no money. The lobby, and everything in it, spoke cash. Richard stood there, filthy, his hands dangling, too overcome with relief to give himself a less helpless demeanour. Staff zipped past with looks of withheld judgment, expatriates glanced over their shoulders as they came all squeaky clean from the tennis courts, businessmen turned away. As he sensed the doorman approach, Richard strode across the lobby, hoping to see a sign for the Gents. He found one, but he saw another sign too, and he followed that one instead. It took him through the hotel and out the back of the building to the gardens.

If ever there was a right time for loutish behaviour, this was surely it. Richard didn't stop to think; his senses took over. He walked across to the swimming-pool and stepped right into it.

Cool – clear – water! Sizzling like a red-hot pan, he allowed himself to sink to the bottom. Every atom in his body exulted. Water gushed in his ears, bubbles fizzed around his skin, and his temperature dropped with a fresh blast.

The first thing he noticed when he floated to the surface were cleavages. Three of them, belonging to expatriate women in swimsuits who were leaning forward on their sunbeds waiting to see what emerged in the wake of the splash, while the tail end of a waiter rushing into the building presaged the consequences. Richard nodded at the women, then noticed all around him a cloud of murky water. He looked at it, and at them, and said, 'Well, it's been a long day,' then suffered the ignominy of being too weak to haul himself out of the pool. Instead, he had to abandon the attempt and swim to the steps to get out.

Trailing water in his wake, he made his way inside the building to the Gents, where he leaned over the gold taps and poured water into his mouth. He could hear it falling into his empty belly, like torrents coming over the Aswan High Dam, as he drank and drank. When he looked up, partially satiated, his dejection was compounded by his reflection in the mirror. Now he could see what those women had seen: five days' worth of beard, bloodshot eyes, lips caked with blood, and hair so matted that it had scarcely even got wet. But what Richard saw, more than the dirt, was the hunger on him, the thirst. He pulled off his shirt, dunked it in cold water, and was washing his armpits with it when an Arab businessman came in behind him. His white robes swishing about, he glanced nervously at the half-naked apparition standing by the sink as he dried his bejewelled hands, and Richard stared blankly. He could smell the man's cleanliness, his aftershave, even his fine leather briefcase. He had probably been enjoying a refreshing salad in the buffet and was about to do a business deal over Turkish coffee and mints.

After the Arab left, Richard shivered as he pulled on his shirt, the cool air attacking the water in it. Somehow he had to get a room and lie down. His spirits had been recharged that morning, knowing that he was nearly in Khartoum, but here he was, hours later, countless hours later, still in this unpredictable state. Every time he thought it was over, another obstacle presented itself.

'We always wake up,' he told his reflection. 'Even the worst bloody nightmares don't go on forever.'

And things *had* improved: he was now cool, and he was near food, even if he had no access to it. Taking a deep breath and holding his head high, he opened the door and walked right into a waiter and a clerk.

'Him, him!' said the waiter. 'Jump right in pool!'

The clerk, an Indian with the good looks of a film star, looked Richard up and down but seemed uncertain what to say. 'Sir?'

'Yes?'

'Are you ... a resident here?'

'I soon will be. I'd like a room, please.'

The Indian blinked very quickly several times and said, 'Very well. Come this way, please.'

'Thank you. I will.'

They walked back through the lobby, where the clerk took up his position at reception. 'You wish to check in?'

'Please.'

'And how long do you wish to stay?'

'I'm not sure.'

The man looked around the lobby. 'You have some luggage?'

'No. Do you have a vacancy?'

'Yes. Yes, we have rooms.' The Indian busied himself behind the counter.

Richard glanced around the lobby with an air of conceit, his hands clasped, his trousers depositing a pool of water at his feet. As soon as he got to his room, he'd order something to eat and make calls – ask Bob, his boss, to send him money, contact some diplomat about his passport, and try to get through to the hotel in Wadi Halfa. Then he could sleep. No longer bridled with the sense of dispossession that had beleaguered him for days, he could hardly conceal his delight.

'May I have your passport, please?'

Richard was ready for this. 'I'm sorry,' he said lightly, 'I don't have it on me.'

'You have no passport?'

''Fraid not.'

'But you cannot check in without your passport. The authorities insist—'

'I know that, but my passport is at the British Embassy.'

'Sir?'

'I've had to apply for a new one, so if you could just give me a room …'

'I'm afraid that is not possible. It is our policy to—'

'I understand that,' said Richard tersely, his nerves too frayed for courtesy, 'but policy is going to have to take a running jump because I need a room! So if you'd just give me a key, I'll get you a passport as soon as I have one.'

They eyed one another.

'That is not acceptable.'

'All right, so why don't you contact someone from the embassy and I'll speak to them, and they will explain about my passport.'

'The embassy is closed, sir.'

'So what do you want me to do – sleep in the street?'

'I'm very sorry, but the police insist we take passport details from our guests.'

'I know that, but can't you make an exception? Look, all my stuff has been stolen: my passport, my money, my belongings. Why do you think I'm standing here looking like a melting yeti?'

'I am most sorry for your difficulties, but—'

'So do something about it. Give me a room!'

The man wobbled his head. 'This is beyond my—'

Richard thumped the counter. 'Yeah, and it's beyond mine too, so let's call the manager.'

'I was about to, sir.'

The manager appeared a few minutes later. He was a Scot. He had a tightly trimmed red beard and a disarming smile, and was not very much older than Richard. Leaning over the counter, he looked at Richard from head to toe and said, 'You must be the gentleman who jumped into the pool?'

'Er … yeah. Sorry about that, but I, eh, well, I was very hot.'

'As are we all. However, we don't all take quite the same measures to cool down.' Still smiling.

'Yeah, I know but—'

'Had you checked in first, you would have been most welcome to avail of our swimming-pool—'

'Like I said, I'm—'

'Instead of abusing our facilities and alarming our paying guests.'

Richard felt deeply weary. 'Are you going to give me a room?'

'I understand you're not carrying a passport?'

'No. I've been robbed. I was on the Wadi Halfa train and a bloke stole my knapsack and I've just walked all the way from Abu Hamed—'

The Scot looked confounded. 'Walked?'

'Well, that's what it feels like anyway. I actually got a lift, but I've hardly eaten in four days and you just have to help me out! I need a room, something to eat, and then I'll get on to the embassy about my passport.'

'The embassy is closed until tomorrow morning.'

'I know that,' said Richard, needing to strangle someone, 'and as long as they're not available, I have to rely on you!'

'I appreciate that, but it isn't as simple as you seem to think. Should the police do a spot-check on our books and discover that an individual is staying here without papers, they could make things very awkward for us.'

'I'm only asking for a room and a meal, for God's sake. I'm starving to death!'

'Starving? I don't think so.'

Richard whimpered with frustration. '*Oh, God.* All right, so maybe I'm not actually *starving*, but I am dehydrated and knackered and the last thing I need right now is a squabble about pedantics!' He raised his hands in apology. 'I'm sorry, mate, but I'm at the end of my rope, you know?'

'I can see that, but if you were so desperate for our help, jumping into our pool, fully clothed and very dirty, was hardly the way to attract a sympathy vote. We expect a certain degree of decorum from our guests and—'

'Fine! I can do that. I can be decorous!'

'That's as may be, but checking into a hotel without identification is a serious offence. For you as well as for us.'

'So if you can't book me in, could you at least make some calls for me? I need to get on to London to ask a friend to wire me out some money.'

The Scot hesitated.

'Listen, I might look like a vagrant, but I'm actually quite well bred underneath all this shite. I work for an architectural practice in London – I'll give you their number, if you like – in fact, I'll give you my parents' number, my sister's, my boss's, my dentist's girlfriend's mother's number! There are half a dozen people who can vouch for me if that's what you need, but for pity's sake, how many tourists are wandering around Khartoum looking like Jesus after his forty days in the desert?'

'Ah,' said the Scot dryly, 'but then Jesus didn't go about hurling himself into other people's swimming-pools, did he?'

So he has a sense of humour, this man, thought Richard. *Thank God.*

'I'll have to speak to the manager,' he said.

'What? I thought you were the manager!'

'Sorry. Assistant manager, for now. I'll see what I can do.'

He left Richard standing, open-mouthed, at the desk. Businessmen checked in and out, signed their credit card slips, picked up their leather briefcases and moved on. Would that it had been so easy, Richard thought. He waited, dreaming of the shower, the food, the clean sheets – all a mere lift ride away. Surely they would not deny him? Surely they would have some sense of responsibility towards a fellow European? But then a terrible thought followed: because he was white, he expected different treatment from what he knew a Sudanese man would receive if he came in, penniless and smelly, demanding a room.

The handsome Indian clerk returned to reception some moments later and approached Richard. 'I am afraid', he said, 'that without the sanction of the British Embassy, we cannot verify your claims and therefore cannot risk checking you in without proper identification.'

'… You're not giving me a room?'

'I'm sorry.'

'Bollocks!'

The clerk tidied some papers.

'So what am I supposed to do now?'

No response from the busy clerk.

Richard glared at him. 'Well,' he said, 'do please thank your Scottish colleague for being so helpful.' He spun around and headed for the door. There was no point tantalizing himself with the Meridien's comforts any longer, and he was afraid that if he saw the contemptible Scot he'd take a swing at him for being too gutless to get rid of him personally. Not knowing where he meant to go, he stormed out. It would soon be dark, but it was imperative now that he should find the Acropole and see if they would take him in. At least they might remember him. If not, he could maybe try to find the man-in-the-street who had given him tea. He was a good man. He might even feed Richard, take him in for the night. *A Westerner looking for charity in a place like Khartoum*, Richard thought wryly, *this has to be a first.*

This was the absolute low point. It was unacceptable to him that things could go so awry because of a missed train. Drawing attention to himself had aggravated his situation, not improved it; he could no longer sit out the night in the lobby of the hotel as he might have done otherwise, hoping not to be noticed. Instead, he had to keep walking.

He remembered something from the Kitchener book. During the construction of the railway, Kitchener had written to his solicitor in England bemoaning that in 'this damnable country' God had put every conceivable obstruction in his way. Richard knew how he felt.

He yearned for a phone book in roman script. There was no other way of finding the numbers of the diplomats who were responsible for him. They were supposed to help tourists in trouble, but what bloody good would they be to Richard if they didn't even know he existed? And why had that Scot not had the common decency to make one phone call on his behalf? Why?

His resources, such as they were, and his optimism, had been wiped out. As he moved slowly along the driveway of the Meridien, it occurred to him that he could sleep in the garden, under a bush. That was it. That was the thing to do. And if they found him, then perhaps they would better appreciate how destitute he actually was and would make those calls. His pathetic condition would drive them to it. He loitered, trying to see where he might dip into the greenery to hide, but the doorman was watching him. Richard cursed. There was nothing for it but to go for a walk and come back later, when they had all forgotten about him, then he would slip in discreetly and – forget the garden – take a lift upstairs and sleep in one of the corridors until he was found. If he were not found, he would at least have the energy, the clarity, to know what to do the next day.

He went back onto the street. His drying clothes scraped against his skin, and the longest day went on being long.

Then he heard footsteps running behind him and a voice calling. A voice with a Scottish accent. Richard turned to see the man who wasn't the manager coming after him.

'Sorry,' he gasped, when he caught up with Richard. 'I've sorted it for you. If you come back up to the hotel, we'll give you a room and make some calls.'

10

'Where were you off to?' the Scot asked as they made their way back to the hotel.

'I was just asking myself the same question. Your colleague came back from the manager and threw me out.'

'I had a word with the boss myself. I'm Andrew, by the way. Andrew Shandy.'

They shook hands. Richard made a mental note never to forget this stranger who had saved him from destitution. They walked into the lobby without speaking. Richard had been living on his wits for days and, finding himself at last in someone else's hands, his mind went blank. He was content to be led about like a shaky puppy. Andrew grabbed a key at reception.

'We can't check you in properly. We're breaking the law doing this, but if we can get the embassy to take responsibility for you, we should be okay. Meanwhile, here you go.'

Richard stared at the key dangling in front of his face. He felt neither elation nor even sharp relief; it was too late for that. It would take time to get back from the edge. Besides, he was too preoccupied with thoughts of food. He knew what he wanted: tea and toast. Nothing more, nothing elaborate; no three-course feast as men apparently crave when they fall out of prison or come in from the blizzard – or the desert, for that matter. All he wanted was some toast.

He was still gazing at the dangling key.

'Maybe I should take you up,' Andrew said, leading him to the lifts. 'By the way, I'm sorry for having a go at you about being starving. It's just that I see so much affluence passing through this lobby, so much arrogance, that it sticks in my craw sometimes. This country is in sorry shape.'

Richard was beyond replying. He followed Andrew along hushed corridors to the room, the very sight of which moved him. All the surplus amenities of Western culture that lay before him had acquired surreal importance; it wasn't simply the need to be physically spoiled, it was the reassurance that he belonged somewhere. He belonged in the world of the television set, the fridge and the flush loo – these were the props of his own civilization, and however surplus they were to survival, they were the things that brought him home. He moved towards the large, neat bed.

'How long has it been since you ate properly?' Andrew asked.

'I honestly couldn't tell you.'

'What do you fancy?'

'Toast would be great. Just tea and toast. My system wouldn't cope with anything else.'

'I'll see to it. And I'll get you something for those burns.'

Richard's forearms were red, the skin stretched; his face felt like a mask that had been glued to his head. 'Thanks.'

By the time Andrew had closed the door behind him, Richard was asleep.

He woke in the middle of the night, in his air-conditioned lair, every part of him cooled. It was 12.15. A tray lay on the table, the food long since gone cold. In spite of several hours' sleep, his head was still spinning. Thirst and exhaustion fought a battle over him. Deep micro-sleeps full of vivid images of food created a burning sensation in his belly, but he was too weak to move, so he kept falling asleep again, until thirst eventually won out. He dragged himself up and drank the bottle of water on the tray, then called room service. His appetite was dormant but his mind greedy. After drinking more water found in the fridge, he fell into the shower.

Nothing short of food could have taken him from the delicious pelt of water that sluiced away the congealed scum of five days on the road, so when a rap came on the door, he reluctantly got out.

The mere sight of the toast rekindled his appetite, and before the waiter had left the room Richard had ordered more food. He had two pots of tea and ate everything they brought him – toast and eggs and chips and even desserts. It was the midnight feast of his dreams. Then he fell asleep feeling sick, but planning to eat more as soon as he woke.

When he did wake, not long afterwards, he threw up everything he had eaten. His body punished him for punishing it, but at least it had had the courtesy to wait until he had privacy, water, and above all, his own bathroom, because he spent the rest of the night in there, racked with cramp. Later, as it grew bright outside, he lay on the bed feeling crushed, a great weight of exhaustion pinning him down, too stupefied to think clearly, to consider what had become of Frances. As the day progressed, he lost track of time and had barely enough wit to keep drinking, for even that was a chore, an effort beyond him. When he slept, it was the horrible sleep of the sick, interrupted by episodes of acute disorientation.

The phone rang. Richard kept waking, sleeping, waking, until it stopped.

Andrew appeared at the end of his bed. Then he was gone again.

It was a hangover. He was with his brother, on the boat. On the Shannon.

Voices. Someone else talking. *Sunstroke. Drink the whole of the Nile to get better.* Water forced down his gullet. Dark again.

Another night, long and lonely, but the next day Richard slept more easily. When he woke, it was evening, and Andrew was standing at the foot of the bed again.

'Hello, my favourite friend,' Richard mumbled, his mouth rancid.

'Sorry for barging in, but I have to keep you hydrated. How are you feeling?'

Richard groaned.

'I'm afraid I had to call in our doctor yesterday. You had me worried. And, eh, he made me eat humble pie – said you probably saved your own life by jumping into the pool. If you hadn't, you would have cooked from the inside out.'

'That's what it felt like.'

'He was amazed you got here at all.' Andrew poured Richard more water. 'Out in that sun, after days of deprivation, your body temperature would have been going into a danger zone, he said, and then the proteins in the body start to fry—'

'Yeah, yeah, I was there.'

'Anyway, you're going to feel flattened for quite a while, apparently, and you'll have to take a whopping great dose of anti-malarial medication to make up for what you've missed.'

'Andrew, look, I don't know what to say. I'd still be out there if you hadn't taken me in.'

Andrew chuckled. 'I was doing Khartoum a favour.'

'How long … what day is it?'

'Sunday.'

'Oh, fuck.' Richard struggled onto his elbows. 'I have to see someone from the embassy.'

'The Third Sec came around yesterday, but I had to send him away. He'll be off duty by now. I'll get hold of him first thing tomorrow. You're not up to it, anyway.'

'I am. I have to—'

'You have to rest. That's all. Maximum rest. Or you'll be paying for this for a long time. Now drink another litre of water for me. There's a good lad.'

After Andrew left him, Richard sank back on his pillows, fretting. It had been six days since he had left the train. Six days! Frances would be insane with worry. He rang reception and asked if they could get him the numbers of every hotel in Wadi Halfa, but was informed that they would be unable to get that information before morning. And no, they told him, they did not have a countrywide telephone directory in roman numerals.

Richard hung up and fell into a deep sleep.

He woke the next morning in a panic. Another night had gone by and he still had not contacted Frances! He immediately got hold of Andrew.

'You sound a little better,' said the Scot.

'I am, thanks, but when's this diplomat turning up? I really need to see him.'

'About eleven, if you're up to it.'

'I am. I need his help.'

'Don't worry. He'll look after everything. Meanwhile, is there anything I can get you?'

Richard thought about it. He had effectively not eaten for a week. 'I could manage a light breakfast, I think.'

'Good. I'll see to it. And I have some English newspapers if you'd like?'

'Yeah, great. Thanks.'

'Anything else?'

'Well, now you ask, a toothbrush would be blissful.'

'Sure. I'll send out for the basics. What do you need? Shorts and a few shirts?'

'Definitely, if that's okay?'

'No problem. Anything else?'

'Don't think so – or were you going to offer me a woman?'

'Not in this part of the world, no, but you might like to tidy up that accumulated facial growth before this diplomat laddie turns up.'

'God, yes. Better get me a razor too.'

'Done. Oh, and be warned. He's a bit eager, is Webster, a bit officious, but he's a good lad underneath.'

Charles Webster, the Third Secretary at the British Embassy, was not at all so easygoing as the friendly Scot. No doubt he saw Richard as yet another careless tourist, travelling in Africa without enough intelligence to move from A to B without getting into trouble. That was certainly the impression he gave.

A man in his thirties, he had a stern countenance and a square jaw, and he stood by the window with Andrew, expressing little concern for Richard's health. 'It was rather foolhardy, wouldn't you say, to carry your money and travel documents in the same bag? Even in more predictable parts of the world, tourists are specifically advised to separate their papers so that they can avoid getting into the very situation in which you now find yourself. It's basic common sense.'

This stung, but there was nothing Richard could say.

'And you say your knapsack was on the seat beside you – within reach of a passer-by?'

'I was inside our compartment.'

'By the door?'

'Yes, but—'

'The open door?'

'Of course. We'd have suffocated otherwise. Look, we were led to expect that the Sudan is very safe in this regard.'

'It is, in comparison to some places, but people get robbed, of course they do, and I would have thought that falling asleep with a bag on the seat was something of an invitation.'

Richard was stumped. He had expected a gentle pat on the hand, a 'There, there, you unfortunate sod, we'll take care of this.' Instead, he was getting the third degree.

'You're Irish?'

'Is that a problem?'

'Not at all, but I'll have to brief your people in Cairo.'

Richard was sitting on the bed with a towel wrapped around his waist, while Webster, cool and clean in his pink short-sleeved shirt and white trousers, wandered about the room making him feel like a naughty little boy. This was his patch. Everything that happened to Richard subsequently depended on him, and they both knew it.

'I take it you were travelling alone?'

An image of Frances suddenly came to Richard, clear and sharp.

He saw her asleep on that bench in the compartment, unaware that he had gone. What would she have done when she woke? What would she have thought?

'Were you alone?' asked Webster again.

'No. I was with my girlfriend.'

Andrew started. 'God, I'd no idea.'

'And she didn't disembark with you?'

Richard looked up at Webster. 'Obviously not. She was asleep when it happened, and even if she hadn't been, there wasn't exactly time to have a bilateral discussion about the most sensible course of action. If we'd both been awake, I would have let the bag go and we would have come back to Khartoum together, but in the split second when I saw the kid take off, I thought I had to go after it. It had my passport, airline ticket, travellers' cheques – I couldn't get out of the Sudan without it.'

'And you didn't hear the train leaving?'

'I did, but when I ran for it, it was like running straight into a jet engine.'

'So where is your girlfriend now?'

'I have absolutely no idea.'

Webster sighed, looked out at Khartoum and said, 'So now we have a missing tourist on our hands as well.'

'Look, you have to find her. It's been days!'

Perhaps it was the pathetic vision of Richard standing in the dust watching his train leave with his girlfriend on it, but Webster was all right after that. He softened. 'Yes, that's certainly a priority. What do you think she would have done?'

'I don't know. She doesn't even know where I am.'

'If she has any sense, she'll sit tight in Wadi Halfa until she hears from you. Do you know where she might stay?'

'There's a hotel opposite the station. I can't remember what it's called.'

'I'll make enquiries. What's her name?'

'Frances Dillon.'

'Very well. I'll track her down and let her know you're all right, and I'll advise her to come straight back to Khartoum.'

'Thanks.'

'As soon as you feel strong enough, you need to get some passport photos taken. Bring them along to the office and we'll do the necessary paperwork and send the lot to your embassy in Cairo. They'll issue a new passport, but it will take a while, and we'll need to apply for another exit visa to get you out of the Sudan, so you're going to be with us for quite some time. As for money, you should ask your bank to wire out whatever you'll need. I'll give you the name of the bank they should send it to. Meanwhile, as far as we're concerned, you can stay here for as long as you can afford to.'

Richard didn't care about affording it. His days of roughing it were over. Some of the money he had put aside for a deposit on a flat would have to meet this bill, because he certainly wasn't moving down-market, not even to the more than adequate Acropole, after what he'd been through. And when Frances got back, they could enjoy together the huge double bed, the air-conditioning, and all the luxuries that were anathema to her concept of travel.

'I'm sorry to hear about your girlfriend,' said Andrew after Webster had left. 'Do you think she'll be all right?'

'I hope so. Fran is only good at moving on; staying makes her fret. She'll go frigging mad in Wadi Halfa. It's hot as hell, there's nothing to do and she hasn't a bog where I am. The hotel is just four walls in the desert. Wadi Halfa is no more than a staging post.'

'Poor lass.'

Richard went over to the window. 'Yeah, but she came here looking for excitement and she's certainly found it now.'

'Meantime, you're stuck in Khartoum with time to kill. What are you going to do with it?'

'I'll do what I've been doing for the last three years: wait for Fran.'

Andrew went back to work. Richard sat in bed, staring at the wall, thinking about Frances. Now that he was well enough, he was able to concentrate on her predicament, but he couldn't begin to imagine what it must have been like for her to wake up and find him gone from that train. This was certainly the most outlandish of the mishaps they had suffered over the years, and it was also the last straw, as far as he was concerned. He had done enough at Frances's behest. He had journeyed on many stuffy, overcrowded trains to far-flung spots; he had suffered more stomach bugs than he cared to count, had stayed in more spartan rooms than he cared to remember. Thank God they were done with it. Frances had had her way; they had had their adventures. In fact, Richard had had enough adventures in the last week to keep them going for a lifetime. More than ever before, he looked forward to the normal life that lay ahead. No more dust and deserts and railways leading nowhere.

That afternoon, Webster phoned. 'Bad news, I'm afraid. I got through to Wadi Halfa – to a place called the Nile Hotel – but I was too late. Miss Dillon has already left.'

'What?'

'There are currently no foreign women in Wadi Halfa.'

'But she *was* there?'

'Oh yes, she was there all right, but not any longer. So I contacted SRC, the railway corporation, and they told me that a train left Wadi Halfa this morning – five days behind schedule, as it happens. Presumably Miss Dillon is on it, because another train got into Wadi Halfa on Saturday, and since you weren't on that one, she probably decided to make her way back to Khartoum.'

'Jesus. She'll be doing that journey for the third time in two weeks.'

'Yes, but she'd hardly stay down there indefinitely on the off-chance you might turn up, would she?'

Indefinitely? Frances didn't know the meaning of the word. 'I wouldn't have thought so. When is this train due in?'

'When it's due is a bit academic, but barring breakdowns, it should turn up sometime on Wednesday.'

'Great.'

'I'd be a lot happier if we'd had the chance to reassure her before she travelled. She must be beside herself.'

'She'll be fine. The train will keep her head together. She's better off on the move. Staying in Wadi Halfa any longer would tie her in knots.'

The next morning, still seeping with relief that his own trials were over and reassured that Frances's worries soon would be, Richard bought a pair of swimming trunks in the hotel shop and went down to the pool. Clean and blue, it was simply too inviting to resist, and even the sunshine looked benevolent from the cool interiors of the hotel. In fact, the sun was just as violent as it had been four days before, and when he ventured out, his scorched arms stung, as if spattered by hot fat, for his reinstated respectability was no shield against the extreme heat. Stretched out beneath a parasol, exposing only his legs to the white glare, he listened to the water lap about the pool, to the splashing of swimmers and the soft voices of expatriate women; he inhaled the sharp, clean smell of chlorine and perversely enjoyed the burning sensation on his shins. This excess was all within his control. He had learned about control, and what it meant to be without it, and when he could bear the heat no longer, he dived into the pool.

His body still racked after its ordeal and his energy levels nonexistent, he spent the day by the pool, regaling other guests with his adventure and dramatizing more than necessary the hardships he had encountered, as well as the difficulties Frances would have to endure before they could be reunited. That evening, he sat about with the extended overseas community, providing an interesting distraction and fresh fodder for their gossip, while they, in turn, provided an interesting distraction for him. They gave him a third perspective on the Sudan. With Frances, he had had a periscope's view of the country. The only Sudanese they had met had been taxi drivers and waiters; the only foreigners they had spoken to were other tourists, whose main interests were landmarks, transport, health. The experiences they sought were the boat, the train, and seeing the twin Niles merge. The Sudan was the means, not the purpose. But at Abu Hamed and on the way to Khartoum, Richard had spent time with the Sudanese, had briefly lived with them, and learned, and now he received another education – the Sudan, through the eyes of the Westerners who lived there. They expounded on the difficulties of life in Khartoum. The summer heat. The dust storms. The illnesses, of course. The power cuts and poor facilities. When pressed for positive aspects, they mentioned the people, the low crime rate and, paradoxically, the weather.

Disinclined to hear a catalogue of complaints repeated in a chorus of different voices, Richard asked about the political situation. 'Nimeiri sounds like quite a character,' he said.

An American engineer, Judd, chortled. 'That's for sure. He changes political shirt more often than he changes underwear!'

His nodding wife, Marigold, giggled.

'Former Communist ally,' mumbled Hugh, an English academic teaching at the University of Khartoum, 'and now America's best friend.'

'He's a regular Houdini,' said Judd. 'Survived more coups than you could count.'

Marigold nodded.

'But he won't survive much longer, in my view,' said Hugh. 'There's a lot of opposition to him in different quarters. Always has been, but the government is bloated with American money now and is utterly corrupt. It's bound to blow sometime, especially as things aren't going well in the South.'

'Oh?' said Richard.

'He had a lot of the support in the South', explained Hugh, 'because he helped bring about the ceasefire in '72 – in fact, the loyalty of Southern troops helped him survive those coup attempts, but that support has been badly eroded. Two years ago he suspended the Southern Regional Assembly, which—'

'It's about oil, Hugh,' said Judd, in a low, patronizing voice. 'They have oil down there,' he explained to Richard, 'and Nimeiri promised a refinery in Bentiu, which would have brought a lot of benefits to the Southern folk, but he's reneged on that, and then the Jonglei Canal got dumped on them. Huge project, French-built, down in the marshes, ecologically unsound, and the only people who are really going to benefit from all the extra water it drains off are the Egyptians!'

'All in all,' said Hugh, 'another cock-up. There's even talk of a mutiny among Southern troops. Some say the ceasefire is breaking down.'

'No way, we won't let that happen,' said Judd. 'There's more US military aid and know-how coming into this country than any other in Africa. We won't let them mess up.'

'Indeed,' Hugh snorted derisively. 'And all because there are a few commies across the border.'

The discussion went on, the expatriates sliding rumours about like pieces on a chess board, debating, dissecting, and mocking, also. By the time Richard went back to his room, he knew more about the complexities of the Sudan than he could ever have learned sitting on one of its idiosyncratic trains. Odd, he thought, how people travel far and wide but mostly only *see* the countries they go to; they never truly absorb the realities of a place. Frances was a bit like that, hopping from spot to spot, like a butterfly, never grasping anything other than a railway timetable … But these thoughts of Frances, as he lay in bed, weighed him down with guilt, for while he was swanning about in air-conditioned comfort, sipping cold drinks and enjoying stimulating conversation, Frances was crossing one of the most torrid plains on earth. Even for her, being entombed on that train yet again must have become an ordeal – although if anything was going to cure her of rail-lust, this should certainly do it.

The night before the train was due, he scarcely slept. It had been ten days since he and Frances had sat in a stupor together, ten days since it had all abruptly ended and he was gone and she was gone and they hadn't even had time to blink at one another. At the very point at which they had put their separations behind them, they suddenly ended up not even knowing where the other was. This trial almost over, Richard slept fretfully, and when morning finally dawned, he kept to his room, staring at the wall, counting the minutes until it was time to go.

At four o'clock, half an hour before the Wadi Halfa train was now expected to arrive, he walked up the road to Khartoum Central spruced up in smart new clothes which he hoped would offset the sight of his peeling nose and lip sores. It would be a delirious reunion. There would be no recriminations about the knot Frances's wanderlust had got him into. It would be untarnished relief and delight. He knew exactly how she would look at him when she saw him standing on the platform, safe and well, and yet he couldn't wait to see her expression. It had been easier for him – he at least had known, more or less, where she had been since they parted – whereas Frances would have endured ten desperate days of anguish, and Richard hoped the shock of losing him might make her more enthusiastic about having him. She might even agree that it wouldn't be so bad, after all, to live the kind of life where this sort of thing couldn't happen.

The station was redolent of their arrival in Khartoum. Although it seemed longer, it had been only two weeks since he and Frances had disembarked in a flush with the crowds, and Frances had led the way out to the streets, her blonde curls bouncing behind her in spite of the accumulated sand that should have made them lank. Richard had followed in her wake, feeling white, and small, and spoilt, with only one word in his head. *Africa*. Egypt had been too Arab, too ancient, to feel African. Wadi Halfa had been too hot to be anywhere, except Venus perhaps, but Khartoum was Africa undiluted and it had given him an unexpected thrill. It had challenged, even frightened him, because he seemed to be at its mercy.

Or had it been foreboding that had unsettled him that day?

Things had changed since then. He liked Khartoum, with its leafy colonial boulevards and low-rise charm. Compared to the havoc of Cairo, the Sudanese capital was a country garden, with two rather exceptional streams running through it, and there wasn't much that could faze Richard now. He was used to Africa, having crawled across its dry belly to save himself, and by making his own way from Abu Hamed he had moved into Frances's league, for the ten days without her had changed him. He had ceased to be the reluctant tourist. He saw things differently now. No longer holding a camera pressed against his nose, he saw beyond the exotic veils and twinkling eyes to the lives behind them. Between Abu Hamed and Khartoum, he had been marked. Altered. Not by the white lunar landscape, but by helplessness and thirst, and reliance on those who had rescued him. All this had left a groove, and Frances would instantly see it. Richard wanted her to see it; he wanted her to know that he was sorry for shutting out the world that fed her.

He had planned the evening ahead: they would celebrate with a good dinner, a long swim and hours spent cordially in bed. Richard was impatient to hear how Frances had coped, and he looked forward to describing the minutiae of his misadventure in order to draw unrestrained sympathy for his troubles.

In all this excited jumble of thoughts, one thing never occurred to him: that Frances would not be on the train.

He spent an unhappy evening at the station. When the train finally slithered in and its cargo of dusty passengers emptied out like sand from a bucket, Richard couldn't see a solitary tourist amongst them. It was all a jumble on the platform. There was no oppressive anticlimax, as often comes in with a long-distance train, for although passengers were weary and travel-worn, they were also cheerful, as if this was one big chaotic celebration. Even in that heaving, suffocating mass of people, Richard was sure he would find Frances. His heart racing, he pushed his way through the crush, desperate to see her, to pick her up and swing her around and tell her how he loved her.

He searched that train, that station. He looked into every carriage, through every window. He walked the length of the platform countless times, scoured the concourse, stood for an hour by the entrance watching every face that came and went.

Andrew's jaw dropped when Richard returned to the hotel alone. He had put flowers and chocolates in the room and did not have the time to retrieve this romantic presentation before Richard went up there, dejected.

As soon as Andrew got off duty, they took his Land Cruiser and went to the Acropole and the Hilton and to five other hotels to see if Frances had checked in, but drew a blank in every one. Back at the Meridien, they sat for a while in the car park.

'What now?' asked Andrew.

'I don't know. I don't understand why she didn't go to the Acropole.'

'*You* didn't.'

'Ah, but I was looking for you,' Richard joked half-heartedly.

'You really think you missed her at the station? I mean, it's hardly Waterloo.'

'Do you know how many people travel on that train? Thousands. She could easily have slipped through when I was looking in the opposite direction.'

'Fair enough, and if that's the case, she won't remain unnoticed in Khartoum for long.'

Another restless night followed. Instead of enjoying hours of abandoned love-making, Richard agonized. It was like being on a mental merry-go-round, except there was nothing merry about it. Had he really missed Frances at the station? Could they truly have walked past each other when they should have been drawn like natural magnets to one another's side? If so, where in Khartoum could she be? And if not, why had she not been on the train? There were so many answers to that particular question that he refused to entertain them, but every now and then, the confusion blanked itself out and one thought took centre stage: they had lost one another. In Africa.

It was absurd, and terrifying.

The following morning, he went straight to see Webster to tell him he had missed Frances at the station and that she might turn up at the embassy looking for him. Afterwards, he went again to the Acropole to double-check that she had still not turned up or left a message. She had done neither. Richard returned to the Meridien despondent, and tried to drown his apprehension in several glasses of Coke, but no amount of fizzy drink could blot out his worst fear.

Andrew sidled up to the slumped figure sitting by the pool. 'No sign?'

Richard shook his head.

'It must be like waiting for her to turn up for a date.'

'I wouldn't know. We never had dates.'

'I see.' Andrew pulled up a chair and sat down. 'You're a fast worker.'

'Not really. It was just the nature of the thing. I never took Fran out to dinner or tried to woo her over candlelight. I never even made love to her in a Volkswagen Beetle. All we've done since the day we met has been to book into hostels in weird and wonderful places. The romance is all in the location for her.'

'But you live in London?'

'*I* live in London. She lives everywhere.'

Andrew frowned. 'How so?'

'She's … you know, footloose. While I've been doing sensible, obvious things like finishing college and getting a job, Fran's been giving the obvious a very wide berth. I have to work for a living; she has to travel to survive. She does whatever it takes to feed herself and get to the next stop. I just turn up for the holidays.'

'How long's this been going on?'

'Three years.'

'Three years,' said Andrew, impressed. 'That's something. Where did you meet?'

'She picked me up in a café in Hamburg.' Richard chuckled. 'I didn't know what had hit me – this gorgeous girl comes up to me saying, "You have got to be Irish!" Funny, for someone who stays so resolutely out of Ireland, she's very sentimental about it. She goes weak at the knees if she sees an Irish flag on a rucksack, and always has to have her *Irish Times* when she can get it, but just try and get her back there.'

'Still, you've held it together, against the odds. Every relationship I've had has been compromised by my lifestyle – no harm, maybe, since it isn't much of a life for a family – whereas you've maintained a long-distance relationship for years. How's it done?'

'With difficulty, believe me, and I don't recommend it. Being pig-headed helps, of course, especially if you're dealing with someone like Fran – Frantic Fran, I call her. She insisted that our first summer together was no more than a passionate holiday fling, and I tried to go along with that, but I couldn't hack it, so I had to change her mind. That Christmas, I flew out to see her in Turkey and got so hooked that I arrived back in college two weeks late and in major debt. The way it started was the way it went on. Twice a year I went out to wherever she was and we'd go off on one of her mad trips. It was good craic, at the time. When you're a student, travelling seems to be the only thing to do, but you get pretty weary of it after a while.'

'Some never tire of it.'

'Yeah, I wish I'd known that then, because Fran never seemed to arrive anywhere. As soon as she got where she was going, she wanted to be somewhere else. By the time I left university, my college loan looked like a lottery win. Dad had to bail me out.'

'And people say love is free,' Andrew mused.

'Ha! Love is very bloody expensive if you fall for the likes of Fran.'

'I'll bet your father was pleased.'

'Actually, he didn't mind too much. He saw it as an investment. I'm the youngest of four. My two sisters never travelled anywhere until they went to Australia and didn't come back, and my brother never travelled, but he's never worked either, so Dad was trying to get the balance right with me. He thought Fran was good for me, that if I bummed around and saw the world, I'd work it out of my system and settle down sensibly – and rather closer to home than my sisters. He was more right than he knew. Fran wore me out.'

'So she lives in Turkey?'

'Na, she left Turkey ages ago and went to India. She could see the writing on the wall – that I'd never be like her – so she tried to go beyond my reach. It was like hanging on to a kite long after it had gone out of sight, but I wouldn't let go.'

'You really are a stubborn bastard.'

Richard smiled. 'You'd understand if you saw the kite in question.'

'Doesn't she ever miss home?'

'On the contrary, Fran hates going home. We spent last Christmas in Dublin with her Mum and that was really nice, I thought. Going nowhere, doing nothing. No maps or timetables; no bleeding rucksacks. Just a few walks by the seafront and curling up to watch telly together. Simple luxuries. It gave me a taste for a different kind of life for us, but after a week, Fran was like a pan of popcorn. Couldn't wait to get out of the place.'

'Sounds like a bad case, right enough. Most of us expats talk about nothing except getting home.'

'She has this hang-up about becoming lost in the crowd. Faceless.'

'I can understand that.'

'You can?'

'Don't get me wrong – I love my holidays in Scotland. It's great to spend time with family, see a bit of mist on the hills, have a few drams, but nobody knows me very well back there and I like that. They don't know about my life here. They think it's weird and wonderful, but what I most enjoy about being abroad is that it gives me a reprieve from responsibility and extraordinary privacy. I like that. It suits me.'

Richard grinned. 'Where were you when Frances needed you?'

'A girl after my own soul, sounds like!'

'Absolutely. Although if I were you, I'd be having trouble with these Sudanese women. They're stunning.'

Andrew caught his eye. 'As it happens, I am having trouble with these Sudanese women. One in particular.'

'Oh, dear.'

'Hmm, right now I'm trying very hard not to fall in love with a young lady from a deeply conservative family.'

'Well, you're wasting your time. I tried not to fall for Fran – I knew she'd be bloody difficult – but when someone like that gets hold of you, you might as well give in.'

'That isn't an option. I'd leave the job before I'd get involved with Nazreen.'

'But it might be worth the trouble. It usually is.'

'Not in this case. For me it would be trouble, for her it would be expulsion from her family. Exile.' He forced a laugh. 'And even I'm not worth that!'

Richard looked at him. 'You're already hooked, you poor eejit.'

'You can talk. You're still traipsing around after Frantic Fran.'

'Ah, but I'm not. She's coming home with me this time.'

'You got around her?'

Richard sighed. 'I thought I had, yeah.'

Andrew glanced at him, not understanding.

'Where the hell is she, Andrew?'

'Maybe she missed the train?'

'Unlikely.'

'It happens to the best of us.'

'Not to Fran. She forgets to get off trains sometimes. She never forgets to get *on*.'

'Fine, but she isn't here, is she? She hasn't gone back to the Acropole and she hasn't shown up anywhere else. If you ask me, she must still be in Wadi.'

'Not according to Webster. Anyway, give me one good reason why she would stay there any longer than she had to.'

'She thinks she has to. She's waiting for you to turn up.'

'Except she'd already waited several days and seen a train arrive without me. She wouldn't have hacked it any longer, not when the train was there for the taking. She'd be physically incapable of letting it go without her.'

'Maybe, but something prevented her from getting to Khartoum. Anything could have happened.'

'Anything *has* happened, Andrew, and it happened to me, so why didn't she come back to find out what?'

Andrew had no answer to that. He stood up. 'Better get back to the grind.'

'Jesus,' said Richard sitting forward.

'What?'

'I've just realized where she is!'

'Where?'

'Abu Hamed. It's obvious! It's the only place I could have got off – she'd have worked that out – so she took the train back that far and got off to look for me. To fetch me. It makes sense, doesn't it?'

'Heck … yes. That makes a lot of sense.'

'And Suleiman will tell her I'm okay. If she asks around for me, he'll tell her what happened. He might even put her up in his little bunker until the next southbound train! That's the one she'll be on, I'm telling you. She'll be on the next train in!'

The next train from Abu Hamed came in at midday the following day. Andrew went with Richard to the station and stood by the entrance, keeping guard over the exits, looking for a white face amongst the crowd, while Richard went to the platform. The Wadi Halfa flock unravelled as it came through the building and dispersed as it left it, becoming a mere sprinkling on the city crowds.

In the quiet aftermath, Andrew went to the platform hoping to find a young couple wrapped so tightly about one another that they had quite forgotten him. Instead, he found Richard halfway along the train, his forehead against a carriage, his hands on the peeling wooden slats. Andrew put a hand on his shoulder, then moved away and waited.

Back at the Meridien, Andrew got the number of the Nile Hotel in Wadi Halfa and called it. Then he went to find Richard. He was outside, walking around the garden.

'I hope you don't mind,' Andrew began, 'but I took the liberty of calling the Nile Hotel again. Just in case they missed Frances the first time, when Webster called.'

'And?'

'According to the guy I spoke to, all the foreigners ... well, he said they took the ferry last week. I asked about a girl on her own, maybe ill, maybe waiting, but he insisted that all the tourists who had been in the hotel had left the country. I don't know what to make of that, do you?'

Richard looked as if he'd been winded. 'Shite.'

'Although it would certainly explain why she wasn't on the train.'

Richard turned on him. 'What are you suggesting? That Fran woke up and said, "Bother, wonder where Richard's got to?" and carried on regardless? Into Egypt? This is my girlfriend we're talking about! My partner. Not some bird I picked up along the way!'

'Right. Fine.'

'Listen, I may not know where she is or what she'd do in this situation, but I can tell you what she wouldn't do – she wouldn't go on without me. The Sudan is a very large country. I'm witness to that. If Frances isn't here already, then she'll roll in from the desert in a day or two. If I can do it, she can. She's the genuine article. A real nomad. She's like a camel – she has enough hump to keep on going until she gets to where she wants to be, and I just have to sit tight until she gets *here*.'

*

The next day, frustrated and disgruntled, Richard went to see Webster and told him about Andrew's call to Wadi Halfa.

'We should make enquiries in Cairo then,' said Webster. 'I was about to do so anyway.'

'She isn't in Cairo!'

'If she went on—'

'She wouldn't leave this country. She doesn't know what's happened to me.'

'If she went on, she would certainly be in Cairo by now.'

'And how am I supposed to find her in a city of twelve million people?'

'You set out from there, didn't you? She might have gone back to your hotel to wait for you.'

'In Cairo? How would I have got to Cairo?'

'It's a contact point, that's all I'm saying. She's evidently not in Khartoum.'

'Not yet.'

Webster raised an eyebrow. 'She could still turn up, I suppose, but I'm inclined to go with what Andrew heard from the people in Wadi Halfa – that all the foreigners took the ferry. She might have had her reasons, Richard. It might have seemed wiser than turning back. Meanwhile ... I feel duty-bound to notify your people in Cairo that she's missing.'

'*Missing?* Jesus, you don't think she's been raped or abducted or—'

'You said she's travel-wise and well able to defend herself, didn't you?'

'She has a green belt in karate.'

'Good, good, so she's probably fine – but we'll notify Cairo all the same.' Webster made his way to the telex room, with Richard on his heels, and sat down at the machine to type the message himself. 'Anything you'd like to say?'

'"Have mislaid my friend. Have you got her?"'

Webster shook his head wryly and prepared a more officious message. Richard looked over his shoulder.

'RE: Richard Keane – Passport Application.

Further to Mr. Keane's passport application, we wish to advise that the young lady with whom he is travelling, Miss Frances Dillon (Irish), has not yet returned from Wadi Halfa as expected. It is possible that she has gone on to Cairo. Could you please find out if she is at the Longchamps Hotel? If so, advise urgently. We need to establish her whereabouts.'

Webster stayed on line after sending the message, dinging the other end for an immediate reply. Every time he hit the key, a little bell-shaped symbol appeared on screen, indicating that he was holding. After a moment, Cairo asked them to stand by while they rang the Longchamps.

They sat, waiting, Richard's eyes hard on the screen, longing for a positive outcome, but several minutes later the following reply came up:

'Sorry. No Miss Dillon at Longchamps, but we'll make more enquiries and keep you informed.'

'Thanks. Charles Webster.'

The telex numbers came up, and the line shut down.

Richard moved into Andrew's place in the suburbs that afternoon. Holding out in luxury until Frances turned up was all very well, but now there was no estimated time for her arrival, nor even any certainty of it, and the cost of staying at the Meridien had become prohibitive. He couldn't squander any more of the savings which he still hoped would become a deposit for their first home, so, with his few clothes in a plastic bag, he moved into Andrew's spacious bungalow. Here, he could also avoid the foreign community who congregated at the Meridien. They had been looking forward to meeting his girlfriend, to hearing the other side of this extraordinary story, and when she didn't come there was even more interest. Expats were talking about them all over Khartoum.

To make matters worse, word soon got around that the elusive Frances had taken the Aswan ferry, in spite of the fact that her lover had disappeared in the Greater Nubian Desert, and although Andrew never told his friend what the gossipmongers were saying when they lounged around the hotel, Richard knew they were having a field day. Love, romance, desertion! Women took to stopping him, frightfully sympathetic and full of ideas about what they would do in his position. He couldn't afford to be too embarrassed – the more people who knew about him, the easier it would be for Frances to find him – but he prevaricated now when asked about her, and insisted that, in her place, he would not have boarded that train for a third time, but would have continued on to Cairo where they could meet up when his passport came through. No one believed him, of course, and as days passed, it became humiliating to be seen as a man who had been so spectacularly jilted.

'And have you?' Andrew asked, when Richard said as much that Saturday evening when they were sitting in the gardens of the Sudan Club, surrounded by expatriates, waiting for *Gandhi* to be shown on an outdoor screen.

'Course not. It's a question of the proverbial needle in the haystack, except that in this case the haystack happens to be Africa.'

'There's something missing here, Richard. She should have been on one of those trains. Impulse should have brought her back to starting point, but it didn't.'

'You know, I couldn't help noticing that.'

'Don't bullshit me, man.'

'I'm not.'

'You are. You have been all week. You keep saying she'll turn up, but you've looked like a man swamped in doubt ever since you met that first train. You said she'd turn around in this crisis, but she didn't, so why aren't you freaking out? I mean, shouldn't we be worried about the well-being of a young lassie wandering around Africa on her own?'

Glancing at the people taking their seats around them, Richard muttered, 'She'll be fine.'

'Damn it, Richard, stop knocking me back. The embassy people don't know what to make of you. Webster says you're behaving more like a man who's been stood up outside a cinema on a cold night than a bloke whose girlfriend's gone missing in the Sudan.'

'What do you want me to say?' Richard hissed. 'That I have been jilted?'

'I'm only worried about the girl.'

'There's no need to be.'

'How do you know that?'

Richard scowled. Then, with a deep sigh and his eyes firmly on the blank screen ahead, he said, 'Because things were getting shitty between us. That's what you want to hear, isn't it?'

Andrew nodded slowly. 'I wondered.'

'Fact is …' Richard took another deep breath. 'The fact is that I can't be certain that she'll come back here or … even try to find me. She's probably far beyond Egypt by now.'

'Surely not?'

'I'd like to think not, but as days go by, I have to accept that with all this time to herself and me out of the picture, she might just grab her chance and take off.'

'But you told me that you were going home together.'

'Yes, but I didn't tell you that I forced her hand. I made her choose, because it was getting crazy, you know? Fran's never seen my office, met my friends, and she doesn't even know what I have for breakfast on an average Sunday morning. Not that she cared about any of that. She just wanted to do it her way and I went along for the ride, but there came a point when I wondered where we were actually headed. My job's demanding more time and I want to give it my best shot. I'm ready to settle down and I thought Fran should too. I thought it was time she took a good hard look at what makes her so restless.'

'What *does* make her restless?'

'God knows. You could blame her gene pool, I suppose. She has a lot of her mother in her. That so-called creative streak that prevents her mother from concentrating on her daughters for more than two minutes is the same streak that keeps Fran flitting about. As for her dad, he was an easygoing type, by all accounts, satisfied with his job in the civil service, with his pint after work and following the hurling, but Fran saw him as dull and unambitious and she's terrified she'll turn out like him. She loved him a lot, but she once described him as a small man, whereas I think he was a man who knew how to make himself happy. I never met him, but he seemed content with his lot. Fran, of course, thinks contentment is a dirty word.'

'It's the most reliable form of happiness.'

'It's the most witless form of happiness, according to her, because it eclipses experience.'

'It also eclipses pain,' said Andrew.

'I tried telling her that. I kept saying that she's too solid for complacency to sink her, that even out of motion she still exists, but she didn't believe me.'

Andrew didn't know what to say.

'Anyway, whether by heritage or circumstance, she's as flighty as a bird. I don't think she has ever finished a project in her entire life, and I might be just another such project.'

'Och, don't be so gloomy.'

'Why not? She could have come back to Khartoum blindfolded if she'd wanted to, and anyone trying to abduct her would get his neck broken.'

'But she has a life with you to look forward to.'

'Except she *wasn't* looking forward to it. She was dreading it.' Richard shook his head. 'This trip was her last fling. Egypt was … like a honeymoon. Christ, I was happy. And in the Sudan *she* was happy. On her train. On that line going through the middle of nowhere. It's so bleak, you know? It's hot and dry and breathless, but it's packed and busy and like a moving party. Fran was entranced. It brought into focus what she was giving up because of me and she couldn't stand it. Tension mounted. Resentment, recriminations, the lot. And then I fell out of the fucking carriage.'

'Hmm. I don't think much of your timing.'

'Fran won't either. And now … well. I held her by a thread and I'm not sure that thread will stand the strain. Given this unexpected glimpse of freedom, she might not be able to help herself. Wandering around the Sudan or Egypt or wherever the hell she is, at the mercy of her passions, there's no knowing what she'll do. I know she loves me. I'm just not sure she loves me enough to carry this through on her own.'

Richard was waiting as he had never done before; waiting, waiting, wanting the impossible. No matter how much he wished it, he couldn't make Frances materialize before him, as happened in his dreams, and without her he felt as denuded as he had in Abu Hamed.

And yet, one particular phone call could bring to an end much of this. He had been putting it off for days because he didn't want to know the answer, because there was hope in limbo, but with Webster muttering about getting the Sudanese police involved he could no longer avoid making that one conclusive enquiry. On the Monday that he should have been back at work, he went to the embassy to see if his passport had arrived and asked Webster if he could make a call to Egypt. He had to contact the Abu Simbel Hotel in Aswan, he explained, and ask if their rucksack was still in the storeroom. If it was gone, then so was Frances. It was that simple.

With Webster's help, he got through to the hotel quite quickly. Richard told the receptionist that he had left a rucksack there some weeks before and asked if his girlfriend had picked it up yet.

'Many people coming and going,' the man retorted. 'Many luggage stay here!'

'Please. I need to know if my bag is still there. Could you check the storeroom? It's a blue rucksack, not so big, not so heavy, and we left it just inside the door.'

'I am sorry, sir. I cannot leave the desk. Very busy here. You call back.'

'I can't do that. Please—'

Webster took the phone from him and spoke in Arabic, then said to Richard, 'He's going to check.'

'What did you say?'

'I pulled rank.'

The Egyptian came back to the phone some minutes later. There was no blue rucksack in the stores.

That evening, Richard sat on Andrew's terrace. He had already been crushed, twice, at the station, but like a stick insect his limbs had kept moving. Now he felt dead in every extremity.

He was trying to decide what to do next when Andrew pulled up in his Land Cruiser and came running through the house.

'What's up with you?'

'Get into the car,' said Andrew. 'There's a lass – an Irish lass – who's just checked into the Acropole.'

Before they had even reached the car, Richard had asked when Frances had arrived, who had seen her, how had she got there? ... Andrew had no details except that some expats had been speaking to this lady, and the news of her arrival had filtered back to him at the Meridien. 'I came to fetch you right away.'

'Just when I'd given up all hope, she turns up! Typical bloody Fran! Christ, I've waited for this. I tell you, mate, this has been like living without any blood in my veins. I mean, Jesus wept. But things are going to change. I've learnt my lesson. And I'll tell her. I'll tell her tonight. Wherever she wants to go, I'll go too. Stuff London, stuff career. I'm not letting her out of my sight ever again.'

Andrew slowed at traffic lights and tried to put the brakes on Richard's excitement. 'It might not be her, Richard.'

'For God's sake, how many Irish women are likely to be travelling around Sudan alone?'

'Not many, but you've taken a lot of falls recently and it's a long way down from where you are right now, so get a grip, man. Cool it until we get there.'

He was wasting his breath. Richard continued in the same vein until they reached the hotel. After they had parked the car, he bounded forwards, but Andrew pulled at his elbow. 'Richard! It might not be her, for crying out loud!'

'Don't be ridiculous.'

'You have an Irish girl staying here. Frances Dillon. Could you page her please?'

'Irish?' The receptionist checked the register. 'Yes. Room 33.' He picked up the phone.

Richard clenched his fists in triumph.

Andrew smiled. 'Maybe I should leave you to it?'

'No, no, you have to meet her!'

He walked around in circles while they waited. When the lift dinged, they both spun around as a young woman emerged.

It was a cruel twist, and one that Richard could have done without.

The woman went to the desk. The receptionist nodded towards Richard.

Richard stood, staring.

'Richard? said Andrew, confused. 'Frances?'

She grimaced. 'Em, no.'

She was a journalist from Belfast. Richard didn't really take her in. After explaining their mistake, Andrew insisted on buying her a drink. Richard sat, saying nothing, looking at her, not seeing Frances.

Wherever Frances had gone to and whatever she was doing, they were suffering one thing in common at that time: not knowing. Not knowing where, when, how, why. Scooped out of each other's lives, they had been left hanging, devoid of information, of certainty, for day after day, then week after week, until it would become month after month and year after year. It was something he would have to get used to, but that night in Khartoum he couldn't stand it any longer. He thought that he simply wouldn't be able to bear another night without her. In the Gents, he hit his head against the wall, hard, but the frustration lingered, like an internal rash he couldn't scratch, so he went back to finish his drink. Events were beyond his control and had put him sitting there, with a girl he had never seen before and would never see again, a girl he had believed was Frances, come to find him at last.

He knew then, and Andrew knew, that Frances never would come to find him.

three

11

'One of us is lying.'

Her voice dropped from the upper berth with all the weight of a dead body. It wasn't what I had expected her to say. In fact, I thought she might finally be contrite and admit to a monumental error of judgement. By her account, getting onto that ferry had been the only thing to do. In his eyes, it was worse than impetuous; it was desertion. This was a bitter pill for her to swallow, but I thought she might apologize and come clean. Instead she said clearly and without emotion, 'One of us is lying.'

'Apparently.'

Frances hesitated. 'And one of us is telling the truth, so why go on like this?'

'That doesn't follow. We could both be lying. At a push, we might both be telling the truth.'

'Unlikely.'

'Is it? Something might have got in the way, Fran. Something beyond our control.'

'Like what?'

'I don't know. Maybe there was an international conspiracy against us?'

'Yeah, and maybe some desert djinn spirited you out the window.'

'That's exactly what happened,' he said ruefully, 'except I went out the door.'

'Very funny.'

I longed to move. My back was aching, but they were speaking quite loudly now, convinced by my near-comatose state, and I didn't wish to discourage them by squirming around.

'Look, there could have been some mix-up at the embassies,' said Richard. 'A genuine administrative error of some kind.'

'You think maybe the people in Cairo issued you with a passport while I was sitting right under their noses bleating for you? Come on, Richard, that just doesn't make any sense!'

'I'll tell you what doesn't make sense. You getting onto that ferry when you hadn't a clue what had happened to me. That makes no bloody sense at all.'

For a while, they retreated into their corners to consider. I heard Frances fumble about; something crinkled and I fancied that she was opening a bar of chocolate. I thought I could even smell it. *Cruel.*

Irritated, perhaps, by her retreat into chocolate, Richard suddenly lashed out: 'Honest to God, Fran, how can you explain taking off to look for me in another country?'

'I'm not going over that again.'

'No, because that could be tricky, couldn't it? You might get something mixed up next time around.'

'There is nothing to mix up. I was at that embassy in Cairo and they were no more issuing you with a passport than they were issuing one for Margaret Thatcher!'

'Fuck it,' he said, his voice rising. 'After all I went through to persuade you to live with me, why on earth would I jump off a train in the mid-afternoon heat, in the belly of an absolute wasteland, to get away from you? It doesn't wash! There are a lot more comfortable ways of terminating a relationship, if that's what I'd wanted to do, but I *didn't*. You, on the other hand, were giving up your precious arsing-about with undisguised reluctance, so if anyone was going to make a break, you're the one who was most likely to!'

'I know that! And that is precisely why I am determined to prove that's not what happened! When I said I'd give it all up, I meant it. No matter how difficult, I intended to go through with it, and I've spent the last four years wanting to tell you that I kept my half of the bargain!' Her voice was louder than at any time since she had entered the compartment. 'Wanting to be with you didn't make it easy to abandon my whole *raison d'être*, and I don't apologize for admitting that it wasn't. At the time, I happened to think you were worth it and I wasn't going to give up on us just because you'd fallen off our bloody train!'

She tried to pause, but indignation caught up with her, her words running on of their own accord. 'I don't know where you damn well went to, but you owe it to me now to tell me why I woke up on that train and found you gone!'

Four years had been purged. She had probably screamed this at him a thousand times in her mind, day after day, night after night. Every time she got onto a bus, or chopped a carrot, or sat in traffic, she had probably practised all this in the hope of one day vindicating herself.

The train shuddered and we all moved with it. The vibration, constant in my limbs, threatened to render me unconscious if I was not immediately distracted. My eyes had stared into the darkness for hours, picking up every little movement, every light flashing past the window, but now my eyelids were heavy, in need of rest. I willed Richard to speak.

'Fran,' he said calmly, 'did I love you so badly that you could think me capable of ditching you like that? You must know I wouldn't do that kind of thing to anyone, but with *you* ... I wasn't physically capable of getting up and leaving you.'

'You were in a fury.'

'Maybe, but if I *had* walked away, I'd tell you now just as I would have told you, face to face, at the time. But there was no reason to do so. Yes, you were being a horse's ass. Yes, you were making me pay, daily, hourly, for wanting to be with you, but even if I had wanted to dump you, why would I do so in such a spectacularly uncomfortable manner?'

'To punish me.'

'Don't be ridiculous. I'm not vengeful. And abandoning my girl-friend in the middle of the Nubian Desert simply isn't my style. I thought you would have known that.'

'What I knew and what I expected of you proved to be of no value to me then and is irrelevant now. You are lying to me, Richard. That's all the proof I need about what really happened.'

'But why would I lie? Why, in God's name, would I leave you in the first place?'

'Because', she said quietly, 'I wasn't worth the trouble anymore. Remember? That's what you said. I can still hear the contempt in your voice. "You know what, Fran? You're just not worth the trouble anymore." Those were the last words you spoke to me and you can't withdraw them, you know, or cancel the effect they had. My would-be reasons for running out are written all over the wall, but you weren't without motivation either. You hated it when I taxed you with emotional acrobatics. You loathed conflict and I gave you little else in the Sudan. And it might have been even worse back in England. You'd been after me like some prize catch but you got me at a price you hadn't reckoned with. Maybe you wouldn't leap off a train to escape me and maybe your bag *was* nicked, but given time to reflect, you might very well have realized you'd taken on more than you really wanted, so however you went about it, you made sure we didn't make contact.'

'You underestimate what you were to me.'

'I could say likewise.'

He gulped back whatever drink he had up there. 'Really? If you loved me so much, how come you dreaded the prospect of living with me?'

'Not living *with* you. Living the way you lived. Look, let's not go round that particular roundabout again. We've already paid too dearly for it, taking different exits to get off it.'

Richard tapped his empty can against something metallic, and the sound provided a monotonous diversion from the suspended conversation.

'I don't know what to say,' came Frances's voice eventually. 'Whatever went before, whatever happened to you, I was in Cairo, trying to find you. It makes no difference now. Contrary to expectation, my life did go on without you, but back then I didn't think it would. I dreaded living in England, I'll say that over and over again, but it was preferable to losing you. I got on to that ferry because I was tired and confused, and because I thought it was what you wanted. I wish you'd tell me now that it was, then we could laugh off the whole sorry business.'

'You'd forgive me so easily?'

'I just want to know what happened.'

Richard snorted derisively. 'You mean you want me to admit to something which never took place in order to make you feel better about your own choices. Well, I won't.' He jumped down from his berth and opened the door. Light shone into the compartment.

Stalemate.

The train raced. I dropped into a momentary dream, which vanished as soon as it appeared. A flash of normality. The familiarity of my London flat and a face I knew, a voice I knew. Not these faceless voices, unhappy and full of query and distrust. In the lull, sleep touched and tempted me, and the trusty shackle of the train's wheels enticed me away from this drama. A wide black pit opened beneath me, inviting, drawing me in, and this complicated affair being acted out overhead ceased to be of so much interest. It would dissolve and be lost in sleep, and when I woke I would no longer care about this curious story of Cairo and Khartoum. I slid gently towards the great hole. Yes, I would cease to intrude on these people, on their private misfortunes and speculations. I would allow myself the sleep that drew me with every somnolent rattle of the bogies. It was none of my business anyway.

But as I drifted off, I became aware of discomfort. I couldn't put my finger on it. Having finally dissociated myself from the two voices that had held me mesmerized, I was being gently rocked into restful sleep – but that sleep remained at a frustrating distance as the sensation I tried to ignore increased. The truth dawned: I needed to pee. Within seconds the black hole of unconsciousness had vanished and a curious dilemma replaced it. I could, of course, get up, nod at Richard in the bright light of the corridor and squeeze past him to go to the lavatory. However, that might lead them to conclude that they had disturbed me, which would compel them to move away from the compartment to continue their discussion in anonymity elsewhere; alternatively, they might remain silent in my presence. I deserved no better than the latter, but my curiosity had been reawakened and now asserted itself like a growth inside. I was convinced that, before dawn, the clot would eventually seep out and we would discover what exactly had happened on the Nile Valley Express. I could not risk missing that moment.

I hesitated also on their account. It was vital for them to maintain their privacy if they were to survive this meeting, and if another person intruded, the spell would be broken. The next morning, they could go back to their separate lives intact only if they had met as in another world, where the mystery that had tormented them had been discussed without witness or loss of face. Individually, they had probably dreamed of an opportunity like this – hours of unrestrained access to the other – because if they had met in a crowd, the pressure of their past would have been intensified, and not necessarily resolved.

My bladder ached. I wondered what to do.

And then Frances spoke. Her voice seemed strangely close to me. She was leaning over her berth to reach him in the corridor. 'Richard?'

His form reappeared in the doorway, a handkerchief bulging out of his front pocket.

'What about proof? One of us must have some kind of proof of where we were when—' There was a sudden movement overhead. 'Of course! My passport.' After much shuffling about, she handed it to him. 'There. Have a look. See what date I left Cairo!'

He didn't move. 'I don't intend to check up on you.'

'Oh, but you have no compunction about accusing me! Take it. I want to be cleared. I don't greatly fancy the charges of desertion and deceit.'

'You don't want to be cleared. You want to nail me.'

'That too.'

He took the passport and turned towards the passage to read it.

'Look for Heathrow – May nineteen eighty-three.'

'So you went to England. Why wouldn't you? The flight was booked. But ... Oh, fancy this: you *did* go to England in eighty-three, and since then you've been in ...' he turned the passport around 'Bahrain. Oh, and Turkey again. What's this? Spain? Greece ... Seems very little has changed. You're still moving around like a lost soul.'

'Give me that!' She reached down to snatch back her passport.

'I rest my case. Your own evidence supports it.'

'No it doesn't! For all you know, those could be holidays. It proves nothing. *Your* passport, on the other hand, could settle this once and for all. I'd like to see it.'

His thumbs began tapping against his belt.

'Give it to me,' said Frances.

His thumbs joined the fingers in a fist in his pockets.

'Richard?'

'There's no point showing you my passport. It won't prove anything.'

The atmosphere in the compartment was so stretched I thought the air would crackle. Had we finally reached the climax? The truth? If Richard's passport had not been issued in Cairo, total doubt would be thrown over his account of events.

'I have a different passport now,' he said. 'I got a new one last year. At home.'

Frances gasped. 'You don't seriously expect me to believe that?'

His body twisted slightly, like a small boy caught misbehaving.

She jumped off the berth to face him, but after a pause said quietly, 'How could you do this? Fabricating some bloody story that made my heart bleed? And how *could* you walk out on me like that? Anything could have happened to me. Anything could have happened to *you*! I might have had all the diplomats in Africa looking for you!'

'Why didn't you?' he said calmly. 'At least then you might have found me. Instead, you moved on. What kind of loyalty is that, Frances?'

'Loyalty? You left me and you won't even admit it!'

'I won't admit it because I didn't do it!'

'So show me the passport to prove it!'

'I can't. That passport got mangled. By Frank. He scribbled all over it and tore some of the pages out.'

'What? Who's Frank?'

'My nephew. Orla's kid. He got his hands on it when we met up in Dublin last year. Wrecked it.'

'You cannot be serious?' she said with a chuckle. 'I've heard more bullshit tonight than I know what to do with.'

She had finally caught him out, and he knew it, and I was sorely tempted to contribute to these proceedings by leaning out of my berth to say, 'Right, well, that more or less ties this thing up, don't you think? Now would you excuse me, please? I need to go to the lavatory.'

Then Richard said lightly, 'I do have proof, though.'

The stuffy air reverberated. It was as if a small explosion had gone off inside the compartment.

'Proof?' she said.

'Yes.'

'You can prove that what you've told me is true, in spite of the fact that your current passport was issued in Dublin?'

'More or less. I can prove my general whereabouts when all this was going on.'

'You really expect me to believe that in four years you lost two passports — one taken out of your hand on a train and the other scribbled on by your nephew?'

'It might not suit you to do so, but yes, I think you ought to believe me.'

'Why?'

'I have a letter. Well, I had a letter, which not so much proved my intentions as yours.'

'... Go on.'

'Ironically,' he hesitated, 'just when you were about to give up the world, it seems I took it on. Not so much out of despair, as out of hope. I really thought I could find you.'

12

Richard left Khartoum as soon as his exit visa had been issued. Andrew told him to cut his losses and get back to work, but he wasn't ready to give up and London just wasn't the right place to go. It was, he believed, the last place on earth he'd find Frances.

Andrew disagreed. 'It's the one place that she can be sure of finding *you*. She'll show up eventually, and you'd better be there when she does.'

But Richard was not convinced. She could have found him in Khartoum, had she wanted to, and besides, he would immediately be sucked under the mill if he went back to London, with no means of getting out again. He had taken all his annual leave; he wouldn't get another day off before Christmas. Besides, going home was the sensible thing to do, and he was no longer so inclined to be sensible. The Nile Valley Express had disabused him of all those notions of security and prudence. It was delaying the inevitable, perhaps, slithering away from facing the facts, but he persuaded himself that if he was ever to trace Frances, he had to do it her way. After making his farewells to Andrew and Khartoum, he flew to Cairo.

He went straight from the airport to the Longchamps Hotel, and when he walked into the lobby he knew instantly that Frances had been there – with him over a month before, yes, but since then also. After checking in, he went to the balcony for a cold drink and gathered his thoughts. Returned to a bustling semi-Westernized metropolis, he felt more naked than ever without credit cards, and although his salary had just hit his bank account, his financial situation was tottering. This little misadventure was draining his savings, and much of the money he had intended for a deposit on a flat now sat in the coffers of the Meridien Hotel. The relief of stumbling out of the desert into the lap of luxury had cost him, but the Meridien had been his oasis. Or was it Andrew who had been his oasis? Richard missed the Scot already; he even missed Khartoum, as he sat on the little sunny terrace off the Longchamps restaurant. Cairo was a very different prospect. He'd forgotten about the noise; the heave; the way the buildings seemed to be held up by the muggy air compressed between them.

Work, meanwhile, was getting tricky. His friend and immediate boss, Bob Holden, had agreed to give him another week off. He thought Richard mad, chasing a girl to Egypt, but agreed to cover for him a bit longer, so he had only days in which to get a lead on Frances's whereabouts. He convinced himself that she was in Cairo. She had loved it when they had been there together, and now that her money would be running out, she couldn't go far without finding a job. That would be no hardship to her – she would do the rounds of language schools looking for teaching hours, and if that failed she would try offices where English would be an asset. Airlines. Travel agencies. Richard had his work cut out.

But his first step, the next morning, was to call Rome. He rang the small English-language school in Trastevere where Frances had worked for six months and spoke to her pal, Karen. He explained that he was calling from Cairo.

'I'm sorry, who is this?'

'Richard Keane. I'm a close friend of Fran's.'

'Oh, yes. Richard. Hi. What's up?'

'I, well, I was wondering if you've heard from Fran recently?'

A pause. 'She's with you, isn't she?'

'She was, yeah, but I'm afraid I lost her halfway up the Nile. I thought she might have been in touch with you.'

The silence at the other end was loaded. Richard imagined her shaking her head, thinking, *So she couldn't do it after all.* 'Karen?'

'Sorry, I haven't heard a word from her. What happened?'

Richard went over, once again, the events of the last weeks. The more he said, the more stupid he felt for ever believing Frances would settle down with him.

'What about her mother?' asked Karen. 'Have you tried her?'

'I don't want to alarm her. She's on her own and—'

'Her sister then?'

'That's one of the reasons I'm ringing. I can't remember her surname. Do you know it?'

'God, no, I'm afraid not.'

'Did Fran give you a contact address when she left Rome?'

'How could she? She didn't know where you two would be living. She said she'd send me an address as soon as she had one.'

'Fuck … Listen, I'll keep looking for her here—'

'That's a good idea. She'd like Cairo.'

'But if you hear anything, would you call me?' He gave her his number.

'I suppose she *is* all right,' said Karen. 'She wouldn't be ill somewhere?'

'Every trace I've covered suggests that she took the ferry to Egypt, which means only one thing.'

'She bolted.'

He hated her for saying it.

Cairo became hotter. On oppressively sultry days, he went from language school to language school. He went to aid agencies, airlines, foreign banks, tour companies, and he sat around the Longchamps a lot, waiting. Watching the lift. Finally, six days after arriving and three and a half weeks after being separated from Frances, he dialled her mother's old number. The new occupants of the house gave him a new number. When he got through to it, the crackling line did not make the conversation any easier.

'Frances?' her mother called out. 'No, I don't know where she is. I never know where that girl is. She's off travelling with her boyfriend. Who's speaking?'

'This is her boyfriend. It's me, Richard.'

'Oh, Richard.' A short silence, and then, 'Given you the slip, has she?' Richard detected pride in her voice. If he ever saw Frances again he must remember to tell her that her mother did love her and was even proud of the way she lived. 'I could have told you,' she said to him. 'You were wasting your time trying to get her to settle down. You were tying your own noose, dear.'

There was mild amusement in her tone. A parent's conceit: *I told you so*. Richard struggled. He could ask her to tell Frances he was searching for her, but pride stopped him. He was already pathetic in Mrs Dillon's eyes; he didn't wish to plead. Besides, she was right. Frances had given him the slip. Let her at it.

He left a message and rang off. Enough running.

13

A cold voice dispelled the clinging vision of a warm, sweaty Cairo.

'For God's sake,' said Frances, impatiently.

Her voice startled me; I had become so involved in Richard's search for her that I had drifted away from the compartment. They had climbed back up and were sitting on his berth. 'You said something about a letter,' she said. 'Can we get to that?'

'Did your mother ever tell you I called?'

'She mentioned it. She said you rang to let me know you were all right. I was deeply reassured, obviously. What about this letter?'

'That was about a month later. Karen and I kept in touch, and when the letter came—'

'She wrote to you?'

'No. You wrote to her, remember?'

The stillness overhead indicated that Frances did remember.

Richard went on. 'Karen phoned me. Told me she'd heard from you. That you were okay. Fine. Settled in London. You even gave her an address.'

'Jesus, you mean you *knew*? You knew where I was and you didn't come? God, why not? Even if we didn't get back together, we could at least have put an end to all the fretting. Why didn't you do me the small justice of coming to see me if only to set my mind at ease?'

'I couldn't.'

'Why not?'

'Because ... because I was still in Cairo.'

I frowned. Frances must also have frowned. 'A month later? Why?'

Richard's voice croaked when he said, 'I was working there.'

'Working? What do you mean, working?'

'I mean I live there. I never left.'

'... You live in Egypt?'

'Yes.'

'You're having me on.'

'Nope.'

'What about your blessed career? That fancy job.'

'They gave me a final deadline. I missed it.'

'You were fired?'

'Like I said, I missed the deadline. I'd already taken more than my full quota of leave.'

'But you *loved* that job. You wouldn't give it up for anything – not even for me.'

'Seems I did give it up for you in the end.'

'I don't understand.'

'I know. It was wildly out of character – for the person you knew, at any rate – but all that achievement and dosh, what was it for? To buy a house and go home to find it empty every day? To take expensive holidays, with Club Med Singles perhaps? I wanted those things for both of us, Fran. Half the bargain didn't amount to much.'

'I'm not the only woman in the world, for God's sake.'

'You were to me. But there was more to it than that. When we met up in Egypt for that last trip, I really thought I had it made. There I was in my mid-twenties, with a great job, solvent enough to buy a place of my own and about to settle down with the girl I loved. And I'd done it all with my eyes closed. I'd even travelled the world without noticing because my eyes were honed onto those blonde curls of yours. I was a follower, I went with the flow – into college, out of college, into a job, out to you. But in the Sudan, I was forced to burrow deep into my own resources, and you know

211

what? It got me all revved up. Going back to London would have been going back in more ways than one and I had the cop to see that. When I went looking for you, I met people; I got a feel for Cairo that I'd missed on our whistle-stop tour. I'd been in Africa for almost two months by then and I ... well. London seemed grey in comparison. Dull. Everything you'd told me it was. Also, I dreaded the prospect of going home with my tail between my legs. After all the fuss I'd made about finally persuading you to come back, I'd have to turn up without you and I wasn't much looking forward to it.'

'The hunter coming back without with his prey?'

'So I was immature and arrogant, what of it? Anyway, two days before I was due to leave, I got talking to this English guy at the hotel and it was like a window opening up. He was living in Cairo and his flatmate was going home, so he was looking for a replacement. Before I knew what I was doing, I'd taken the room. Before I knew what had happened, I had a place to live and a job in one of the language schools I'd been pestering. I took a leaf out of your book.'

After a moment, Frances said quietly, 'You've taken all the leaves out of my book.'

'Without meaning to.'

'You've stolen the very lifestyle you made me give up! I agreed to stop travelling because *you* wanted a dreary little life in Putney, and all for what? For the great pleasure of being left with a huge gorge in my life! I should never have given in. I should have kept my hand! It's too bloody much to find out that after denying me what I wanted, you went and took it all for yourself!' She jumped down and stood by the door with her back to us.

'Why did you take that ferry?' Richard hissed. 'We could have found each other if you'd only hung on. If you'd only turned back!'

'Oh, but then I might have interrupted your great love affair with *my life*!'

'We could have lived in Cairo together.'

'I spent a year trying to tell you that. You wouldn't listen. Your career wouldn't withstand a break, you said, couldn't take the damage I might inflict on it, but you ended up forsaking that career in the course of one conversation with a complete stranger! You've managed to take all the things that meant most to me, including yourself!'

Richard came down and stood behind her. 'I didn't mean it to work out that way. Honest, Fran. At first I stayed because I didn't know what else to do. Anything was better than coming face to face with all my petty little plans, with the way I'd fucked things up, but then Egypt got into my bones. It was amazing.'

'Good thing you got off the train then!'

'Ah,' he said quietly, 'but look at what it cost me.' He touched her elbow.

'Fuck off.'

He made her turn around. 'Jesus. You look fantastic.'

'And you look ill. I hope you are.'

'I'm not used to these northern climes.'

'Don't rub it in.'

'Fran, for what it's worth, I understand now what you were fighting with on the Nile. I understand how much I was asking of you. It just didn't register at the time. It couldn't. I was too caught up in my own agenda. I'd got my way, that's all I cared about, but I was drawing you away from the pivot on which you spun and that was a mistake. If only I'd known what I was up against … Sometimes, when I'm spinning on that same pivot, I get the buzz you used to get and I realize what an ass I was.'

'That's the most sensible thing you've said all night.' She brushed past him and sat by the window in the dark. 'So, you knew where I was and still you didn't come. You think this is proof? You're bloody right it is. Proof that you didn't want me anymore.'

'Hmm. That brings us back to the letter.'

My bladder was now seriously distended, but in order to allow myself relief, I would have to barge past Richard at the door, wearing a suitably drowsy expression, and miss out on his 'proof'. Like Frances, I was sceptical about the second passport, but her own account was by no means above suspicion. An inherent allegiance to my own sex struggled to support her case, but the harsh facts rendered it too often suspect, so every time one of them spoke, I switched sides as effortlessly as a cat looking for a warm lap. Of course, I didn't have to believe either of them. They were strangers who would vanish from my life at Innsbruck, and regardless of how they resolved the matter, for me it was ultimately no more than enormously entertaining.

Richard stepped up on the berth opposite mine and brought down a bottle. He offered Frances water. They drank; my bladder throbbed with every gulp. Then he continued.

'Karen phoned me often to see if I'd heard from you. She got our postcard – the one we posted from Aswan – but with the vagaries of the Egyptian and Italian postal systems combined, it took ages to reach her. A few weeks later, the letter came. Karen rang me immediately.'

Frances didn't appear to react.

Richard sat on the bench beside her. 'Do you remember what you wrote?'

She didn't stir.

'Because I remember it well,' he went on. 'I always will. "Richard is fine," you wrote. "Richard is back at work and delighted to have me here. And I'm pretty happy to be here too …" On and on you went, about our lovely life together. The flat we were going to buy; your job options. You made a mockery of everything I had offered you in good faith and I just couldn't fucking believe it. I'd known you to be slippery, unpredictable, but I'd never known you to be so blatantly dishonest. Nor had Karen, and she didn't like being taken for a fool, because if I hadn't contacted her first, she would have believed all that stuff. She would have been happy for you. She suggested I write and tell you where I was, but there was no point. You'd made yourself pretty clear, and besides, I knew that if I put pen to paper, I'd end up grovelling, begging you to have me back.'

The train rushed through some unseen part of northern Italy.

'If only you had,' said Frances quietly.

'Oh, if only. If only you hadn't left the Sudan.'

'So that's why Karen sent my things over without so much as a note.'

'Yup.'

'And that's why I've never heard from her since.'

'What if you had? How long were you going to keep up the charade – the happy life you were living with good ol' Richard?'

'I planned to tell her the truth when I had sorted myself out. Anyway, I don't see how any of this proves anything.'

'It proves that I contacted Karen to try to find you and that you had something to hide.'

'I wasn't trying to hide anything.' Frances's voice had no feeling in it, as though she no longer cared what he thought, what conclusions he reached. The fight had gone from her, probably because she had lost it anyway. She moved to the door and leaned against the edge of it, then slid down the jamb and sat on the floor with her back to me. I could have reached out and touched her.

'What did you expect me to write?' she asked. '"Dear Karen, You'll be longing to hear how Richard and I are getting on, but I can't tell you, because Richard isn't here. I don't know where he is. I haven't seen him since the Sudan and I don't know what to do. I don't know where he is." I couldn't write that. I tried, but it wouldn't come. It was too bleak, too true. After all the drama of finally giving in to this man who was so determined to have me, it was too humiliating to admit that he'd left me. The joke was on me. So I wrote to her quickly, to ask her to send over my stuff. It's all I was capable of at the time.'

'Really,' said Richard dryly. 'Karen worried about you, you know. Cared about you. She deserved better than a heap of lies.'

'I know that, but for what it's worth, I fell into a very black depression when I got to England. I felt as if I'd been dismembered, lobotomized. It was hard enough living it, without having to write it down.'

'And this address you gave her? You're still there, are you?' His tone was provocative.

She looked up. 'What do you think, Richard? You seem to be so sure of my every movement from the moment you left, why don't you tell me where I've been all this time? Tibet? Xanadu?'

'I have no idea, but I do know that you never lived at that flat. I went there when I got back to London. The landlord had never heard of you. He said you'd never lived there. You might have gone to England initially, but you certainly didn't stay.'

Frances gave a curt laugh. 'Well, you're right about that. I didn't stay in England. An old school pal of mine was renting that flat. I stayed with her for a bit when I got back from Egypt.'

'And then? Where did you go then?'

'Oh God, we could go on like this all night. Why should I tell you every detail of my life between Cairo and Florence? It won't change anything. We're just a couple who didn't make it. Our lives moved on, and it's where we've ended up that matters, especially since we both seem to have arrived somewhere we didn't expect to be. Knowing whether we ended here by choice or circumstance is of no consequence now, and even if we could resolve it, I'll still be the same person when I get off this train tomorrow morning as I was when I got on.' She stood up and went back to the window. 'Although maybe a little sadder.'

Sitting right opposite me, Richard rubbed his fingers across his brow. 'And me?' he said. 'Where will I be in your thoughts tomorrow?'

'The same place you've always been: filed away under Doomed Affairs.'

He shook his head. 'Is that all it was?'

She turned. 'All right, so it was some great love story, but we were still doomed from the start. I knew it. You knew it. I mean, honest to God, Rich, we went from the Greek Islands to the confluence of the Niles – and there wasn't this much realism attached to any of it. It was high romance. Unsustainable. We would have had a bitter end if we'd tried living a daily routine, wondering where all the fun had gone to.'

'You seem to forget that I loved you enough to traipse across continents after you and that you loved me enough to forsake your traipsing.'

'But that wouldn't have been enough, not nearly enough, to save us from the deadly drawn-out process of seeing something disintegrate, with no means to stop it. We were spared that, at least.'

'I wish we hadn't been. Even gradual disintegration would have been preferable to losing everything in one moment, without even knowing where it went. We didn't have the luxury of failing, Fran, and we don't have the satisfaction of having tried. Instead, there's this question mark hanging over us like a great meat hook. If my knapsack hadn't been snatched, you wouldn't have absconded. I would never have let you. Jesus, when I think of the little gobshite who robbed me! He's the "circumstance" you referred to. He turned our lives upside down.'

'If there was such a boy, he didn't change anything; your decisions did.'

'Jesus, how many times do I have to—'

'Oh, relax! Come on, Rich, it's finished. Done with. And in the heel of the hunt, we finished off the picture rather appropriately, if you ask me. In fact, that's where you stand in my mind: you're the man I lost on a train in the Nubian Desert.'

'So it makes no difference to you that we met again?'

She sighed. 'My curiosity has been disappointed, but whether that will matter next week or next year … I doubt it. I won't think of you any less or any more or any differently than I do now. Meeting again might have resolved something, but nothing earth-shattering or important, just something that mattered to me once. In the end, circumstance has won the day, either way.'

'The adventurer turned philosopher?'

'Merely turned realist. You spent three years trying to make a realist out of me and you finally succeeded by stepping out of that carriage. And that's what counts. Not why you stepped out, but how you changed things when you did.'

'… I've often thought about us meeting again,' said Richard, rubbing his palms together. 'I longed to ask if you ever reached any end, ever got to where you were going. Did you?'

'I got some place else.'

'Where?'

'Are you going to believe me?'

'Of course.'

'You're blowing fairly hot and cold tonight.'

'I'm warmer than you think.'

Frances sighed, and then spoke in a flat, disinterested tone. 'I didn't run away to the East or anywhere else. I went home, and I've been there ever since.'

'Dublin?'

'Mmm.'

'You've been in Ireland all this time?' he asked incredulously.

'More or less. Apart from the odd holiday or business trip. For a long time, I was afraid that if I got onto a train again, I'd never get off.'

'But you managed to drag yourself onto this one …'

So much for the warm spell.

'Yes, I did,' she replied curtly, 'because there is nothing to keep me on it anymore. And since you seem to be so interested, whenever I come to the Continent in the future, I plan to travel by train where possible, if that's quite all right with you?'

'You can't blame me for being sceptical. After all the resistance you put up, you're telling me you went off and settled happily back home – as soon as I was out of the picture?'

'I wouldn't say *happily* is the word. I did it because you left me no choice. I was broke. And devastated.'

'Don't pile it on.'

'Why not? You are. But I will give you this much: you were right. However questionable your timing might have been, you did the right thing. I'm going to the loo.'

How *could* she? The very word made my internal muscles seize. How could she walk freely down the passage towards that haven of relief, leaving me to suffer on in acute discomfort?

As Frances moved away, Richard took several deep breaths, then went out to the corridor, but if I got up, he would turn towards me, and I didn't have the courage to see or be seen by those eyes. He probably wouldn't give me a second thought. He had no way of knowing that I had been listening to every word he had spoken since Florence, but I knew, and throwing myself into the bright lights of the corridor would be like throwing myself before the Grand Jury. It would be written all over my face: guilty. Guilty of eavesdropping, spying, peeking – worse. Curiosity had been stronger than my bladder thus far, but now shame took over and controlled my ailing body, making me powerless to get out of bed. So he stood, looking out beyond his own reflection, and I lay on. Then, after a jerky movement of anger or irritation, he moved away from our door. I saw his legs drag in an unconscious stroll. Where was he, I wondered? Was he on the Wadi Halfa train or on the streets of Cairo or making love to her on a felucca in Aswan? It was of no consequence. Shame, curiosity, self-control could decide no longer. Before I knew it I was out in the corridor, heading with some difficulty towards the toilets. When I came back, I might have to face them both, acknowledge them, be acknowledged by them, but if that was to be the end of my accidental witness to this reunion, then at least I would be able to reflect upon its contradictions in bodily comfort.

As it happened, when I emerged from the lavatory I was able to make an inconspicuous return to the compartment. Richard was at the far end of the carriage with his back to me, speaking in earnest, no doubt to Frances, who stood out of my line of vision. I slipped under my blanket. Now, all I could hear was the sound of a night train, rocking, hissing and crackling across the lines beneath me. This was dangerous. I could easily fall asleep, left alone with no one to listen to, lights flashing in regular bursts at the window, emphasizing the monotony of sensation that drew me towards slumber. I was missing out now and, short of walking down to the couple and introducing myself, there was nothing I could do about it. If anything was said at the end of the corridor that would point the finger, I would miss it. Any prosecuting clue would evade me and I would be left to ponder two conflicting truths or one indiscernible lie.

I wondered what time it was, and where we were. I tried to put the night into some kind of perspective, some context of time and place, but failed. I had been hypnotized away from the Innsbruck train and scarcely knew it. My eyelids drooped heavily onto their sills; I was being rocked to sleep by crushing disappointment. It was a frustrating way to spend a night and, seeing no alternative, my mind gave way to my eyes and dropped away from the train.

'... Deirdre encouraged me to find a job. She thought it was the answer to all my problems.'

I woke. It had been a short, deep, sleep. The two came back in chatting, apparently cordially. It was impossible to fathom how long I had been out exactly. Beyond the window, there was still no hint of dawn.

They clambered up to his berth – he gave her a leg up, handling her as comfortably as if they had never parted – where they settled, quite relaxed, making no attempt to whisper. To them, I must have seemed a long way away, down there near the floor. Like someone shut away in a drawer. I wondered how he had regained her good humour and persuaded her to talk on, but talk she did.

14

London alarmed her. It was all green lights, a mad race to make it. Deirdre, an old school friend, welcomed her warmly, in spite of the fact that she had not seen Frances for years and didn't have much choice when she arrived homeless on her doorstep, and it was fun, at first, to see each other again and giggle over the things they had done at school. But it could not be long before reality reasserted itself, and within days Frances had hit the floor. She had no job, no life, no income, and she had no inclination to do anything about any of it. She knew that she would have to see Richard, to face him down, before she could contemplate embarking on life without him, but she dreaded the prospect of doing so and kept putting it off.

It was Deirdre who gave her the push by insisting that the lethargy that had engulfed Frances would lift only if she took a more active role in terminating the relationship. It was because she had been made powerless, Deirdre asserted, that Frances remained inert, and so, eight days after arriving in London, and four days after Richard was due back at work, she made her way to his office.

She had never seen him in his office, had never even seen him in a tie, but seeing him at all made her bowels rumble and her fingers dither. She planned to say to him that she merely wanted to ascertain that he was all right, and then she would leave, with more dignity than his behaviour in the Sudan had allowed her. He would not be expecting her, nor would he particularly wish to see her arriving at his desk, but she was determined to let him know that she had come back to England, as she had promised she would.

She felt ill by the time she stepped into the cosy reception area of the practice. *Strange*, she thought, *he walks through here every day.* Her fists gripping her bag so tightly that the leather straps might have been the rope on which her life depended, she asked the receptionist for Richard Keane.

'I'm afraid Mr Keane isn't available. Can anyone else help you?'

Frances put her hands on the desk to support herself. To whom, she wondered, was he not available? To any girl with thick curly hair and a deep tan that might come hounding him? 'No. I need to see Richard.'

'He isn't here, but you could speak to Mr Holden, if you like?'

Frances nodded. The famous Bob Holden. Richard's buddy. He would do. She could tell him everything and insist that he make Richard meet her.

When she was shown to his office, Bob had his feet up on a cabinet and was swaying lightly in his chair with a phone in each hand. She stood by the door while he finished one conversation, and then he spoke into the other receiver and seemed surprised there was no longer anybody at the other end. 'Oh, well,' he said, hanging up. 'Nice talking to you too.' He beamed at Frances. 'Hi!'

'Hello. I'm, em, looking for Richard.'

'Richard?'

'Keane.'

'Ah. Keane. Our Foreign Correspondent. He's away, I'm afraid. Can I help?'

Her throat closed. 'He's still away?'

'Yeah, he's been held up overseas, but I can deal with anything that might be outstanding.'

'No, no, it isn't business. I—'

Bob exhaled. 'Thank heavens for that! Half his clients are breathing down my neck! You haven't heard from him by any chance, have you?'

Before she could think of what to say, he added, 'Of course not. You wouldn't be here if you had.'

'Where is he?'

'Ah. He's somewhere around there.' He pointed towards Africa on a map on the wall. 'I can't keep track.'

'Is he all right?'

'Yeah, fine.'

'You've spoken to him?'

'Just once, and there've been a couple of telexes.'

A mixture of relief and despair flooded through Frances. She had to sit down. *He has left me. He has left me.*

Bob frowned slightly. 'And you would be? ...'

'He should've been back by now.'

'So our clients keep telling me,' said Bob, scratching the side of his neck, 'but the fact is, Richard had to change his plans.'

'Why?'

He smiled. 'You know, I look forward to asking him that very question! I was in a meeting when we spoke, so it was short and to the point, but he had some story about getting stuck in the desert.'

'He's stuck in the desert?'

'God, no. By the time he called, he was holed up in some swanky hotel in Khartoum.'

The room began to spin around Frances.

'Girlfriend problems,' said Bob conspiratorially.

'Sorry?'

He scratched the side of his neck again. Richard had once told her that this man would make friends with a mugger while he was being robbed, but she was thankful for Bob's indiscretion. 'He's trying to persuade his girlfriend to come back to London,' he stood up to look more closely at the map, 'but he doesn't appear to be having much success.' He turned. 'Do you know her?'

Frances stiffened. 'Who?'

'Frantic Fran. Richard's girlfriend. I don't suppose you've ever met her?'

She shook her head.

'No, well, that's hardly surprising. Nobody has. Sometimes I wonder if she really exists. If you ask me, Richard's been off having holidays all by himself, sad bastard.'

Frances couldn't bring herself to own up; she didn't actually want to.

'But if he doesn't come up with this Frances person soon, we'll really begin to wonder about her.'

'When are you expecting him?'

'Monday, and not a day too soon either. Things are getting sticky around here.' He grinned. He looked like someone who thrived on things being sticky. 'I could give him a message if you like?'

'No, thanks. I'll call back.'

On the way out, Frances noticed a postcard of Luxor pinned to a noticeboard. She stopped. Nobody was looking, so she unpinned it and read the back. It was from Richard. She had watched him write it.

The anticipation of seeing Richard and the subsequent disappointment prolonged her gloomy stagnation. She could not fathom why he had not yet returned to London, but as long as the people who were in contact with him showed no sign of concern, she had no reason to fret. And yet she did fret – about Richard, about what she had driven him to, about her own predicament.

Her efforts to climb out of the hole he had dropped her into were half-hearted. Every attempt to find work was thwarted at interview because she couldn't conceal her lack of commitment; it was difficult to find enthusiasm for a job when she didn't even want to be in England in the first place. She didn't actually know where she *did* want to be, but she continued to search the Appointments pages every day, mostly to pacify Deirdre. Although there was plenty of waitressing and secretarial temping available, Frances had no interest. The more imperative it became to get work, the less able she was to contemplate it. Depression took root. She found it difficult to get up in the mornings and even harder to go to bed at night. She spent the days watching television; it stopped her spending money, stopped her thinking. She began to begrudge Deirdre her life, her flat, her trendy job. In the evenings, Deirdre partied; Frances watched TV.

Every night, putting an end to the situation seemed easy – the next day, she repeatedly resolved, she would take things in hand – but when morning came, the sheer weight of disappointment weakened her resolve and she would find it even harder to get out of her makeshift bed on the living-room floor.

To be constantly indebted to Deirdre was not only soul-destroying but also exhausting. 'I'm sorry, Dee,' she said to her one evening. 'I'm so sorry. I want to go, I really do. I just can't think of where to go to.'

Deirdre smiled insipidly. She clearly couldn't fathom why Frances was so unable to pull herself together, to brush herself down and get on with life, the way she did when a relationship ended, but Frances did not have the wherewithal to do so. There was nothing to get on with, no work to throw herself into, no social life to distract her. She was in a vacuum, and it was a ghastly place to be.

And then one morning Frances finally moved. She stepped out of the morass of self-pity and loathing in which she existed and, while tidying out her rucksack, found Lucy and Sam's phone number scribbled in the back of her diary. She dialled it immediately.

Lucy answered. 'Fran! Where are you?'

'London.'

'Fantastic! Now I can show you the wedding video!'

They met for coffee in the King's Road. Lucy burst into the café like a woman with a mission and embraced Frances warmly. 'It's so good to see you!'

'You too.'

'I was thrilled when you phoned! I thought I'd never hear from you again.'

'You won't get rid of me that easily.'

'I should hope not. You're part of our honeymoon. Like Egypt.

Part of the backdrop.'

'Honestly, Lucy, you behave as if marriage were the Holy Grail. I thought women of our generation were supposed to aspire to something more.'

'Weddings. We're supposed to aspire to more than a big fluffy wedding, but marriage – committing yourself to someone for life – that's worth anybody's salt.'

'Yes, and you made sure you had the big fluffy wedding as well.'

'Of course I did, darling. I had to distract the family with my huge white dress so they wouldn't pay so much attention to my big black groom!'

Frances giggled. 'God, seeing you makes me feel human again.'

'What's been happening? I can't wait to hear the next instalment. Has Richard explained everything? Was he frantic? Did he think he'd lost you forever?'

'Oh, Lucy, stop.'

'Why? What's wrong?'

'I told you in Cairo it was over, and it *is* over.'

'No ...' Lucy's face creased in disbelief. 'He really walked out?'

'Looks like it.'

'My God. That's unbelievable. Why didn't he talk to you first?'

'I don't know.'

'Haven't you asked him?'

'No. And I'm not going to either. Three weeks ago, I went to his office to clear the slate, make it final, but he was still away.'

'But that's good, isn't it? He must have stayed out there to look for you.'

'Oh Lucy, don't start! He's had ample opportunity to find me. He could even have warned his boss that I might turn up in England, that I might get in touch, but Bob wasn't expecting me.'

'What did he say when you did show up?'

'I didn't tell him who I was.'

'Why not?' Lucy asked, exasperated.

'Because if Bob had a message for me, he'd have jumped at the very sight of any woman looking for Richard and he didn't. He didn't even flinch. He made it sound as if Richard was just arsing about out there — but if you ask me, he was keeping his head down. I mean, get this: he was staying in an expensive hotel in Khartoum — the last place I'd look for him!'

'But you still have to see him. There are so many imponderables in all this, you really have to talk to Richard and make absolutely sure—'

Frances's eyes filled. 'I couldn't take it, Lucy. He's made himself clear. Why would I go back for more punishment? To see in his eyes whatever it was that drove him to do what he did? No, thanks. He's pulverized me already, and all I can do for the moment is try to remember to breathe.'

'But he loved you, Fran. I'm sure of it.'

'Maybe. But somewhere between Aswan and Wadi Halfa, he stopped loving me.'

At Lucy's insistence, Frances moved in with her and Sam that night. Deirdre made no attempt to stop her, which was hardly surprising. Frances's extended stay had suffocated their friendship.

But Frances did not stay long at Lucy's. She believed it was a fresh start, the very move that would goad her into finding work, and yet she received no encouragement from Lucy to do so. Instead, over that weekend, Lucy pampered her. She cooked some Egyptian food, which failed horribly, but they laughed as they prepared it, and then they sent Sam out to the pub so that they could watch the wedding video, which Lucy narrated with such irony that Frances laughed most of the way through it. It was fun to see the relatives she had heard so much about, the not-so-subtle natural divide which occurred between the two families at the reception, the over-the-top wedding dress. 'Lady Di move over,' she mumbled. Lucy whacked her. 'Denzel Washington move over,' Frances added with more enthusiasm when Sam was caught on camera, smiling.

Lucy grinned. 'He's okay, isn't he?'

'He's gorgeous. Fed up with him yet?'

'No. And just because you got dumped in the desert doesn't mean you can have my husband.'

The next morning, Frances felt changed, released. 'Right,' she announced at breakfast, 'first thing Monday, I'm going to get my head together and find a job.'

Lucy put a cafetière down in front of them. 'You'd be making a mistake.'

'Eh? How can you say that? I've been moping around London for a month already – and I'm not going to do to you what I did to Deirdre. You kept me sane in Cairo, and the sooner I get out from under your feet, the better it'll be for all of us.'

'About Cairo, Fran.' Lucy poured their coffee. 'I owe you an apology. I'm sorry for being so blindly optimistic. I should never have promised you that Richard would come.'

'You kept me going, Lucy, but now I've reached a standstill and I need to get restarted. I have to make some money so that I can go back to doing what I do best. Now that Richard's out of the picture, I can go further east. Overland from Bangkok to Singapore sounds good to me.'

'Across the Irish Sea sounds better.'

'What?'

Lucy caught her eye. 'Go home, Fran.'

'I don't have one.'

'You do. You just won't see it. Even reduced to this condition, you still won't see it. Why? Why are you so stubborn about it?'

'Because my mother has no time for me and my sister bores me.'

'Good. So there's a challenge for starters. Set things right with them. Don't try to make a life in Richard's town – not even for a few months. You'd always be wondering if he'd be around the next corner. At every cinema, in every restaurant, on every bus, you'll be looking for him, and then one day you might see him with someone else. As long as you're in London, you'll never get away from him and there'll be no getting over him. So go back to where you come from, Fran. You've been everywhere else. It's the only place left for you to go.'

Frances took the night train to avoid the summer crowds. It was uncomfortable and noisy – they never switch off the lights on the Holyhead line – but she relished every moment. Getting onto a train again was like sinking into a hot bath, and even though they were chugging through nowhere more exciting than good old Britain, it was an adventure. A small one, perhaps, or one getting bigger with every mile, she wasn't quite sure, but it felt good. At Holyhead, the sight of the ferry in the middle of the night set her back. It was rather more substantial than the Wadi Halfa steamer, but reminiscent all the same, and for a moment she was thrown back to that night, to Lena and the blood and the horror of it all.

She couldn't sleep, or even sit still, on the Irish Sea. Wandering around the ferry, inside and out, she felt like a fly on the rim of a web; the spider had left it there, hanging, for a long time, but now she was drawing it in to eat it up. And the fly didn't mind.

They sailed into Dún Laoghaire after dawn. Shivering in the cold sea breeze and stunned by hills that were no longer familiar, Frances stood on deck, thinking about a hot wind on a hot day, scorching the very air she breathed. North Africa haunted her still, and she allowed it to, because to let go of it would be to let go of Richard. The bustling, sweet-smelling alleyways of Khan el Khalili and the tearless heat of Wadi Halfa held her in their grip, and she wept for them, and for herself, on that lumbering ship in that grey morning. What was she doing, she wondered, arriving alone in this place?

And then something happened. Africa let go of her, and Ireland, stark and vital and unexotic, began to reel her in. The cold air shook her senses. The skies and the freshness and the Wicklow hills disconcerted her. She saw landmarks she knew, noticed things that had changed. The morning light and the slapping of black water against the hull were reminiscent of something she couldn't yet recognize.

They sailed between the piers. Early morning walkers looked up without interest at the relentless ferry, their dogs bounded with pleasure, yachts tinkled at their moorings, and however much Frances rejected the notion, she knew there was only one home-port and this was it. This was her harbour. For five years, she had been a tenant in the world, but here she was owner-occupier, as she could be nowhere else.

She disembarked in a state of confusion. She had expected apathy to weigh down her every step; instead, something vibrated inside her like a quiet engine.

Everybody from the customs officials to the bus driver seemed to be expecting her, and their cordiality dismantled the fanciful notion that she was a stranger here. They knew she was not. On the empty double-decker bus, the driver joked with the conductor. Frances sat on the bottom deck. She did not stand out; she did not look foreign or sound foreign, and she knew where she was going. To the conductor, she was just another hitchhiker back from a jaunt on the Continent, not someone who had deserted years before, and as he gave her change in her childhood coinage, chatting to her all the while about the good hot breakfast she should have when she got home, she began to sink into the identity of a local. The loneliness of the outsider, which she had once embraced, dissolved in a deluge of familiarity. The postboxes, the trees, the streets – everything she could see was Ireland, as was she.

A door had slammed on her in the Sudan, but on that bus another door opened and, to her own amazement, she found herself willing to walk through.

And Ireland bore no grudge against her.

15

Italy, as we slid on through it, was black and featureless, like a sock with no open end.

'There must be some detail missing,' said Richard. 'Some link that would make all this possible. I want you to believe what I've told you – all of it, not just the bits that sound plausible – and I want to believe you. I want us both to be right. There must be something that could have made it happen this way.'

'You were angry with me long before Abu Hamed. That's what made it happen that way.'

'A mistake in time,' he said, ignoring her. 'That must be it. You must have left the embassy before they heard about my passport. I lost several days when I was ill – maybe there was no overlap? Maybe we hit the embassies at different times? When did you get to Cairo?'

'Sunday. I told you. Sunday morning.'

'And then what?'

'I went to the embassy on the Tuesday.'

'Same day as I did, I think.'

'You *think*?'

'It's four years ago, remember. Besides, a day here or there isn't going to make much difference. You claim there were telexes going backwards and forwards for a week.'

'That's true.'

'So how many people work there? Could someone have reissued my passport without knowing you were looking for me?'

'No. It's a tiny office. Just the ambassador and two women. And don't forget, we got replies from Khartoum. They knew nothing about you.'

'But I was there, Fran. I was there.'

'Then you must have been keeping a very low profile. I wonder why.'

'Why do you so resist the idea that circumstances beyond our control stood in our way? Look at the distances we were dealing with, the technology, the antiquated communications systems!'

'Oh, make up your mind, Richard! You've just spent hours telling me that I left you and now you want to believe that I didn't! Which is it?'

'I wish I knew! But the only way we can cancel out the whole miserable episode is if we're both on the level.'

'Look, if there was some imperceptible factor at work which could vindicate us both, tell me what it was and I'll believe you. In fact, I'll believe everything you've said, from Abu Hamed to Florence, but I will not accept that you made contact with Cairo because I have the scars to prove that you didn't!'

Her voice broke; my throat tugged.

'Fran, listen. I'm hanging about Khartoum waiting for a passport and a telex comes into the embassy asking for me. I'm just an unfortunate mug who came under their wing. If I didn't want you to know where I was, how could I influence a bunch of diplomats to send false information back to Cairo? The fact is, any telex would have been answered long before I even knew about it.'

'Then it appears that your bag was not stolen and that my gut reaction was right. You left me. You had no need to go to the embassy for a passport or an exit visa or for anything else. Pity. That bit about dragging around Khartoum looking for a bottle of Perrier water was very moving.'

'Jesus. You think I made that up?'

'And a lot more besides.'

'Oh, Christ, be fair! How could I have done any of this to you?'

Her answer was to get off the berth, jumping rather heavily onto the ground beside me. Richard immediately followed and stood between her and the door.

'I'm tired, Rich. I'm tired and drained and who knows, if you push me far enough, I might even admit to re-starting the civil war in the Sudan. I made a sacrifice for you, and you would have me say I ran away. I have never been as desolate as I was in Cairo, and you would have me say it was my escape. It was nearly my ruin. Let's not go over it again.'

He stepped towards her. 'But you have to believe me.'

'No, I don't! I don't owe you that privilege. The last time I saw you, you told me that I wasn't worth the trouble and that's what I believe!' She banged her fists against her hips. 'Show me a passport issued in Cairo in 1983 and I'll buy the whole bonanza, but don't ask me, don't *ask me* to compromise myself again.'

They were facing one another, two dark shapes in the dim light, when he pulled her to him and kissed her. She didn't resist. In the middle of nowhere, they stopped for a moment's cohesion. Who knows what came over them? The past, I suppose.

Instead of wanting to curl up and die of embarrassment as they gasped and pressed their hips together, I felt only a mild inclination to file my nails. One also had to hope that this encounter would go no further. Making love on the overnight train to Innsbruck would no doubt be a deeply moving experience for them, drenched in melancholia and memories, but they had already exposed quite enough of themselves to me and I had no desire to further increase our intimacy.

Besides, even my most romantic notions conceded that this lapse in verbal negotiations would be fleeting. This was not the great reunion I had been waiting for, although I had yet to discover if the couple agreed with me. Had their roles and aspirations been sufficiently reversed, the new ones cast in stone? Or might they yet drop back a little and meet once again in the middle? For my own part, nothing short of a great confession would satisfy me now, and as I waited patiently for the outcome of this fresh entanglement I noticed that I was holding my breath, subconsciously more intent on not being there than I knew. God, how they kissed. Frantically and tenderly and quietly, and then frantically again – so much so that I was beginning to wonder if the past had become the present.

When they finally drew apart, Frances stood back and said calmly, 'You regret it, don't you? In a fit of pique, you decided to punish me, and by the time you'd changed your mind, it was too late. Your flat was gone, your job was gone, and so was I.'

Richard turned away, put his hands on the top berth and leaned his head against his arm.

'That's what happened, isn't it? You thought you'd let me stew for a bit, in Wadi or Cairo or wherever I was. You thought it might chasten me, but circumstance got in the way and you couldn't sieve me out of the soup when you wanted to. Africa is too big a pot for games like that, Richard.'

Her words were so condemning, so clear, that I released a long, quiet breath. It was over. Out at last. His story was part truth, part invention, and although he had lied, a little, he was guilty of no more than foolhardy behaviour, which no amount of regret could redress given the distances and the woman involved, who had no ties, no base. No telephone number.

Frances sat down. 'And the reason you can't admit to it is that you can't quite believe you threw it all away.'

I knew, thank the gods, I knew. The frustration of reaching Innsbruck without getting to the bottom of this would have been intolerable, and I felt like walking in on them now, like the detective who lurks behind the curtains while the trap is laid, then unveils himself when the confession has finally been extracted. 'So,' I'd have said. 'Why didn't you say so earlier and we could all have had a good night's sleep?' Instead, I stretched my toes and waited. What a fascinating night, all the same.

Richard straightened up. 'My bag was stolen, Frances. I waited for you in Khartoum and searched for you in Cairo. What more do you want from me?'

My toes shrank back. A train shot past in the opposite direction.

He went to the door and stood with his back to us. Frances slid across the bench, closer to him, and to me. Too close for comfort. She sighed and said, 'It never, ever occurred to me that meeting you again could prove so utterly inconclusive.'

The wheels squeaked and ran beneath us, comforting in their monotony, tireless in intent. I felt deadly tired and longed for some external distraction – voices next door, the sound of another passenger coming along the corridor, anything to remind me that I was not alone here, on half a mile's worth of train, with two resolute ex-lovers, and liars to boot. But there had been no sign of other life all night, as if the train ran only for this couple and would not arrive at its destination until they had reached some resolution, derived some comfort from their encounter. The train was their accomplice, not mine; I was an intruder, and the more exhausted I became, the more I resented these people and the wretched coincidence that had reunited them in my compartment.

Richard turned and slid to his hunkers with his back to me, looking along the corridor. 'I did everything wrong,' he said, 'I know that now. I handled you badly. That hunger, that curiosity you had – I couldn't contend with it.' He chuckled bitterly. 'I was jealous, you know. Your wanderlust was like a rival, and giving in to it would have been like agreeing to live with you and your other lover. I was the bloke with my feet on the ground, but he was the ruddy sky and he had a much better hold on you and a lot more to offer, so I had to bring you down. I had to harness you before you disappeared into the stratosphere. It terrified me that I wouldn't be able to, Fran, and that made me do a lot of stupid things, but leaving you wasn't one of them.'

'So what happened then? What happened to us?'

'*You* happened to us. You were the escape artist, not me. Always moving on whenever you got bored, looking for a bigger fix every time.'

'But you were the fix I wanted! The rest was just … oh, I don't know. I travelled by compulsion. It was an urge, an indulgence. You kept telling me that and you were right. So right. I've often thought since that you had seen through me as no one else had, and now you're telling me the opposite.'

'I was not right. I was selfish and arrogant and I tried to destroy the best part of you. But I didn't know what I was dealing with. Passion. You nurtured it and fed on it and you were entitled to it. It's what drew me to you and kept me there, and yet, with my great gift for tunnel vision, I wanted to strip you of it … It's no wonder I lost you in the process.'

Frances put her hand on his knee.

'I refused to understand you,' he said.

'You were never meant to understand me. It was the very push-me-pull-you that kept us so enthralled.'

'Except that I pulled too hard.'

'And we snapped.'

He put his fingers through hers. 'I'm so sorry, Fran.'

'Don't be. If we hadn't broken up, I might never have found my way home.'

He shook his head. 'You really expect me to believe that you've been sitting quietly in Dublin for the past four years? After the fight you put up?'

'I lost the fight, Richard, long before Abu Hamed.'

'But you went on kicking. Kicking *me*.'

'I know, and I'm sorry.' Her tone lightened. 'But it had become a habit.'

'Yeah, and then you kicked me right out into the Nubian Desert!'

'Without even a bottle of Perrier water.'

They chuckled.

'I don't know how it came about,' she said, 'this change in me. All I know is that I reached a point on that trip when everything began to merge into one pretty pastel. When Egypt failed to excite me on my way down the Nile, I persuaded myself that I was merely numb, because of you, but in truth, something was draining out of me. The need for perpetual motion was making a graceful retreat. It took one step back in Aswan and another in Cairo, and it finally slipped away when I sailed into Dublin and knew that I didn't have to go on anymore. It was hard to lose you just when the compulsion to be everywhere else withered, but in the end I was glad to be free of it, especially when I found the right place to be.'

'What about the right person? You still think in terms of place, location. Surely the right partner is what counts?'

'If tonight has proved anything, it's that we weren't right for each other.'

'Tonight has proved nothing. We might have learnt. We could have done things differently if we'd had time to work it out. Proper time. Not just holidays.'

'We would have made a shambles of things.'

'Since I'm not the one who gave up,' said Richard, 'it's easy for me to think otherwise.'

'Oh God, there you go again! If only I could prove to you what I did at the time – short of going back to Cairo with you!'

He stood up. 'Now, that sounds like an excellent idea. I'd like to see if the lovely Sabah is the same miserable frump I dealt with when I needed to extend my visa.'

'What about the ambassador? Did you ever meet him? His name was Doyle.'

'Yeah, I've met Doyle.'

'Well, there you are! I haven't invented him.'

'There's any number of reasons why you might have gone to the embassy.'

'I went because I wanted you back!'

'Right. Fine. So let's agree that somewhere along the line some unknown factor prevented us from making contact.'

'No. Let's not have scapegoats in the air.'

'Why won't you accept that it was out of our hands?' Richard asked.

Oh no, I thought. *Not another round.*

But I sensed a smile when Frances replied, 'Because you don't deserve to get off so lightly!'

He chuckled, and the tension dissipated.

'This is just too weird,' said Frances. 'Meeting again like this – on a train of all places!'

'It's no more surprising than meeting in a restaurant in London or on a street in Bombay, is it? It just has to be the same place at the same time.'

'Yes, but the same carriage!'

'But if we'd got into different carriages we would have travelled all the way to Innsbruck on the same train and never even known about it. Now *that* would have been weird.'

Frances pulled her hair over her shoulder and fiddled with the ends of it.

Richard sat down with her, opposite me, his head leaning forward, like hers, because of the berth behind their heads. He was very close to me. I closed my eyes and swallowed so loudly I was sure they'd hear.

'It's like sharing a cabin with a corpse,' he whispered.

Why he saw fit to whisper at that point was anybody's guess, but I went even more rigid and broke out in a cold sweat.

Frances sent another chill through me when she said, 'I did that once.'

'What?'

'Slept with a corpse. Someone died when I was on a sleeper in France. We were all getting up in the morning, but this woman lay there without moving. She seemed perfectly peaceful, so we didn't think anything of it. Eventually the blinds were up and people were ready to go and she still hadn't budged, so one of the ladies tried to wake her. She was taken off at Marseilles.'

I considered moving to reassure them that this eventuality was not about to repeat itself, but I wasn't absorbing their attention as much as I fancied.

Richard took her hand and fiddled with her fingers. 'How's your Mum? Still as distracted as ever?'

'Worse, I'd say. She's getting on.'

'Was she surprised when you came home?'

'Not so as you'd notice. She worried about how we'd both fit into her new little mews, but I moved out as soon as I got a job.'

'Doing what?'

'The usual – teaching English – and then I set up my own business.'

'You're joking.'

'No. Why?'

'I just can't see you as a cut-throat businesswoman. The suits wouldn't suit you.'

'They don't. I wear jeans. But I can show you my brochure if you like.'

'No,' he said, wearily. 'Enough of evidence and testimony. Just tell me about it.'

'I work as an agent for language schools. Using my contacts overseas, I hoover up foreign students who want to learn English and enrol them in Irish schools. I've set up quite a network now, and I get a percentage of their fees from the schools.'

'So all your moving around has paid off?'

'You bet. I've just harvested another ten Florentines for the winter term and I hope to do the same in Austria. The income isn't great, but—'

'—you get to travel. Hence all the visas in your passport.'

'Yeah, but I was going to say I'd love to set up my own school. It's big business, you know, and Ireland is very attractive to the Spaniards and Italians, who like their kids to go to a Catholic country with good family values. Even the Arabs like Ireland because it has a strong religious tradition.'

'What about Egypt? Wouldn't that be a big market?'

'Maybe, but the Gulf States are more profitable. They have cash.'

Richard shook his head. 'Who'd have thought it? The wandering hippy has a killer instinct.'

'You believe me now?'

'I don't know what I believe, but your Dublin accent certainly has an edge it didn't have before.'

'Yeah, well, the aimless soul belonged somewhere, after all.'

'I used to think it belonged with me.'

'Sorry.'

'Jesus. What the hell did we pass up?'

'Something that never really came our way. We only thought it had.'

'I can't believe that. I should have been willing to get off my ass, to—'

She put her hand to his face. 'Don't. It's so long ago.'

'It isn't long ago. It's tonight.'

Frances fiddled with her hair, pulling on the ringlets.

'Fuck it,' said Richard quietly. 'Fuck it, anyway.'

She leaned against him, her head on his shoulder. 'So, what about you? You haven't really given up designing, have you?'

He sighed. 'I had to, for a while, but I couldn't stay away from it for too long, so I put out some feelers and eventually an Egyptian firm offered me work. I was little more than an office boy at first, and I've mostly worked as an overqualified draughtsman since then, but it's been enough to keep my hands nimble and my CV filled in. Now things are looking up because there are some major joint ventures being planned for Cairo, and I want to get involved. I can't afford to stay out of design any longer. That's why I'm going to London. I have an interview next week with an English firm tendering for one of the contracts. If I'm successful, I'll become a true expat, with a ridiculous salary and a rather more affluent lifestyle than I have at the moment.'

'But why are you here – in Italy in the middle of the night?'

'I'm going back the long way.'

'Don't tell me you've picked up my bug for trains?'

'Ah, well, you never know who you might meet on a train.'

'Richard ... you haven't been wandering around looking for me, have you?'

'Let's just say that I've taken a lot of trains these last few years. There must be a dozen ways to get from Cairo to London. This time I came through Rome.'

'Lucky you. I haven't been back, you know, since you dragged me away. I wonder if Karen's still there?'

'She is. I've just been staying with her, actually.'

'With Karen?'

'Yeah. We kept in touch after we lost track of you.'

'Oh.'

'And then she came out to Cairo on holiday last year ...'

'I see. So how is she? Apart from sleeping with my ex-boyfriend, that is?'

'*Fran.*'

'She is, isn't she?'

'How do you work that out?'

'I don't know. I can't see you very well, so I must have smelt it off you.'

'Then you're putting your nose where it doesn't belong.'

'She's ten years older than you.'

'What of it?'

She nodded her head slowly. 'Well. Seems I did you a double favour: I moved aside *and* introduced you to the next in line.'

'It isn't like that. It isn't even serious.'

'Does Karen know it isn't serious?'

Richard turned to her. 'Karen knows I have never got over you. That's all she needs to know.'

Frances put her head in her hands. 'Oh, God. What a mess.'

'Anyway, Karen's still in love with her ex-husband.'

'What? *Still?* But that man's a bastard!'

'You don't know the half of it. Only last year he came crawling back ...'

And so they gossiped for a while about people they had known, updating one another on broken marriages, babies born, expectations unfulfilled, disappointments foreseen. They bantered like two friends who had never been apart. The doubts set aside, an intimacy and familiarity emerged, allowing me to taste, briefly, the closeness they had once shared, which, for all their bickering, they had not been able to keep at bay. Indeed, the distrust dissipated so easily that one couldn't but suspect it, whereas the affection was so unselfconscious that it was above question. Whatever had once held them together lingered around them still, and I fully expected Richard to lurch across the berth and grab Frances again, even though this would make it much harder for them to part within a few hours, as they were bound to do.

Their chat inevitably drifted back to their time together. Musing over a New Year spent in a mountain dwelling in Turkey, which had no water or electricity, Richard said wistfully, 'Makes me want to do it all over again.'

'Does it?'

'Not you?'

'Not at all. But I wouldn't have missed it. I wouldn't have missed out on you, not for the world.'

He didn't lurch, but with the hesitation of first contact, he kissed her again. It was lovely. Stupid, but lovely.

Shirts were being yanked out of waistbands by the time Frances pulled away. 'Stop.'

'Why? It's still there, Fran. All of it. Why can't we carry on where we—'

'Because I'm getting married in March.'

Something rattled in Richard's throat.

'I know,' she said. 'I shouldn't have let this happen, but there's so much unfinished business between us. I never even kissed you goodbye!'

'Goodbye? And I thought we were saying hello.'

'Oh God, you're such a curse!' she said, thumping him. 'A charming, lovable, damnable curse. It's just like you to pop up in a five-by-eight compartment in the middle of the night!'

'Who is he? One of those mad Australians?'

'No. It's someone I met at home.'

Richard said nothing, so she went on.

'I'd never have picked him out for myself. I always thought that if I married, it would be someone challenging, like you, always on my case, demanding the best of me. Instead, I'm going to marry a man who, I don't know, makes me feel good, easy. He looks after me. He loves hurling and cats and he's got a big bushy beard ... not really my type, I suppose.'

Richard looked out towards the corridor; he didn't want to hear this, but I did. She was speaking to me – girl talk – about the man in her life. Her voice had become lighter. Spongy.

'Everything is straightforward with him. We grow our own veg and go hillwalking at weekends. At night, we go to bed with mugs of cocoa and fight over the duvet.'

'Sounds a bit dull,' Richard mumbled, 'but if he makes you happy ...'

'I have never been so deeply happy and contented.'

Richard went out to the corridor. My heart thumped against my chest so loudly that I expected one of them to bend over, look into my face and say, 'Having a good listen then?'

Frances stood up and leaned against the doorjamb that had supported one or other of them so often during the night. 'Richard, we had the kind of relationship that had nowhere else to go. It was too demanding. It sapped all our energies and would have left us with nothing to live on. We were never meant to argue about who should worm the cat or buy the milk; we weren't cut out for mundanity. You swore it was what you wanted, and yet it would have denied you everything that Egypt has cultivated in you. Our affair was an extravagance. I adored you. I even loved you. But I have no idea whether I liked you enough or even knew you well, because when we were put to the test, we had no faith, no insight into one another. We still don't.' After a moment, she added, 'I've found something else now. Comfort and simplicity. An untroubled mind and an easy heart. Domestic love. It's worth a thousand passions. Wadi Halfa has taught me that.'

She turned, but Richard, coming back into the compartment, grabbed her elbow. He took her other arm and then her hands. 'Let me take you down the tracks again. You've forgotten what it's like. You've forgotten the buzz, the thrill of driving across the desert at sunset. I can show you all that again!'

She leaned her forehead against his. 'Tell me that you left me, Rich. That's all I want to hear.'

'I can't, Fran. I can't.'

I had to move. I was so stiff I thought I'd break. I turned my head into the wall to stretch my neck and clenched all the muscles in my legs, extending my toes. I lifted my head, fractionally, again to stretch my neck, and noticed that the night was no longer black. Outside the window it was now a deep blue. Dawn was not far off. Not long after dawn, we would reach Innsbruck. For a moment, I enjoyed the sensation of returning to reality. Closing my eyes, I willed the strange night and its strange story away. I tried to dismiss it, since it had so engulfed me, but with the couple standing near me, clinging to one another, I felt nothing but sorrow.

I tried to sleep.

She had told us about Cairo, described the embassy there, before she knew about his passport. If she was making it up, she had walked right into a trap. But as truth it held together well, so how was it possible that his passport was issued from that embassy when she was sitting there waiting for him? It did not add up. And what about the Khartoum end? Could a careless telex operator have sent negative replies to Cairo without making clear enquiries about whether such a person was in the city or not? Richard clearly didn't think so, but he held an important advantage over Frances and me: he knew what we did not. There was every likelihood that the British embassy in Khartoum was a busy office with a large number of employees, many of whom would not have been aware of the tourist who had fallen off a train, but as long as Richard was the only one of the three of us who had possibly been there, he could not be challenged.

Ignorant about so much, I pondered instead on my gut feelings to see which way I swayed. Trouble was, I swayed neither way, rather both at the same time. If they didn't agree about so much, it might have been clearer. If Frances had not admitted that by nature and inclination she was very likely to bolt, and if Richard had not spoken about how close their last row had brought him to abandoning hope for their future, I might have sniffed insincerity coming from one berth or the other. Instead, my otherwise sound intuition told me nothing. It was all very clear and unclear. Both arguments were reasonable. Had he wanted to leave her, he would surely not have done so in such a personally tortuous manner. Had she wanted to escape commitment, why did she end up living the humdrum life she had so dreaded? Or did she?

The real question was this: how could either have treated the other with such contempt four years before and repeated the insult this night on this train?

I ought to have slept in another carriage.

One thing was sure. Having spent the whole night talking, and listening, none of us felt any better for it. Even though so much remained undisclosed, the silence beside me was permeated with sadness for what had been lost, for the great romantic adventure that had been brought to an end. Whatever the truth, the Nile Valley Express was now being mourned and I was so entangled in their story that I mourned it too. In fact, I felt entirely depressed. It would not occur to me until much later that I came out of that carriage worse off than any of us. The one who may have been lying was the only one who knew exactly what had happened, while the one who was telling the truth also knew where stood the lies. I, on the other hand, had no idea which of the stories I had heard, which of the pleas I had listened to, was genuine. Worse than that, I never would know. For that reason, I looked at the brightening sky with some relief and wondered what would happen at Innsbruck.

After kissing her again, Richard moved to the window. 'How long will you be in Innsbruck?'

'No time at all. I'm staying with friends in Salzburg. They're picking me up and taking me straight back to their place.'

Without turning from the window, Richard said, so quietly that I scarcely heard him, 'Stay in Innsbruck for a few days.'

With dawn and our destination so close, he had little left to lose.

'No.'

'Come back to Egypt with me.'

'No.'

He turned. 'Come back with me?'

'... No.'

16

The brakes squealed and woke me as we pulled into Innsbruck. I sat up, suddenly, like someone who has slept through their stop, and looked around. There was no trace of my night companions. Like a dream, they were gone in the morning.

'Damn!'

I got out of my berth, pulled on a sweater and shoved my sleeping bag into its cover. The corridor was full of people ready to disembark. I stuck my head out and saw Richard's shoulders at the far end of the carriage, near the door. It was like waking to find your best friends had left without you. I retrieved my runners. My hands shook. I couldn't untie the laces and cursed my lazy habit of shoving off my shoes unopened. I pulled my haversack from under the seat and stuffed my gear into it. The train came to a halt, lurching forward, dragging all those bodies within to an unwilling diagonal slant, then throwing us back with the jolt which everyone expects but nobody is ready for, causing mild tumult in the corridor as people overbalanced on one another. Then all motion stopped and everyone went still.

We had arrived.

I resumed my frantic cramming. Already people were moving towards the doors. I cursed. I could not believe that I had slept through all the noisy disturbances that come with early morning – the travellers falling out of their berths, shuffling along to the lavatories, calling out to one another. I had missed the rising mood of anticipation as a journey nears its end, of passengers looking forward to arrival, to stretching beyond the confines of limited space.

I must have fallen asleep after my passport was checked. Frances and Richard, in the corridor at the time, had seen the border guard coming and stepped in for their documents, which were checked outside the door. The guard then leaned in and shook my shoulder. In a passable imitation of a deep sleeper, I handed over my passport. The couple in the corridor were waxing lyrical about the scenery on their side of the train, but from my horizontal position all that could be seen was the slatey lower half of mountains. High above, I knew, there was blue sky, but down where we were meandering cautiously through an Alpine gorge, it was dark and cold. The voices behind me described silvery bits glistening in the early sun and snow trailing off halfway down the rocks, but I remained bound to my position by a curious form of embarrassment. If I moved, they might look in and my shameful face would betray me by admitting that their privacy had been abused, that the isolated world they had inhabited all night had never existed. The granite masses shunting visibly through my restricted view did not give way to warmer slopes, and sleep must have edged over my undiverted eyes.

By the time I had pulled on my haversack, I was alone in the carriage. However important it had been not to be seen to see them, I was now desperate to cast my eyes over these two ordinary people who had disturbed my night's sleep with their extraordinary tales. I wanted to put faces to the voices and the only way of doing so was to merge with the crowd, then cast an eye over my shoulder as I passed them on the platform. But even more vicious was my determination to see how they parted, *if* they parted. I believed I deserved to witness the outcome, to intrude on their leavetaking. I could not miss it.

I quick-stepped down the platform through the people emptying off the train. Everyone seemed to be part of a couple. I looked frantically for Richard's black shirt, then came upon it so suddenly I almost kicked his heels. I had a curious impulse to put my hand on his shoulder. *Hang on, you two. Wait for me!* Instead, I dropped back. They were walking slowly, as others rushed past.

Frances was slight, petite, beside his bulkiness. They were walking so slowly that, in order not to appear obvious, I had to stop and lean nonchalantly against a pillar. I wondered would they leave the station together. Could she, in the early hours, have agreed to try again? Surely, surely, this man loves her more than her boring, puts-out-the-cat fiancé? So what if Richard abandoned her on a hot train at the mercy of two garrulous Australians? We all make mistakes. Was he, were they, not worth another chance, for who could resist fate when it had thrown them together on a train just as it had separated them? Surely this was meant to be. If she turned away again, was it not likely that it had been she, after all, who had turned away before?

Bahrain. Oh, and Turkey again. What's this? Spain?

Their demeanour suggested that it was unlikely that they would walk off, hand in hand, to enjoy a romantic breakfast in an Innsbruck café. Their very bodies spoke despondency. My hands shook. If they stayed together, when would I give up? What would satisfy me? Would I follow them, stalk them, or would it be enough to know they held out against the night's deliberations?

That passport got mangled.

They were delaying it. They dragged their feet at the slowest pace until the platform had nearly emptied. It exasperated me that I couldn't hear them anymore, but they were scarcely speaking anyway. They couldn't have had much left to say, except for the truth of course, the truth which had not come all night and which I was certain had not been spoken while I was asleep. That was why they were moving slowly. Nothing had been resolved, nothing had changed, but there was still time. A little bit of time.

Come to Egypt with me.

No.

When they neared the barrier, my heartbeat accelerated. I had worked myself into a warp about these people, and I was fully aware that my sense of perspective had long since run off the tracks. Instead of enquiring about the next train, I was leaning against a pillar watching two strangers walk past a locomotive. In the cold light of day, what the hell did I think I was doing?

They passed the barrier and moved into the bright, white station. I followed. Two young women walked swiftly across the concourse, calling to Frances. Seeing them, Richard veered away from her and headed towards the exit.

Frances called 'Richard!' but her voice stagnated in the vast arena, stopped on her lips and went nowhere. To anyone else, it might have sounded surprised, casual. To me, it sounded bewildered, and final.

In response, he lifted his left arm in a half-wave, and dropped it without turning.

Victoria Station

There was a general strike on in Belgium. No form of transport was available from one end of the country to the other – and I was sitting on the border in Luxembourg. Like a great block that would not budge, Belgium sat between me and a hovercraft to England. But bad news for me was good news for the Luxembourgeois. The private sector was working overtime – minibus companies were running a round-the-clock service into Belgium and private citizens had become taxi-drivers overnight. All I had to do was sit on the pavement outside the station in the evening sun and wait for someone to drive me to Brussels.

I was sick. Sick at heart, left mourning something I could not identify. It was like leaving a cinema after seeing a film that has left you bereft, involved, impossibly connected to a fantasy that sticks to you, because it has made you ache for an experience you never had, but which you feel the want of. A void sat inside me which I longed to fill. I needed to get home. To touch firm ground.

By the time I got to Brussels the strike was ending, and on a warm Sunday afternoon I embarked on the last leg of my trip. It would take seven hours to get to London. Seven hours until I saw Saul again. He had waved me off on a Saturday morning three weeks before, insisting that he would meet me on my return at eight o'clock on this Sunday night at Victoria Station.

Anticipation made the final journey drag. I distracted myself by going over, again, the particulars, the intricacies, the timing and the possibilities of what I had heard between Florence and Innsbruck. I picked at every detail like a surgeon seeking a weakness in a mass of tubes. The words went around and around. In there, somewhere, there had to be a clue that I had missed. Richard and Frances were both so clear about where exactly they had been that April four years before, whereas I had no recollection of where I was at the time – but of course, nothing out of the ordinary had happened to me then, whereas for them, days and details had been branded into their memories by events. And yet, there should have been a chink. Seepage. I couldn't find it.

We arrived at Ostend in the evening sun. I bought a Jetfoil ticket and several bars of Côte d'Or chocolate, then waited in the terminal unable to kill time painlessly. I had one minor concern. In our carefully laid plans, there was one eventuality which Saul and I had not accounted for: the Belgian strike. As a result of it, all the trains were running behind schedule and I was now due to arrive at Victoria an hour later than anticipated. I was as certain as I could be this would not deter Saul, but I tried to ring him anyway. There was no reply, but he would surely make enquiries and be informed about delays. Somehow, I could not begin to doubt he would be there.

The journey to London was disrupted by a large crowd of English football supporters who had come over to attend a match in Holland. Unfortunately, for them and for us, they had got the date wrong – there was no match – so they compensated for their disappointment by drinking the entire weekend away. It was amazing they had even made it to the Jetfoil, but they appeared to have done so by moving about in a thick throng, supporting one another by standing close together. The disadvantage of this support system was that if one of them fell over, they all did, and this is exactly what happened when we were disembarking in Dover. We were led off the vessel into a series of narrow corridors which seemed to be swaying independently of anything else. It was some kind of interim platform, but to the ardent football supporters, who thought they had stepped onto terra firma, the movement was disconcerting. One of them fell over and, like an over-ripe cheese, everyone else pressed into the tight passage went over with him. The chain reaction must have gone all the way into the customs building.

On the London train, the fans sang, cheered, and fell about the carriages, but even this loutish behaviour didn't succeed in taking my mind from the sluggish efforts of my watch.

Finally, Victoria Station. This was the moment I had anticipated for weeks. Saul would be free now, would be mine. He had promised to see his girlfriend while I was away, to finalize things, so that as soon as I returned, we could begin. With these thoughts in mind, I was smiling when I made my way towards the barrier.

I could not see his bearded face as we walked along the platform. In fact, nobody seemed to be waiting for anybody. The concourse was clear. I wasn't unduly concerned until I actually crossed the barrier and saw that he really wasn't there. Standing alone in the middle of that huge station, which grew quieter as passengers dispersed, made me feel very small. My tongue in my cheek, I tried not to look like someone desperately looking for someone; eyes left, eyes right, head still. He was nowhere to be seen. I began to shake. Pride made me move. I wandered about. Up the concourse, down the concourse, my thoughts racing. I had totally misjudged this. My optimism had been way off-beam. How had I been so confident that he would show?

I glanced at the station clock. The sensible thing was to wait twenty minutes and then go, but I had never to date been sensible with men. This time I would be. After all, he was already an hour late.

I wandered over to a wall and tried to stand inconspicuously, overcoming the difficulty of leaning nonchalantly against a wall with a haversack on one's back. I'd had practice in Innsbruck. I went over our arrangement. If he had arrived on time, surely he would have waited the extra hour? But if he had not yet arrived, then what could have delayed him? A woman? *The* woman, probably. The one who was supposedly getting the heave-ho on my account. Damn him. The only person getting the heave here was me. *Damn him.*

He had been so enthusiastic and insistent! But three weeks is a long stretch, and in my ill-timed absence he could easily have wandered back to old warmth. Three days with me, two years with her. What hope had I?

There was no point in waiting. I had been stood up. It was Sunday night; I could go straight back to my flat and feel sorry for myself in private. The prospect sent a shiver down my spine. A lonely quiver. My famous homecoming. How I had dreamt about it! In little *chambres d'hôtes*, on a beach near Cannes, on the rumbling trains, I had imagined this reunion. This beginning. Instead: my flat. It would be cold and full of the traces of the torrid morning we had spent there before he took me to the station. The prospect of its emptiness, a reflection of my life, was so different from what I had envisaged that I kicked the wall behind me. If only I had prepared myself for this.

The clock indicated that I had five of the allocated twenty minutes left, but there was no reason to delay any longer. I glanced out at the dark autumn night and at the outside staircase that led down to the Underground, then scanned the station carefully and, still seeing nobody familiar, headed for the exit, feeling heavy and disappointed. Making my way down the steps, I wondered why I had believed this would work. I had really thought ... I stopped. I would give him the full twenty minutes.

I ran back up and into the station. Nothing had changed. My eyes flew across the concourse yet again. There was a crowd of people at the far end, but no one looking for someone looking. I didn't waste time. It was almost half past nine and the evening ahead, alone in front of the television, was becoming more familiar to me than that odd previous plan of dinner and love-making. Vaguely, I wondered what to do about food.

I went outside again. It was chilly and my pack was heavy and I wanted to be home. Over the entrance to the stairway, large green and yellow signs were marked District and Circle. I went down.

At the bottom of the steps, the Innsbruck train came suddenly before me. I stopped dead. The Innsbruck train and the two people who had lost each other. By accident, perhaps. By design, possibly. In a moment, the story retold itself. The true culprits were time and place. Again, I felt the couple's loss and felt it deeply. Time and place. Either way, that is what it came down to. The wrong time. The wrong place. I turned again, went up the steps and back into the station.

He was standing in the middle of the concourse looking up at the Arrivals board. He had his hand to his forehead and his hair stood up in dishevelled ends. Even from behind, he looked hassled, as if he'd been tearing around the station meeting every train I could possibly have been on. Except the right one.

I came alongside him and followed his eyes to the board. Not immediately, he glanced at me, and then looked again. 'There you are!' he grinned.

And I grinned. Then, both chattering at once, we made our way out of Victoria Station into the brisk, busy and almost winter evening.